DEDICATION

DeArmond, Spencer and Skoog

CONTENTS

ROGER GOES TO TOWN

I'm in the grocery store and my cart is loaded. This time I have everything. Including four boxes of Name Brand Cereal: Cap'n Crunch Berries, Frosted Flakes, Golden Grahams and Lucky Charms. Lucky Charms is my favorite disparate food. Marshmallows? For breakfast?

No store brand salami for me today. I have the Gallo Family Pack. I skipped the Oscar Meyer hot dogs and went straight for the Nathan's. The Nathan's Family Pack. I loaded up two cases of Mountain Dew. Not Mountain Breeze, Mountain Mist, or Mountain Drop. Mountain Dew. Two cases. My kids love Mountain Dew.

I have the cart stacked beyond a reasonable capacity. It's heavy. I'm pushing with my left hand and hip, holding things in with my right, and using my shoulder to hold my phone to my ear.

Why am I shopping like I've got three loaded EBT

cards? It's because of Fire Day. Let me introduce myself and explain.

Hello. My name is Roger Clines. I'm an average white American (French\British), middle-aged (55), slightly overweight (well, maybe 30 pounds too much?), married (first time!) with children (three), gainfully employed (engineer with the city). I hold a Master's Degree (Civil Engineering), am a registered Independent (corrupt two-party system!), and I'm a fairly high functioning drug addict. Five years ago, I never would have admitted the addict part. It wouldn't have occurred to me that I had a 'problem.' I have been using drugs since age fifteen. Pot, Vicodin, mushrooms, LSD, Cocaine, synthetics. Whatever.

Through all of my drug use I have never experienced withdrawals from a particular drug, other than the hammer of a cocaine comedown once or twice. I'd smoke a bowl of weed before work, maybe pop a 7.5 mg Vicodin (the sweet spot pill for me – the big ones) or a 50 mg Tramadol (a special low buzz – the little ones). Come home from work, have a drink or two. A bowl or two. Some cocaine on the weekend, or while on vacation. My marriage was stable. It was never the junkie nightmare this drug use would paint on television. No open sores, or missing work or crazy screaming matches at home. I have always been good with people, and work has never been a problem.

All of that said. The drugs. The drugs are starting to stack. I'm beginning to crack. It's been a slow-moving fracture. I've been observing it like a team of scientists watching seismic printouts. Noting a spike of activity here, a slow run-on split there. I'd stop a drug for a day wondering if I'd pushed it. Would I get sick? Irritable? I once thought to myself: If I can quit all drugs for 24 hours and not get any withdrawal symptoms then I'm good. Yes, that's ridiculous, and yes, I know better now, and yes, I knew better then. The point is that I have been thinking exactly like a Lifetime movie drug addict, while my life has been rolling along like a Disney film.

Until today, when I heard a few words in my kitchen. What I heard converted the day from Monday into Fire Day. It really fucked me up. I don't know how a normal parent would have handles things if they had been there. I'm pretty sure they wouldn't have used it as a justification to lose their mind. Like I said, I've been thinking like a drug addict. A couple of years ago my Vicodin/Tramadol source moved to Omaha. I don't know why he left. I went a while without, but I missed them. I loved to take them at work. They kept me up. I looked around for some sort of replacement and I came across kratom. It's a plant that grows in Southeast Asia. It isn't technically an opioid but it makes you feel the same. And it's natural. Just like pot. Pot never caused me any trouble.

I ordered some online. It came as a loose milled-leaf powder. There were several options for ingestion. Put in capsules. Mix with orange juice. Parachute. That means putting it in a piece of toilet paper and wrapping it up and swallowing the whole package. At first, I was putting it in capsules, but it took twelve capsules to fit my starter dose of two grams. The pills taste horrible no matter how well you wipe them off. Digestion is unreliable so you don't get a consistent buzz. You sometimes shit some of them out whole. By the time I was up to five grams a day I was mixing it with orange juice and slamming it. It tasted like hell. Bitter, green hell-tea with the consistency of mud. I'd slam five to seven grams in the morning and sometimes another five to seven grams at night.

Kratom. It's a strange word to pronounce correctly. Think of one hillbilly pointing at two hound dogs and saying, "Get them hounds off the porch and crate 'em." Kratom is intensely versatile. It jazzes me up when I need a boost, or chills me out when I want to relax. If you take enough of it, you can experience the 'heroin nod.' Tolerance becomes an issue quickly and you have to keep taking more to get the same buzz.

I was taking 28 grams, twice a day at its peak. Mixing that shit up in orange juice and slam. I've talked to some people who say they've learned to like it, to associate the taste with the high. But it's vile. After I drink it, I can wipe the back of my hand across my mouth and it comes away gritty and muddy. The smoke shops around here carry the drug in capsules. I buy from them in between online orders. I always pull the capsules apart and dump them in a single serving orange juice bottle. Sometimes, when I'm opening the capsules, I will accidentally drop one in the juice. There is nothing to do but carry on and curse yourself. Then when you slam the bottle of bitter mud, there will be a sludgy, snotty surprise where the gel cap has partially dissolved. Shake it up. Drink. Wretch every goddamn time. And I love it.

What I love most about drinking it is the fierce come-up. I'm amped in ten minutes. When I dropped kratom cold-turkey and didn't experience any negative effects, I figured I had outsmarted it. I waited a few months and then started again at two grams a day. Lately I take it and ramp up to seven grams, then take a couple of weeks off and begin again at two. See? Responsible drug user.

Back to Fire Day. It wasn't just what I heard. It wasn't just an audio assault. Fire Day also attacked my sight. My eyes and ears were screaming in pain. My senses registered infernos. Fire as far as the eye could see. Fire as far as the ear could hear. Fire as far as my body could feel.

The speaker of the words that ignited Fire Day is my son, sixteen-year-old Charlie Clines. While he's a big kid, standing at a little over six feet tall, I feel compelled to tell you he's not a football player, nor a weightlifter. He's not particularly athletic at all. Unless you consider eating a sport. I've seen Charlie eat and it's not a sport. It's a goddamn job and he's a professional. He's committed to it. Locked for life apparently. He said to his ten-year-old brother Benji, and this is verbatim, as the words are seared into my cortex:

"I know I eat a lot, but when I was younger, I trained myself to eat a lot. I mean a lot. Now that I'm older I don't need the fuel as much, but it's a habit I will probably never break."

And then he turned around and saw me.

He said casually, "Hey Dad."

He saw me standing there slack-jawed, in silent fire. Like one of those poor guys in that quirky 1970's sci-fi film, Scanners. Where the victims are frozen in a silent and terrible rigor. And then he popped off a 'Hey Dad' like we were at the park in spring at a Cline family reunion passing each other at the food table. Me grabbing more beans, and him grabbing a Mountain Dew from the ice chest.

When I told you all I saw was fire, that's true. But in the few seconds between the audio assaults from Charlie and the flames that consumed my vision, I saw horrible things. It was a one-two punch. Words that confound and then sights that delight! Charlie's Fire Day statement deserves to be broken down and examined, but I haven't had the time. He trained himself? Maybe the Fire Day Speech could be weaponized. You need to know a few things before I can tell you what I saw. Backgrounds, histories and such.

I do the grocery shopping for the family. I also do most of the cooking. I don't wash dishes and I don't do laundry. I don't clean the bathrooms. I just do the grocery shopping and the cooking. My wife hates grocery shopping and I love it. My wife hates cooking and I love it.

While I'm mostly your standard idiot, I'm near savant-like at remembering the prices of grocery items. Deli-sliced turkey for lunches, 4.99. And I think they have a nice butter chicken simmer-sauce for 5.99 at the corner. I used to plan large meals for low dollars. I can feed a family of five breakfast and lunch daily, six dinners a week (nothing on Saturday night) with desserts two nights a week, for one hundred dollars. A hundred bucks a week for five people! I consider myself to be a semi-professional grocery shopper. I can stretch that dollar, baby.

Even these days, when we are a foot above water versus face in, I rarely purchase name brand items. At least not for the kids. Sometimes I buy Oreo's or Nutter Butters and smuggle them to my room. It's not that the kids don't deserve it. They deserve the best. The kids are great. But if they've seen the item on television it disappears on Day One. Every. Time. All of it gone. Entire box of Cap'n Crunch? Gone Day One. Cocoa Pebbles? Gone Day One. Yoplait yogurt? Gone Day One. It's crazy how fast it goes. I can replace each item with a store brand item and presto, it becomes food instead of gold and it goes at a more predictable rate.

A week prior to Fire Day, I bought some honey. I had never bought honey before and wasn't expecting it to be so pricey. I stood in the store looking at the little golden bear. 8.99 for three ounces. I fought the urge to check the bank balance. It's just some honey. Man up. I pulled the trigger on the honey. I told myself I would hide it in the spice cupboard behind the lard. That way, my wife could actually have some of the honey before the kids sucked it all up.

My wife Abby had loved the honey. She made some tea and we talked- I didn't have any. I don't like tea and I don't like honey. They both taste like dirt. But it was a lovely night. I remember thinking to myself, half joking: The honey brought us together. Solid purchase. Note to self- always keep some honey in the house.

Now that you know how and why specific foods have different meanings to me, I can explain.

Chompin' Charlie was standing in the kitchen facing the cupboards, fussing over something. His brother was looking up at him adoringly, picking up important life tips. I walked in as Charlie finished up and commenced the audio attack.

"I know I eat a lot, but when I was younger, I trained myself to eat a lot. I mean a lot. Now that I'm older I don't need the fuel as much, but it's a habit I will probably never break," says Charlie as he grabs his dishes and turns around.

In that red-hot moment, I glanced at his dishes. The plate had three frozen burritos. Expensive steak and three-cheese burritos. Three average-sized frozen burritos. While they were burritos of average size, they were also burritos of extraordinary cost. The good ones with steak and three types of cheese.

The plate also had two honey-battered corn dogs. They were the individually wrapped ones. I've never liked buying corn dogs at the grocery store. They come thrown together in a single plastic bag. They get freezer burn and take on a freezer-ice flavor. They are only good the first time you open the box. Recently I found a place where I can pay a little more and buy them individually wrapped. I don't really care about this when it comes to the kids, but if I want a corn dog, I don't want one out of a grubby-hand box.

But you know, who gives a shit about a goddamn individually wrapped corn dog when it is just going to end up on a plate alongside a second corn dog and three steak and three-cheese burritos? And some Cool Ranch Doritos, even though he claims to dislike them.

"These suck," he had told me one day, as he shoved

some into his mouth. I like Cool Ranch Doritos, so I keep buying them. He keeps eating them.

So yeah, his plate was ridiculous, but the plate alone didn't hurt me too much. I'm a father of three. It takes more than an excessively wasteful plate and an idiotic comment to make me lose my shit. Two out of ten pain, you bastards!

What twisted me was the plate, the comment and the bowl. Oh God. The bowl.

Good ol' Charlie had a bowl of vanilla ice cream with various toppings. Every meal needs dessert. This isn't Russia. I could see some chocolate syrup. I could see some type of dark fruit preserves, most likely blackberry, and some strawberry syrup. Not the strawberry fruit topping but the strawberry, day-glow pink syrup. While chocolate syrup, synthetic strawberry Nestle Quik syrup and blackberry jam are all definitely on the table for ice cream toppings, I question putting them all together. I could be hypersensitive, or this could be the whole drug addict in me speaking, but this grouping of toppings makes me suspicious.

I question motives. Having a treat? Making a statement?

And for the last detail. The final stitch. The entire mess had a golden sheen. The vanilla ice cream was golden and shiny. The blackberry jam had a thick glaze covering it. Even the chocolate looked weird, like it was covered with polyurethane and glossed up for display. I glanced towards the garbage and saw an empty honey bear, dropped on its head.

Charles Clines had him some honey on that fine

sundae. A nice chocolate syrup, strawberry syrup, blackberry jam and fucking all-the-goddamn-honey sundae. A feast. Three steak and three-cheese burritos, two honey-battered corn dogs, Cool Ranch Doritos and a super neat sundae.

Now, let's do the whole thing in sequence. Between the family and the drugs and the poor diet and the lack of exercise and the kids and the career and the age and my general mindset, I am no good at remembering the wrongs. I completely space the hurts. Most of the time when someone says something hurtful to me, or I get wronged in a relationship, within a week or two my brain has purged the details and is ready to move on.

Forty years ago, a young me met a cute girl at a party. It was the very first party I'd ever been to, but I could tell that the girl had been to many. She took me up to a bedroom and without saying a word took my virginity. I fell in love. We even lived together after high school in one of those apartments downtown that sit over rarely-visited specialty shops. It was a tumultuous and messy relationship and she kicked me out every other weekend.

She'd yell and scream vicious, red-line-crossing, deal-breaking, point-of-no-return things, and I would leave, tail between my legs, vowing to leave her forever. By the following morning the details would be blurry and I'd end up getting back together with the psycho. I could not remember any details and lost every argument. So, and this is hilarious, I started to make a list. She did this! Don't forget! She did that! Don't forget! It wasn't a complete list, but I managed to keep some type of list going. Kept it in my wallet. One day she found the list. I walked in just as she pulled it from my wallet. That was the end of Roger and psycho girl, and my wallet, but just the beginning of my inability to recall the dark details.

I can remember every detail of this. I was robbed of my senses in the maelstrom and I still remember each agonizing second. I didn't need a video or a notebook to document.

Here is Fire Day, in agonizing detail.

It's Monday evening. I had just gotten home from work. I stopped before pulling into the garage and walked the empty trash cans back from the curb. I also checked the mail. There were lots of bills. There are always so many bills. We have a little table in the entryway from our attached garage where we drop the mail.

I set the bills on the table, and made my way down the hall into the kitchen. Charlie was preparing something at the counter, pontificating to his younger brother, who was staring up at him, rapt.

"I know I eat a lot, but when I was younger, I trained myself to eat a lot. I mean a lot. Now that I'm older I don't need the fuel as much, but it's a habit I will probably never break," said Charlie as he grabbed his dishes and turned around.

He noticed me.

"Hey Dad," he tossed over and carried his food out. His younger brother Benji was hot on his heels. Benji was a cute kid, with a broad, smiley face and a lock of curly chestnut-colored hair.

"But how do I know how much food I should eat

for my habit?" he called after his rapidly departing brother.

Well, that's it. That's the Event. That's Fire Day. I tried every way I could to inflate it but, in the end, it's a pretty short story. Kid made stupid food, said stupid shit. Why was this different than any other day? I don't know. Maybe it was the honey. Maybe it was the drugs. But that's the moment that set me on this path.

And now you are back with me at the grocery store, yes? The cart is laden with name brand, family-sized goodies. The type of stuff you could maybe afford but don't feel right justifying. Three pints of Haagen Dazs vanilla. Four pints of Haagen Dazs pistachio. They have pistachio now! Or maybe they've had it for a while, but I've never seen it. I grabbed some of the Blueberry Cobble Cheddar. The little block with the blue swirls that is 12.99? I got one of those. On the label it says: Creamy White Cheddar Blended with Blueberries and Cobble Flavor. Crafted by Master Cheese maker Kerry Henning. Now doesn't that sound neat? Blueberries and Cobble. Cooked up by the zany cheese genius Kerry. It's got actual blueberries, but no actual cobble. Artificial cobble flavoring, and everyone still applauds? Kerry must be on to something. But what is "cobble?" A fancy way to say "cobbler?"

The rolls of pancetta/mozzarella/basil that are shrink wrapped and cost about eleven bucks each? Three of them in the basket. Let the kids go nuts.

Uncrustables! I got four boxes. Two strawberry and two grape. I don't know about you, but I love them. I always feel guilty buying them. They cost 4.99 for four little peanut butter and jelly sandwiches. That's 1.25 for each teeny PB and J. I rarely buy them because they are decadently priced for something that can be made so cheaply.

I have tons of stuff in my shopping basket. From today on, we eat like the Rich Kids of Instagram. I keep a good mental total of my basket and today I am around 637 bucks. I could not fit another item into the cart. Its 8:34 p.m. now and I'm still in shock from the Fire Day. It shook me. It scared me.

Maybe it's the horrors of today, or the kratom. I took seven grams today at 8:00 this morning with a three-gram bump after lunch. I am high out of my mind for sure, but I'm hanging in there. Facing family, watching kids eat, going grocery shopping. These are not ideal times to be fucked out of your gourd, but for the most part, I'm always fucked out of my gourd. Maybe if I laid off the drugs for a bit, I wouldn't be so stressed out. Maybe I'd have better judgement. Maybe the whole honey thing wouldn't have hurt me so badly.

You tell me. Most likely you aren't a walking pharmacy. Would the honey thing have hurt you?

The last thing I haven't worked out yet is what I'm going to tell my wife when I get home. I will figure that out after. Right now, I'm going to walk the cart right out the doors. I'm taking all this shit. I'm still wearing my office clothes; I definitely don't fit the profile of a thief. I don't think they will even notice me if I act casually. I am going to just put my cell phone to my ear with one hand and wrestle this cart right out the front door in front of everyone. I am betting no one even notices me if I do it right. Gotta play it off legit.

I can pull this off. Maybe you can get behind this too. It would be helpful for me if I wasn't the only person who thought this might work. Yes, I'm stalling. Not going to lie.

When I was younger, around 20-22 my friends and I all lived with our parents and had nowhere to get high so my buddies' Nissan became the hot spot. We would drive around town regardless of time of day and smoke pot. We used a red, plastic, foot-long bong my old friend Vinnie named The Red Death Ray. Smoking a bong, driving down the freeway at 1:30 in the afternoon? No problem. We were so damned fearless and casual about it. I don't recall ever thinking that it was a bad idea, or that we might have gotten caught. Looking back, I think it was that fearlessness that carried us. Cops never noticed us because we never acted like we were doing anything wrong.

I'm going to channel that shit and play it off legit. Just going to walk right out of here and no one is going to notice me, or stop me, or say boo. That's the plan.

Are you onboard?

See you on the other side.

FANTA AND THE ONION FIELDS

I am sorry it took so long to get back to you. I swore to myself I'd let you know the second I had everything packed up and the coast was clear. But I didn't. I just whooped and hollered all the way home. I walked out of there like I owned the place. I was a little concerned about pushing a cart laden with goods and no shopping bags, so I readied a lie about going green-plastic bags are bad for the dolphins. But no one even looked at me twice. I kept the cell phone to my ear the whole time, trying to keep up a charade of 'oh shit I got an important family call and got so worked up I walked out straight away.'

No one came running out of the store after me. No strange looks or employees scouting me – everything worked out. No one had noticed. I considered a few lies for my wife but when I got home, I thought I was so super cool for bringing home the free gilded bacon that I just told her. She helped me bring in armfuls of items. We danced with honey and fine hot dogs and those awesome pickled green beans they sell in the liquor section called "Dilly's." They are awesome and are 11.99 for a seven-ounce jar. In total, it was an amazing experience that became my new normal. Go to a new grocery store. Load up. Walk out like it's your daddy's store. Feed family for free.

After a few months of La Vida Loca Shopper's Sweepstakes, the risk became too much for my wife and she tearfully begged me to stop. I was talking to her about the Fanta 12-packs I saw at a store not too far away. The packaging is colorful and they'd looked yummy all in a row. They had red for strawberry, purple for grape, yellow for pineapple, orange, and blue for berry. Next time I go, I said, I'm going to get all of them. She broke down and told me that she was afraid. This is getting ridiculous, she'd said. Here and there was fun, she'd said. I'm worried you aren't going to come home one of these times, she'd said.

I know how I must look to you, considering all the drugs and chronic shoplifting. I look bat-shit crazy. But I think I'm still mostly like you. I care about my family. I don't want my wife to worry, or be afraid that I might not come home. Like I'm some bank robber who could get shot at his next heist. I didn't work so hard at family and career to risk an arrest.

"How would we pay the bills if you go to jail?" she'd said.

That sealed my fate. The thievery had to end. I'd made her an accomplice.

I should have noticed how uncomfortable she had become. She was going to the store, just to grab a few things. She never did that before. She had been trying to beat me to the punch.

She started saying things like "Oh, please don't go steal trash bags, we don't need any. I just picked some up at the store on the way home from work."

I had been stealing too much, too often and it needed to stop. Abby was right. I was becoming paranoid, and while I downplayed the risks to my wife, I was worried too. Before heading home with my booty, I would drive around the block a few times to make sure I wasn't being followed. I knew I had to cut back. I loved the feeling so much I couldn't bring myself to say I'd ever quit. Cut back, not quit. Just like with the kratom. This is dangerous! Red alert! Well, thinks Roger. I better cut back.

I had been understanding when she talked to me. I promised it was over. I agreed it had gotten out of hand and pledged to buy our groceries like any other honest citizen.

At the store that day, looking at all the Fanta, pretty and inviting, I could only bring myself to get one. They are 7.99 for a 12-pack. I got the orange. If you are paying for something to drink, don't get Fanta. Fanta is fun if you bring home five brightly colored 12-packs at once and stock them in the fridge and the kids eyes pop out. Fanta sucks when you buy it as a beverage to drink.

So, I haven't done it for a while. I pay like everybody else, but shopping has become a bore. It's a big old drag. I feel like a sucker. 4.99? For this? Every time I go to the grocery store, I have to fight the urge to just walk out. It is very difficult to actually pay. I think I've got a problem. If it weren't for my wife, would I have stopped? I definitely do not want to get caught. I feel like every time I get away with it, I increase the odds of getting caught next time.

And still, what's the worst that could happen? Someone comes up to me as I'm walking out and I say 'oh, sorry, I took this phone call and got so distracted...' then I push the cart back in and pay. Easy peasy. Abby suggested perhaps the store's loss prevention would notice me. But I move from store to store. Well, what if an employee gets transferred and notices the same creep stealing? What if they call the cops and the cops go to all the stores and ask for security footage and discover you shopping like your dad owns the chain?

It seemed far-fetched, but all you have to do is live to the age of thirty or watch television to know things turn on a dime, and all it takes is for one particular person to see one particular thing and blammo! Shit starts to happen. I don't want shit to happen to me. But it has just been so simple and fun. Free stuff is amazing. Ever thought of all the great things you can do with unlimited funds at a grocery store? Every year, when the eggnog hits the shelf my dad will drive to a store or two and grab a few brands, then taste test them. He does it every year. Right before Christmas, I hit up four stores and got my dad ten different brands. Merry Christmas Dad!

Our oldest son Brian, has just moved into his first apartment. He lives with his friend Benny. Benny is a pretty cool kid. They work together at the Holiday Inn in the banquet department. I ran through a store and got them ten boxes of body soap, ten boxes of hand soap, ten packages of disposable razors. Ten of the fancy Old Spice deodorants. I even grabbed ten of the stupidly overpriced Axe pomades, which he likes, but cost 11.49 for a little hockey puck size container. Hell no, I would never buy those. Suave has a cheap tub of hair gel I buy the boys for 3.99. 11.49 for a pancake's worth of pomade? Wild. Cake pans, a casserole dish. Some basic dishes. Yeah, free dishes and cooking tools at the grocery store! Wash cloths. Q-tips. I never buy generic cotton swabs. Q-tips or bust, baby. What is with those swabs with the blue plastic stick? I grabbed two boxes for Brian, and six boxes to take home. Those are 8.99 each. Cereal, laundry detergent, toilet paper. My wife and I brought over six hundred dollars of stuff for the kids. It felt great.

Also, when you don't have to spend money on toiletries and food, it frees up the money for other things. Like more drugs. I had been getting smarter about the thefts too. I would grab one of the giant plastic storage tubs and place it in the cart, then load that. Easier to pull one thing out of a cart and throw it in the backseat versus a million things. I made sure to always park behind a giant SUV, out of camera view and with a straight shot out to the road. I would position the car so that I could walk out while having my fake phone call and do an easy flip to the far side of the car. That way I could load it while watching the store to see if anyone was following or had caught on. I even had a slick method for the phone call. I acted like I was talking about police. Figured that would make me look less like a potential thief. 'What did they say when the cops got there? Is grandma ok? Wait, you didn't call the cops yet? Call the cops now, Philip!'

But those days are gone. I haven't stolen anything from a grocery store in six days now. Ha! I'm six days clean. From theft, not the drugs. I'm still doing the drugs. I have discovered some legal drugs and they work pretty well.

They are called Nootropics, or 'smart drugs.' They don't get you totally fucked up, but they synergize. The smart drug people call a synergizing drug combination a stack. My stack is 200 mg of Phenibut (some Russian Astronaut drug that puts me to sleep if I take it alone) and 200 mg of Modafinil which is a wakefulness 'agent' not a stimulant. I do not understand the specificity of the distinction, but it's not speed. I've never done any meth other than the slight bits some assholes use to cut LSD.

It's been harder to cut out the theft than it's been to stop a cocaine binge. It's in my head all day, just like a drug. I considered stealing a few things the other day, and only thoughts of my wife stopped me. I even thought about stealing some grocery bags so I could then steal the groceries, and put them into bags before I got home so my wife wouldn't know. That's ridiculous, right?

I'm not balanced or reasonable. I think it's because I went through a serious trauma and it's affected me. Have any of you ever heard of Karl Hettinger or The Onion Fields?

The Onion Fields is the name of a book and a movie from the late seventies starring James Woods and Ted Danson. It was actually Danson's film debut. It's based on the true-life story of a Los Angeles police officer named Karl Hettinger. Karl Hettinger and his partner are rolling patrol and they pull over a couple of suspicious guys. The suspicious guys, who had just gotten done pulling off a string of robberies were armed and they got the jump on Karl's partner. Karl's partner says, 'Hey these guys have a gun in my back, give them your gun.' Karl hands over his gun and the two cops are kidnapped, forced into the back of the bad guys' car and handcuffed with their own cuffs.

The thieves drive them out of town to some farmland, where they shoot Karl's partner dead and Karl manages to escape, running over four miles while handcuffed.

When Karl gets back to the police station, he is scorned by everyone and his co-workers blame him for his partner's death. Karl did everything you are not supposed to do in that scenario and the department even made a training video based on him to teach other officers how to correctly handle the situation. You don't give up your gun under any circumstances. I sympathize with Karl quite a bit. What a frightening situation.

The terror of that day where his friend and partner got shot in front of him and the fear of his wild, panicky escape broke Karl down. The death of his career and the disdain of his co-workers put the nail in his sanity coffin and Karl snapped. He started shoplifting.

At first, he was stealing small things like pencils

and candy bars. He got caught a few times here and there but since the items were slight and he was a pathetic cop nothing happened. But like me, his thefts escalated. The third time he got caught he was trying to steal a thousand-dollar racing bike. Like me, he just tried to walk out with it. This was the last straw for the department and he was arrested and lost his job.

You see? Karl experienced an unspeakable violent trauma and I had Fire Day. Humans are fragile. In the end, can you blame either of us?

And since I am working hard to be honest, I've got to point out that when I say I'm six days clean, that's not completely true. I'm six days out from my last five hundred dollar plus cart haul, but not from all thefts.

Yesterday, I was at the self-checkout and the lines were long and the shoppers were rude and the employees were too busy talking to each other to be bothered to help people through. It took forever. I had two 12-packs of soda in my cart and I thought fuck it! I'm not going to pay for the goddamn soda. I scanned all items but the drinks and nobody noticed shit, of course. You don't bag 12-packs. I looked legit.

It's also quite ridiculous to pat myself on the back for paying for some of the items. Like a murderer who is proud he doesn't kill children. Any more. Sigh. I've got a problem.

JUICE BOX KILLER

This is the end. Everything has gone to shit. Yes, I'm often quick to hyperbole, but I now state fact. I'm sitting in the parking lot of a police station. I'm considering turning myself in. No, not for stealing groceries. And no, not for any drugs. Something much worse. I'm not sure what I should do. I'm torn. On one hand, I consider myself to be fairly moral, minus the stealing. On the other hand, I pride myself on pragmatism. I didn't intend for anyone to get hurt. I didn't know what was happening. Hell, I had no choice. I don't know if I should ruin my life out of principle. Everything happened so quickly. I could use your objective opinion as I don't trust myself anymore. The drugs and the fear have got me twisted up. Your vote of confidence would go a long way.

The nightmare started two weeks after I talked with you last. I slipped off the wagon. I had made a smooth exit just like always. I got my wife twelve boxes of tampons and 14 boxes of Mucinex- those boxes are 13.99 each. For eight pills! And I had just popped my trunk. No one was dogging me and I was feeling good.

I heard a sharp voice from behind.

"Merry Christmas!"

At first, I didn't turn around. It was July and I had no reason to think it was directed at me. I loaded the trunk.

"Merry Christmas!"

And this time it was said with so much sarcasm and scorn that I knew someone had caught me.

I spun around. A leering punk, maybe twenty, twenty-one, slunk around from the front of my car. He looked like someone who liked to kill small animals. He was overweight but wore skinny jeans and a filthy, too-small hoody. A fat guy in skinny jeans! That's something you don't see every day. A man with a muffin top. He was wearing a skull cap and his face was blighted with acne. Major, angry sores and deep craters. The dude looked rough. He was sipping on a cherry Hi-C juice box. Fucking random and creepy.

"Every day is Christmas when you thieve that shit, huh boss?"

I have no poker face, but I did my best. I went for casual.

"Whatever," I said. I closed the trunk. The guy had moved in between me and the car door. He pulled a cell phone from his kangaroo pocket. A kangaroo pocket is a front pouch that you can shove both hands into. The kind of pocket you see with hoodies. I'm not trying to be pretentious; I just want to give you a full picture. He held the phone facing me and swiped through picture after picture of Roger Clines prancing out of grocery stores with full-ass baskets with free-floating items.

"How come you don't put your groceries into bags like everyone else? You got a good job. You don't need to steal," he sneered.

I didn't say anything. I was too scared. My thoughts were racing to the top of my mind and then breaking apart just before any logical conclusions. How did this guy find out about me? I never noticed anyone watching me. And why?

I couldn't tear my eyes away from the phone. I considered grabbing it and running. He was still blocking my car door, holding the phone up like a talisman.

"You are lucky I'm the one who caught you. If the cops catch you, your life is over."

"What's your name?" I asked. My mouth felt like I'd just spooned in sand.

He laughed. "I ain't telling you shit about me. I'm just sayin' what you're gonna do."

"What do you want?" I asked. It was nearly as clever as 'what's your name?'

He grinned. His teeth were yellow nubs.

Had he filed them down or is it genetic? I wondered.

"Yeah. It's all about what I want boss. You are pretty good at stealing shit. I've been watching you. Sometimes you hit up three stores in a single day! Props to you. You're a good thief."

I flinched when he said 'thief.' It stung hearing it

from someone else. I can say it all day about myself. I guess it's like the N-word.

"I need you to get me a few things."

He tucked the phone away into the kangaroo pocket and pulled out a grubby piece of notepaper that had been folded up a million times into a tight square.

"What is it?" I asked.

"It's a fuckin' list, boss. Get the stuff on it and meet me at the Japanese Car Wash down on 34th. You got two hours. If you don't show up, on time, with my completed shopping list, I'mma Good Samaritan this video to the stores and the police. You don't want that. What would Charlie think if he knew what you are really all about? Hustle! And see ya." He smashed his drained juice box against my car and it dropped to the ground. He set the list on the roof of my car, turned around and slithered away.

I stood and watched him until he'd disappeared around the corner. Holy shit, right? He knew Charlie. That made it even scarier. How does he know Charlie? I thought. That was bouncing around in my head, punctuating the panic. Oh my god. I'm fucked. How does he know Charlie?

I dove into my car and sped out of the parking lot. I pulled into the bank parking lot across the street and unfolded the note. My hands were shaking so badly I ripped the note in half while unfolding.

128 bottles of Gatorade

1 Visionware bowl

1 Blow dryer

1 Candy thermometer

128 grams of Sudafed

5 gallons of distilled water
18 canisters of Coleman's stove fuel
100 ounces of "Red Devil" brand lye
160 ounces of Drano
60 ounces of starter fluid
5 bottles of Heet
10 rolls of heavy-duty aluminum foil
48 ounces nail polish remover
28 ounces powdered baby formula
100 ounces baking soda

What the hell? I wondered. The fucker is blackmailing me to mule meth ingredients. And how did he know Charlie? So yeah, I was scared shitless. And I got busy. I told myself I would go buy the stuff. There was no reason to risk getting caught over this. I only had two hours, and I blasted from place to place. What choice did I have?

I could go to the cops, which would be very bad for my family. I convinced myself that I was doing this to protect my family, to protect Charlie. But in truth I was doing this because I had fucked up. Because I had broken the law and that had given a proper criminal leverage over my family's future. And I was doing this so I would not get caught. Whatever. In the end, I did it because I didn't see any other option.

I hit eight stores. Did you know you can only buy 24 grams of Sudafed at once? I get it, but hell. That's still a lot of Sudafed. The Sudafed was locked up, so I had to buy all of that. Cost me 680 dollars. I stole the rest of the stuff. I know, right? Even in the heated moment I couldn't resist stealing shit from grocery stores. Especially shit I didn't want, like a million boxes of Sudafed. I fought the urge to call Charlie, but I couldn't resist texting him. Was he okay? Was he in danger? Was I in danger?

Roger: Hey

Charlie: Sup

Roger: Sup

Charlie: eating lunch

Roger: You home?

Charlie: Yep

Roger: Want to grab a burger tonight and hang out?

Charlie: am I in trouble

Roger: that depends. What are you eating?

Yes, I was definitely in danger. But Charlie seemed alright at the moment. I focused and stole like my life depended on it. I didn't know if the tweaker would kill me but he certainly had the power to ruin my life.

I didn't get caught at any store. One store I went back into after unloading my cart and made a second run. Fear makes you bold. I was at the Japanese car wash at 4:00 p.m. on the dot, ready to hand over the stolen merchandise to my unknown blackmailer. It was a tight spot.

Dickhead was thirty minutes late. Those thirty minutes sucked. It was a cacophony of blood terror. Should I wait? Should I leave? Was he going to show? Were the cops going to somehow show up? Had I been caught or setup? I kept having this half-baked fantasy of me taking his phone when he showed up and bolting. If I took the evidence then he would lose his leverage. But I could not imagine myself actually grabbing for the phone. In the speeding fantasies I knew I had to reach inside his gross pocket and rip that phone out, but I'm not known for my aggression. I've never even hit anyone in anger. Not even as a kid. And I've never been hit either. I would do poorly in prison. Quite poorly.

He came from the north side of 34th Street sucking down another Hi-C juice box. This one was orange. Dude likes his Hi-C juice boxes. He walked around to the passenger side and tried the door. I instinctively hit the door locks.

He looked irritated and bored, like this was your average, everyday stickup.

"Unlock the fuckin' door, boss."

I flipped the door locks again. He got in and sighed. It was a long wheezy sigh.

"You get the shit?" he asked.

"Yes, I did."

"Okay cool. Let's go."

I suddenly felt indignant.

"I'm not going anywhere man. I gotta get home. You can have the shit right here and that's it."

He reached into the kangaroo pocket. He had dried food and dirt and schmutz on either side of the pockets, like he'd wipe whatever was on his hands before sticking them in. Maybe he just doesn't like a dirty pocket. Dirty pants, clean pockets. He pulled out a .38. The moment I saw the gun, I thought, 'Oh shit, a gun!' My follow up thoughts were, 'This must be opposite day. An actual kangaroo pouch is a slimy, flesh pouch of mucus, surrounded by meticulously groomed fur. This guy has a slimy, mucus exterior, with a fastidious interior.'

That's how fucked up it is when you have a gun pulled on you. Your brain acknowledges the danger and then instantly tries to divert attention to something completely random.

"Give me your cellphone," he said, and waved the gun at my head.

Of all the things he could take from me. My cellphone. I had pictures of Abby on there! The kind of pictures you tell your wife you are deleting immediately but don't.

I handed him my phone. He tucked it into his pouch.

"Let's go to The Wheel. You know where that is?"

The Wheel is a spot at the north end of our valley. The northern rim is surrounded by dense woods, and on occasion the mountains get too much snow and when it melts, it floods. The floods sweep dead trees down into the valley and beaches them in downward spikes on the hill sides. As you drive towards the ridge, the dead trees look like the spokes of a wheel. There are lots of off-road paths on either side of the highway and its remote location makes it a popular place for kids to get drunk and do stupid things. No decent person visits The Wheel after the sun goes down. It's too dangerous up there.

I nodded, started the car and that is how I got kidnapped.

He directed me north until we were almost out of the valley then had me pull off onto an obscured ATV path. We wound deep into the woods. Time turned to taffy on the drive. I was thinking that he was going to kill me. I was thinking that he was going to hurt Charlie. The road ended about five minutes after it got dark.

"Kill the engine and get out. I need you to load that shit into the shed. Leave the headlights on so you can see."

I sat there for a quick moment. I could smell the guy. He stunk like sour milk. I could see glints of light off the barrel of the raised gun. The glints looked beautiful. Like little stars that disappear when you focus on them. Light is amazing, I thought.

"Get the fuck out and load the fucking shed," he growled.

His voice jolted me from the ADD I seemed to be experiencing in the face of danger (man, I hope that's the drugs, because I used to think of myself as capable and agile under pressure). I popped the trunk and got out. There were smashed juice boxes strewn about. He obviously spent a lot of time out there. The shed turned out to be a large wooden box, with a hinged lid that opened from the top, like a deep freezer.

I took as long as I could to get the job done. If I was going to die out there, I wanted a few more minutes, even if they were stained with awful. I considered taking off and running into the woods, but even if I somehow escaped the guy, then what? He had my car and my cell phone. And incriminating evidence.

He exited the car, his gun trained on me. He casually circled over and reached down behind the 'shed' into a noisy sack. Hand came out with a new juice box. Hi-C grape. I had a vision of this creep's mother somewhere, handing them to him after school.

"Go faster."

"I'm almost done," I said. My throat felt dirty and I couldn't swallow. He was going to shoot me out there in the woods.

I got everything loaded.

"All done," he said and snapped his fingers.

I don't know what the finger snap was about. The guy was a freaky little shit for sure. But the snap pissed me off. It looked like the end, and I surprised myself by growing even the slightest bit of balls. What I said was stupid, but at least I resisted to some degree at the final moment.

"Your shed sucks."

He laughed.

"Nice one! Okay boss, let's go home." He pointed with the gun to the driver's side. "Get in."

It was a ridiculously disparate moment. I felt so much relief at the thought that he wasn't going to kill me that I felt grateful at his mercy and wanted to thank him from the bottom of my heart. At the same time, I resented myself to the ultimate for feeling anything positive towards him.

I got in the car and we rode in silence back down the path and onto the highway. We said nothing to each other. What would I have said? I was thinking about my family. Charlie. My future. What was I going to tell Abby? I was getting ahead of myself. I wasn't out of the woods yet. And some resistance, huh? Your shed sucks? Seriously Roger?

When we entered city limits he told me to take him back to the Japanese Car Wash.

The car wash was closed and the lot was empty. As I parked, he put the gun to my head. He pressed it into my hair.

"Give me your wallet."

I dug my wallet out of my back pocket and handed it to him. He opened it and snatched out my driver's license.

"Roger, eh? Is this your current address?"

I didn't answer and stared straight ahead. I realize that I'd made every concession he had demanded, but I was done complying. He'd have to kill me then. At the damn Japanese car wash. We sat in silence for a few moments.

"You did well today. You asked me my name earlier. My name is God. Do you know why I'm God? Because I do whatever the fuck I want and nobody stops me. Actually, so do you, in a way. A much smaller way. Sure, you take what you want to a point and no one stops you. But I take that further. I complete the climb, boss. I'm like Zeus. I will most definitely use you again. Until then."

The gun went back into the pocket pouch that had my phone, followed by my driver's license. He handed the wallet back to me and the douche actually flashed a peace sign with his fingers. Just like that he was out of the car and disappeared down the street.

I told you guys I was fucked. I didn't even know what time it was. It had to be eight or nine and I'd told Abby I was just going to the store for a few things after lunch. I'd also reassured her I wasn't going to steal anything. My survival instinct took over as I examined my options. There was no way that I could tell anyone about this. I would have to lie about my cell phone. I lost it like an idiot. I could get away with not telling Abby about the driver's license. I'd just report mine lost and order another.

My head was full of ranked issues. I had disappeared for about six hours, blown off dinner with Charlie, and lost my cellphone. I helped someone steal goods to manufacture meth. I had been kidnapped and threatened with a gun all night and had to play that shit off legit. Fucker knows Charlie. Fucker knows where we live. I opened the car door and threw up. It was the stress and the relief and the extra kratom bump I'd done earlier. The stuff intensifies feelings and drama to the max. It was a shitty night to be on kratom, but once you've taken it and it's sat in your stomach for a few minutes, it's an eight to ten-hour ride, no take backs. I simply hadn't considered kidnapping as a potential evening event.

I'm not going to get into how I handled everything that night. I will tell you I lied to everyone. There was no way I could tell Abby, especially not after my promise to go straight. If she knew that I'd been kidnapped and scared for my life her heart would have broken. If she knew that God had nude pictures of her she would have had a heart attack. And if she knew that he knew where we lived, she would go to the cops. I couldn't let that happen. I made a mental concession. I would consider flushing the drugs. I'd think about it. Maybe without them I would be calmer, better equipped to deal. I prayed to God. The other one. I asked him if he wanted me to stop taking drugs. I promised not to steal anything ever again.

And I haven't since. I have stuck with that promise. I've been using like crazy, but the stealing is over. Sleeping has gotten difficult. I used to be the sleep king. Before I stole the meth supplies, whenever I heard people talking about lying in bed, tossing and turning, it was an alien concept. You lie in bed for hours thinking about things? Not me. Ever. I lie down. My head hits the pillow and I'm out. Well, it used to be that way. Now when I close my eyes, I see him. I see the gun. I feel my heart hammer. I've been taking 250 mg of Tetrahydropalmatine, or THP. It may sound super synthetic but it's a natural alkaloid that lives in several plant species that shoves sleep down your throat whether you want it or not. I stack that with a heavy dose of Phenibut (2 grams, about ten times my normal dose). This works so well and so quickly that I wait until I'm in bed before I take it. It puts you out within minutes. Phenibut is the topper that makes the rest of the drugs work and stick all night. The tolerance grows quickly and it doesn't work if I do it more than once a week. But the one night you get is a deep sleep of the dead and it's lovely. It knocks me out solid. You could scream in my ear or flop me out of bed and the sleep is so dense I would not wake up. Heaven. The rest of the nights are a blur of restlessness and nightmares and sweat. I told Abby that I had quit kratom and was going through some vicious withdrawals. She made the saddest sound I had ever heard when I told her.

She said, "Oh baby, I'm so sorry. I know it was easy to get carried away, but I'm so proud of you for quitting. You've got my support." And then she cradled my head in her lap and stroked my hair. I felt like a piece of shit.

Work was tough, but I kept it together and a few weeks passed without any drama. I wanted to casually find a way to ask how Charlie knew God, or if he actually did, but never got anywhere. I spent my conscious thoughts rationalizing and excusing and worrying and then justifying. I worried about being part of making meth. Assuming the jerk didn't blow himself up while cooking it, he was probably going to sell it. What if someone got hurt taking the meth I helped make? What if God gets spun out and runs over a kid? Would that be my fault? Yeah, of course it would. All of that considered, could I live with that? Yes, I most definitely could. I didn't make any meth. I don't do meth. I've never even touched the legit speed like Ritalin or Adderall. No, if that is where things had ended, I would not be considering turning myself in.

Last Saturday, God came to my house. I was in the back yard with the kids. We had just gotten one of those large backyard trampolines and Charlie and I were nearly finished putting it together. We could not keep Benji off of it long enough to get it built. It was a beautiful day and I had a great time. That time in the back yard was the calm before the storm. Abby called out from the back door. She hollered that I had company and I knew instantly it was him.

I'd been living with the possibility of this happening and pushed it away every time it popped up. Nothing I could do about it. Maybe he won't bother me again, I'd think. But I knew. I knew he was coming.

I walked into the house and there he was, juice box in hand. Cherry again. I said casually but forcefully, "Let's go to the garage."

I walked in front of him, leading the way, my skin crawling knowing he was in my house. He was around my family. The kids were feet away. Abby would have questions. When we were alone in the garage, I exploded.

"What the fuck man? This is my house! My family! What the fuck are you doing here?"

"Calm down, boss. I'm not here to fuck with you. I just want to make a deal. A trade."

"What the fuck? Trade? You need to go!"

"Slow down. I want you to hear me out. I got something you want."

He was wearing a different pair of greasy skinny jeans, and the same grubby Hoodie. He pulled my cell phone from his kangaroo pouch. I grabbed it from his hands, surprising myself. I had the phone back! He made no effort to stop me.

"It yours, boss. I want you to have it. There's a lot of good stuff on that phone and I want you to have it as a show of good faith. The deal-"

He took a final pull on his juice-box straw. He crushed the empty between his hands and dropped it on the garage floor. I winced. I don't like trash on the garage floor. Abby and I had spent two long weeks painting the floor with a glossy garage floor paint. It had taken us forever to keep it smooth while it dried - constantly picking up stray leaves and smoothing the paint back.

He pulled out the phone he'd shown me in the parking lot during the shake down. The phone I'd imagined taking from him so many times. Those awful pictures of me in the act, me walking out of store after store with an I-dare-you-to-fuck-with-me look on my face. His leverage. I reached out to grab that one too, emboldened by my previous success, but he danced out of reach.

"The deal. I give you this phone and disappear forever, leaving you to live out your days, unscathed by your brush with the Glory of God."

He stopped there. What did he want? Another run? Should I do it? Anything would be worth getting rid of this threat. Sure, he could easily have copies of the photos but I couldn't think about that. I had to deal with what I knew. I had to destroy his leverage.

"I had a good time with your phone. I especially liked the pictures of your wife. She aroused me boss. I want to fuck her."

I laughed at the ridiculousness. "She would never, and I mean never."

His face tightened and he plunged his hands into the pouch and they each came out with a pistol. "You are gonna get me in. It's not going to be that bad. I will be quick. I'm always quick like that. I'm gonna fuck her, so get that through your head. I can take it from you with these guns and your game is over. Or you can give it to me, and then you get a second chance."

My mind spun. There were two guns pointed at me. I want to explain to you what this feels like. I know I have not come across particularly well and I am expecting to be judged harshly. But until you've had guns trained on you and have faced the end of your family, your career, and everything you care about, you can't fully judge me on form. In the life or death moment, you consider everything. Every possible shot, even the long shots or the distasteful ones or the immoral ones are open for a quick debate.

"How do I get a second chance?" I asked.

"I fuck her. I fuck her tonight. I leave you my guns. Then I wait for you up at The Wheel tomorrow night, and you get to shoot me dead. Your second chance."

"I don't want to shoot you," I said. I didn't. I just wanted him to go away. Forever.

"Well I want to get shot, boss. It's time for me to ascend. And I want a taste of your girl before I split."

He waved the guns at me.

"Figure it out. I'm on a tear and I don't care. I could shoot you now and take her, but that could get messy. Charlie might try and stop me. Might have to shoot him. Might shoot everyone."

I grit my teeth and tried to look tough.

"You are gonna get the fuck out of here right now!"

"Naw," he smiled. "Your God wants some strange. Procure!"

Something in me broke. The guns suddenly meant nothing. I loved my wife. I loved my wife more than my own life and I would do whatever it took to protect her. I charged him, reaching out for the guns.

At its best it was a pathetic lunge and he easily leapt out of my way.

He cocked both guns. Click, click.

"Come on boss. You don't mean it. I know you

don't. You don't wanna die. Do ya?"

Dammit, he was right. And you know how I feel about facing facts. If I died, who would take care of Abby and the kids? And what if he hurt or killed any of them? By now I was certain I wasn't dealing with an average meth dealer. This guy was Travis Bickle'd out of his head. And very dangerous. And all this mess because of Fire Day. I mean because of the drugs. Ugh. Okay, all this mess because of me. Greedy, old me. I had to eliminate him, and I had to do it in a way that protected my family. I had to survive and I had to stay out of prison. For my family. I had an idea. It was an awful, terrible idea. But a practical one.

"No, man," I said, deflated. "I don't want to die. Okay. Tonight, then. One a.m."

"Nice boss!" he said, excited. Seeing him excited was gross. The guns went back into the pouch and he pointed at the garage door button. "Push it, boss. I'll see myself out this door. Tonight, at one."

He looked over his shoulder, waiting for the door to rise.

"Isn't that cool? You found your phone! You can text your boy again! And take more pictures! Your life is almost back on track. Later."

He left on foot. I followed him down my driveway and watched him walk down the street and around the corner. He didn't look back once.

The future yawned in front of me, making me dizzy. What the hell? I was in so much trouble. My family was in so much trouble. I could hear the kids playing in the back. Charlie must have finished the trampoline. I could hear their voices rise and fall. I thought about Abby. She was a wonderful wife, and has always been encouraging and buoyant. Whereas I, Roger Clines, am a drug addict. And I, Roger Clines, am a compulsive shoplifter. And I, Roger Clines, just signed Mrs. Clines up for some late-night cuckold action because some twit with a gun told me to. Some husband and father. I used to congratulate myself for outsmarting the system. For staying ahead of the curve. For beating chemistry. But all I'd done was build a shaky house of cards.

That said. I laud pragmatism. And pragmatism sees some catharsis in wallowing, but that shit's finite. I may be living in a house of cards, and I may be a pussy with a gun in my face, but I didn't get this far in life being weak. I went to work on a plan.

In full disclosure, when God had his guns on me, I had no flex. He could have frog marched me in the house and raped me in the ass in front of my wife and kids and I would have just laid there, terrified. When he demanded my wife and I acquiesced? At that moment, I meant it. It's the guns. I also absolutely diddly damn guarantee you would have done the same.

Think about poor Karl Hettinger. Traumatized by the bad guys and the good guys. They scorned him for doing what the bad guys with guns told him to do. They scorned him, but none of them would have done it differently. I have a hell of a lot in common with Karl now. I get it. There is no choice. Knowing that, I knew I had to avoid being at the end of a gun just as much as dying at the end of a gun. As long as there was no gun, I had room to operate.

Part one of the plan was to use my sleep stack to drug Abby. Before any of you get too ruffled about this, think about it from my point of view. I had to protect her from all of this, or her reward for being awesome would be terror. And I don't want to lose her. Does it matter if it's a sleazy benefit to me to keep this hidden from her? For her own good? Okay, I almost can't keep a straight face saying all this, but that is how it went. None of this could get out. Better no one got raped in the ass in front of the kids. And I had just staved that off. All options valid, when surviving.

Part two of the plan was to kill the freak. The guy needed to go. You don't have to be a drug addict to know that, right?

Part three was to get his body in my car, drive him to The Wheel, and shoot him a few times.

Part four was to clean up whatever needed to be cleaned up. Make sure kids are cool while mom's asleep. Nightmare ends. No more stealing. Cut back on the drugs. Be a good husband and father. Easy peasy.

I mixed three grams Phenibut and one gram of the THP. Don't worry, I read that THP, which can be quite toxic in large doses, is not fatal until four grams. They were both fine crystalline powders, with a slightly bitter taste. I always drank it with orange juice.

Abby wasn't going to want a glass of bitter orange juice, but she did like tea with honey. And honey was sweet enough to completely hide the bitterness and the hot water would dissolve the powders.

Don't be silly. Of course, I had the honey on hand. Honey no longer went in the larder, or the kitchen. Honey lives in my closet with the Oreos. You only need one Fire Day to learn that honey needs to be kept close to the chest.

For the creep, it was easy. I was going to drug some goddam Hi-C juice boxes. Yeah boss!

My crazy skeleton plan worked unbelievably well. Everything flowed and went in my favor. Abby and I had Benji in bed and Charlie contained by about 10:30 that night. Abby loved her tea and was sleeping soundly, snoring and oblivious by 11:30.

I ran to the store and purchased four packages of Hi-C juice boxes: one cherry, two grape and an orange. Purchased, mind you. I was going to spike the cherry. I had seen him sucking down cherry most often. The grape and the orange went into the house fridge for the kids. The cherry was going into the soda fridge. Our soda fridge sat in the garage. I think most people call the garage fridge the beer fridge. But I don't drink beer, or any alcohol really. I'm not against it, just am not a drinker myself. I have plenty of vices without it. The soda fridge is the first refrigerator Abby and I bought.

Immediately after Brian was born our refrigerator broke. We didn't have any money so we went to a rent-to-own place and got an instant fridge. It's been solid for twenty years. The fridge keeps on running. I look at the soda fridge as an avatar for my marriage. As long as that fridge runs, I know Abby and I are good.

I had never poisoned Hi-C juice boxes before, but

everything recently has been uncharted territory, and I was highly motivated. I planned to use the most powerful psychedelic I've ever had – 25I-NBOMe. Users call it N-Bomb. I had only tried this drug once and it kicked my ass. It was 16 hours of white-knuckle horror. Endless leg tremors, nausea and the most intense visual hallucinations I've experienced. It's active at 50 micro-grams (not milligrams) and from what I've read it can be fatal at high dosages. I don't have a scale that can weigh in micro-grams; even my jeweler's scale only tacks milligrams. When I took it, I used a magnifying glass and some tweezers to eyeball out 6-7 grains. I planned to use a lot more than that for the punk.

I had a syringe wrapped in sterile packaging that I'd lifted from my last visit to the doctor. I had high blood-pressure, go figure. The guy made me sit in the exam room for over an hour before he came to see me. I took a few things. Forceps (the scissor looking pliers that lock in clamp positions), a syringe and a reflex-hammer that doctors use on your knee. Even after handling the thing I couldn't tell what material the hammer piece was made of. Some kind of plastic perhaps? It's not completely unyielding, but I couldn't make a mark in it with my thumbnail.

According to the internet, 5 milligrams of 25I-NBOMe is a fatal dose. I dissolved an entire gram in a solution of warm water and sugar. I used just enough water to dissolve the drug. Then I sucked that death-water into the syringe. I opened the pack of cherry and took one for myself. Stuck a straw in it. Had to make the Hi-C look legit.

I folded up the spout-flap corner that no one ever uses for that purpose and slipped the needle between the top seams. I injected half the syringe into one juice box and repeated the process with the next. The flaps folded back down neatly. The finished result was a newly opened pack of eight cherry flavored Hi-C juice boxes, one removed. I planned to be drinking that one when God came in. The next two boxes in the pack were spiked heavy.

By the time I had finished prepping the drinks and cleaning up it was nearly one in the morning. I didn't allow myself to think about what would happen if he didn't want a juice box. I was pretty sure he'd want a yummy, apparently highly addictive and irresistible cherry Hi-C fruit drink. I never bought them for the kids. They cost 5.89 for a pack of eight which means that Benji takes one and Charlie takes seven, and it's gone in ten minutes. The kids would be thrilled when they saw them in the morning. If we made it to the morning.

He tapped on the garage door at one, precisely. Taptaptap!

I had a quick disjointed thought: Maybe I should have drugged the kids too. Or maybe I should have moved the family out. But I was certain he would have been watching us. No, we couldn't run. I was the only one allowed to run. And the only type of running I could do was interference. No big deal Roger, just run interference in the most miraculous way. Follow the plan and he won't even make it into the house.

I put on a smile and forced my body to look relaxed. I grabbed my juice box and thumbed the garage door open.

He was wearing the same dirty Hoodie, but he'd changed his filthy skinny jeans for a different colored pair of filthy skinny jeans. I know people are selling jeans that are ripped these days, but are they selling dirty jeans as well? Is that a thing?

He looked relaxed and smiled broadly when he saw me sipping.

"I approve. You got any more of those? Fucking makes me thirsty."

I pointed at the soda fridge, hoping he couldn't hear my heart beating.

"Don't mind if I do, boss," he said and stabbed the first spiked box with a straw. He left the soda fridge door open. I didn't object. I was waiting for him to get suspicious but he didn't notice anything. He drained the box in one drag and dropped it, smashing it with his foot. He reached into the open fridge and grabbed the second spiked box.

"I love this. Hi-C is probably the only thing I'm going to miss when I ascend." He drained the second box, smashed and dropped it and grabbed another.

"When I ascend, I will partake of Ambrosia. Do you know what that is? Nectar of the gods, boss. Until then, this is the nectar of the gods."

From what I've read, it looks like even a slight overdose of 25I is fatal within 1-2 minutes. I had to keep him talking for a few more minutes to give the drugs time to kick.

"I watched some cuckold videos on the Internet tonight. It honestly looks like fun. We have never done anything like this before. Have you?"

Oh gross, Roger. But he lit up.

"I most certainly have, boss. It's my thing. Do you know of any other way to demonstrate full control over a man? Than to bang his wife in front of him?"

"Threatening a man at gun point?" I asked.

He laughed. "Hot dog, boss! You have a point. But this is on a whole other level. You watch, you are going to like it. Seeing your wife being satisfied by a superior man? Any good husband ought to like that. You know? You are giving your wife the best. You know?"

Yes, it was creepy that he appeared to be selling this as a benefit to me and my wife, but I thought I saw his face droop a bit when he said his second 'you know'.

He laughed again, but his head looked wobbly. He noticed and his body tightened up. His smile melted away and he looked at me.

"What the fuck, boss?" he asked weakly as he slumped against my workbench. His legs swayed and I kicked a folding chair over to him. He flopped into the chair; his eyes glazed over. Then he slid onto the floor. After twenty seconds of mumbling, he started to seize up and shake violently. To make things even easier, his guns and his cell phone rattled out from the pouch and I scooped those up. No more guns, no more God. Now he was just a fat fuck that needed to die. He shook for about 60 seconds, flopping around like a fish out of water. It was frantic and terrifying. He kept smashing his face into the ground and growling. Blood streamed from his mouth. Thirty seconds passed, the shaking stopped, and he lay completely slack on the garage floor. Dead.

I thought about feeling for a pulse like they do in the movies, but he was definitely dead and I didn't want to touch his greasy skin. I decided to bind him, just in case. I tied his hands and ankles together using extra-long zip ties. I popped the battery from his cellphone and shoved the phone into his Kangaroo pocket. I flipped his body face first into my trunk, threw in a shovel and a pickax and slammed it shut. I crept into the house; the kids were all asleep. Checked on Abby and she was sleeping soundly. Her breathing was normal. I rushed back to the garage and that was when my legs gave out and I fell face first. The rush of what just happened had left and I was reeling. Wow. I had done it! What would I have done if he didn't want the Hi-C? Or if he hadn't chugged both of them? I told myself that I would've charged him and taken the guns if he tried to take a step into the house. My body started to shudder with extreme relief. I could see light at the end of the tunnel, even while face down in my garage. I just had to get up and finish the job.

My body, however, refused to move. I panicked when I couldn't get my arms to respond more than a wiggle. Was I paralyzed? I had a friend who told me about almost drowning in the Philadelphia River. He and some buddies had thought they would swim across one day, but they were all inexperienced swimmers and idiots. And probably on something. They dove in, but the river was wide and the current was too strong and they had to turn back. They made it out but only barely. One thing had stuck out to me.

The way Gary had explained their utter exhaustion.

"You know how in movies you see someone who almost drowns but they make it to the side? And they flail around at the shore, reaching for a rock or a branch like a gimp? And they just lay there, half in/half out and then they get swept back in? And you yell, 'You were safe you idiot! Next time get all the way out!' Well man, that shit is real. You are too tired to pull yourself all the way out, even when faced with getting sucked back in. By the time I made it out I had driven rocks under my fingernails. All the way back to the quick man. Just trying to grab. Grabbing for my life. And when I got to a large rock I just laid there and flopped around. If I'd been pulled back in, I would have been done. I couldn't move."

That's how I felt. I was half way to freedom and then I was collapsed, laying in a state of exhaustion on the garage floor, with a nut in my trunk. Eventually the shuddering subsided and I was able to get to my feet. I looked at the time. I had only been on the ground for about ten minutes. Sweet recovery, Roger.

By 1:45 a.m. I was driving up to The Wheel. I was feeling pretty good, considering what I had gone through, and considering I was on my way to bury a man. I managed to find the off-road at the top and the stupid box that God had called a shed. I put on a pair of latex gloves and stared into the dark towards the road and I didn't see anyone. No headlights or movement. It didn't look like I'd been followed. I dragged him from the trunk to the woods behind the box. We went back about fifty feet and I shot him twice in the head with one of his guns. Just in case.

That was it. I didn't feel much. Not a rush, not an urge to vomit. I felt some relief, but nothing else. I buried him out there with his guns and his busted cell phone. Covered his grave with some brush. Everything had worked out like a television episode.

Time for stage four of the plan. Cleanup. I stopped at the community garden plot downtown on the way home. Dropped off the shovel and pickax into their donation chute. They slid down to the other side of the fence into a pile of co-op garden tools. Perfect. I was home by 5:00 a.m. Everything was quiet. I couldn't believe it. I had vanquished my enemy without breaking a sweat. I was worried that killing would bother me, twist me up. But it was barely a blip. It had to happen and that's that. The hardest part of the whole thing was digging the grave. The ground was fucking hard and I was in a hurry. That shit hurts. Both my hands were blistered badly by the time I finished.

After the immediate glow of relief passed, I realized that I didn't know anything about the guy. What if he was a politician's son and people came looking for him? Christ, I hadn't even checked to see if he had a wallet or an ID. I didn't want to know who he was. It was better that he didn't have a name. I decided my only course was to do the best I could with what I had. I was a fucking bad-ass. And my family was home and safe and asleep and happy. It was a surreal feeling. I had destroyed the wolf at the door, and no one could know. I had just been through the most extreme events of my life and could give them no public regard. It was hard enough keeping quiet after I'd been kidnapped. This was different.

I retraced our interactions at my house. Front door, hallway to garage. Garage. Hallway to Kitchen. That was it. I figured short of some of his fingerprints or a hair, there was nothing to really link me to him or his death. Other than possible CC footage. Since I could do nothing about that, I vacuumed the car trunk. By then it was 7:00 a.m. I wasn't tired, despite not having slept. The sun was up so I washed the car. It was early and I had plenty of time to think. Time to make sure I hadn't made any mistakes.

I bought two dozen fresh donuts from Smiles Donuts. The guy who owns Smiles makes fantastic blueberry fritters on Sunday mornings. You have to get there early if you want one. He doesn't make very many and they are usually gone by 8:00 a.m. If you've never had a blueberry fritter, picture an apple fritter only with blueberries. If you've never had an apple fritter, you should get to it.

I took the sim card and battery from my old cell phone and dropped them into the rain drain behind Smiles and threw the phone into the dumpster. That phone could stay lost. I realized that I wasn't being very cautious. I'd just killed a man and didn't even bother to properly dispose of anything. I wondered in the moment if my confidence was a gut feeling, or some sort of byproduct of killing my enemy. Some irrational warrior's rush perhaps?

It was 9:00 a.m. when I pulled back into my garage with the donuts. I was going over loose ends in my head when I suddenly realized I hadn't thought to look for the list! I couldn't remember where I'd put it. I'd been so terrified that day. Had I thrown it away? I had zero recollection of where the list ended up. I flipped open the console in my car and there it was. The meth shopping list. Filthy paper, torn across in half. Just hanging out in the console. Rather than berate myself for being careless, I decided to feel good, because I was pretty sure that was the last thing connecting us. And I had found it. I decided to type the list into Google before I got rid of it. Maybe I could see how much meth five bottles of Drano would make.

The top eight results had headers like "How to Make a Homemade Bomb" or "Make a Bomb Shopping at Wal-Mart." That's when it hit me. There was a bomb! And I had stolen the bomb shit! And I had done an internet search for homemade bomb ingredients! Holy shit there was a bomb, folks. How could I have known? I'm bomb slash meth ignorant.

So, he wasn't a random, meth-head, pervert bumpkin. My mistake. I'd underestimated him, because he didn't look maniacally devious. He looked like a greasy slug on legs. With a gun. Scary, but not thoughtful.

I frantically searched every inch of the house. How big was a bomb? After I was roughly satisfied the bomb wasn't at my house or in my car, I wasn't sure how I should feel. Was I over-reacting or giving him too much credit? Maybe there wasn't a bomb.

I was cool with the kids all day. I wasn't a great actor, but the stakes were never this high. I pulled it off. We watched Home Alone for the millionth time together and laughed like we did the first time we saw it. The bumbling crooks, played by Joe Pesci and Daniel Stern, are hilarious. There is a scene where the tall crook tries to convince the short one that they need a nickname. He wants to call themselves the 'Wet Bandits.' I wondered what my thief nickname would have been if I'd kept stealing, but I came up with nothing.

I was lying in bed with Abby tonight, marveling at how well everything worked out. She had her head resting on my chest and we were watching TV. When I heard about the explosion at the zoo on the evening news, I felt a cold hand tighten around my throat. I shot out of bed gasping for air. I couldn't breathe. My throat wouldn't open. Fourteen people dead, eight children. Twenty-six animals, including a newborn elephant named Sticky. I'm sorry. I don't know the names of the people who died and I don't want to know.

I stalked to the sink and turned on the water. I kept thinking, don't hit your head on the sink when you pass out. I scooped a handful of water into my mouth and forced myself to swallow and my throat released. I sucked in air as I collapsed on the floor. Abby was standing over me, with a look of horror on her face. The phone was in her hand and she was dialing.

"Honey, I'm calling 911!"

"No, no," I spit out. "No, no." I grasped for anything. "It's my sleep apnea. I will go to the doctor again."

She paused the dial.

"Seriously, baby," I reassured her. "It happens every once in a while."

"But you were awake Roger."

"I think I nodded off baby. It's okay. It's okay."

I forced myself to stand. I held her in my arms and strategically squeezed a bit harder than normal to seem stronger than I was. I fooled her. Again.

"Let's get back in bed, honey," I managed. I even plopped down frivolously and patted her spot. "Come on."

I flashed my best smile. I was getting quite good at acting. That said, I had been cashing every bit of good will I'd earned throughout twenty years of marriage. The emotional bank account was about dry. He's stolen that too, the bastard. I had never lied to my wife before this. Maybe he was a god. He played me. How long before the cops showed up? The news caster had said due to the body count and the homemade explosive, the FBI and the ATF were going to be investigating. Ah, I was fucked. How long before they trace the bomb back to me? There have been many points where I thought I was fucked, but the bomb was truly the final fuck.

I laid in bed with Abby until she fell asleep. She looked so beautiful and innocent tonight. So pure. And while she's lucky she isn't a drug addict or a thief, because this shit isn't fun; she's unlucky she married a drug addict and a thief, because this shit isn't fun. That was about an hour ago. I got up, showered, dressed and drove straight here. To the police station.

I cannot bear the thought of not sleeping in the same bed with Abby – we've not been apart a single night of our twenty years marriage. Unless you count last night while I was out a-killing and a-burying. But what I cannot bear even more, is for Abby and the kids to think I'm a mad-bomber. If I get to the cops before they get to me, I will only go down for, I don't know. Could I pull self-defense versus murder? Did I fuck myself for killing him? Would they believe that I didn't know about the fucking bomb?

In the end, I never had a choice. Shit. Okay. I could have never shoplifted. Or I could have stopped when I said I would. Or I could have faced shoplifting shame when God threatened me. I could have gone straight to the cops instead of stealing the ingredients. I could have gone to the cops after I got kidnapped. I could have gone to the cops after he came to the house. But that was the only time I had a clear path, during all of this. After he threatened my wife and my family, he had to die. If I'd gone to the cops then, he would still be alive. And I would not exist in a world where he could be a threat to Abby. On the other hand. The goddamn bomb!

This is a mess. And after talking it out with you, I know what I need to do. No, I'm not going to take responsibility for the goddamn bombing. I haven't gone all noble. Pragmatism is key. And that's the driver. I am weighing the inevitable outcome of staying silent, in which I end up framed as the Zoo Bomber. I'm sorry Sticky. I had no idea.

If I turn myself in, I can say I'm doing it for my family. Which is too little, too late, huh? Well, that's what happened and that's where we are.

But I value my freedom. I value time with my family. Maybe I bide my time and see what happens. Maybe I don't deserve to lose everything I've worked for. Fuck it. I'm going home.

ROGER GOES TO EGYPT

I'm irritated. I know that's a shitty way to say hello.

I'm in the coastal town of Abu Zenima, which is on the west side of the Sinai Peninsula. I can see the Gulf of Suez across the road. The thermometer in front of the Nightingale Market said it is 26 degrees Celsius. I don't know what that means in American degrees. Yes, I realize how ignorant that sounds and I am relishing it. You can label America with any pejorative you want and still lose because there is no Abu Zenima there. Everything here looks dead. There is no green. There is some sparse ground cover and squat trees the closer you get to the Gulf, and nothing east. Nothing. Just barren, rocky, mountainous yuck land. No bushes. No grass. No trees.

I'm irritated because the guy I'm supposed to meet out here didn't show. Or I'm not at the right place. Tarek said he'd meet me at the restaurant. I haven't met anyone here who speaks English well, but everyone has spoken some. I had asked a few people where I could get food and they had all pointed here. The City Cafeteria. I've been waiting in front for nearly two hours.

The people who own the restaurant seem friendly but they keep whispering and pointing at me and I feel like they want me to move on. I offered to buy something while I waited but they refused my money and brought me a complimentary pineapple soda. I have never seen this particular brand before. It's called fayrouz and other than the strange name, nothing about it seems foreign. All writing on the can is in English. It was delicious and tasted like pineapple Crush. When I finished, even though I hadn't paid they practically fell over themselves to hand me another. The second was pear fayrouz. It was also delicious, and I've never had an equivalent soda in the States. I took a picture of the can. Maybe I will order some on Amazon when I get back home. If I get back home.

Yes, I have my phone, but in Egypt they use Class C, E, and F power outlets and my phone requires a Class American power outlet. I haven't been able to plug it in since I got here and my phone is dead. I had made sure my cell phone plan would support calls in Africa. Doesn't that sound weird? It had sounded alien coming out of my mouth. Yes, I'd like to activate cell calling while abroad in Africa. I made sure I had service but didn't think about power. I didn't know that was a thing. I'd heard enough people talk about traveling to Europe to have heard of the power outlet differences but for some reason, it didn't occur to me for goddamn Africa.

It wasn't easy to get here. You have to get shots! I had to get vaccines for Typhoid, Hepatitis A, Hepatitis B, Cholera, Yellow Fever, Rabies and Influenza. I had to register with the US State Department. Nothing ominous or anything, but since they don't recommend nonessential travel to Egypt I needed to register 'in case of disappearance or accident.'

Supposedly Tarek is from the area but no one recognized his name. I think I'm going to walk back up the road to the Nightingale Market. It is about five miles North and it looked like they had all kinds of stuff in there. Maybe they will have a phone adapter I can use to charge up my phone. I'm probably missing calls from him and it is starting to get dark and I know the soda guzzling American has worn out his welcome here. I wanted to leave some money for my drinks, but they looked so offended when I offered earlier that I decided to just bounce. I stood up, said thank you and bowed. Nice Roger. Bow to the Egyptian restaurateur.

I genuflected and took off north.

Why am I walking down the Ras Sedr – El Tor Road at sundown in the city of Abu Zenima, South Sinai Governorate, Egypt? It is because of Water Day. Let me explain.

Things in the Clines house haven't been great since the bomb. I think Abby and the kids have picked up on my misery. I was easily irritated and had started to snap when the kids said stupid shit. And my kids said a lot of stupid shit. Water Day was the apex of stupid shit.

I had just returned home from Costco where I witnessed a sign of the apocalypse. I was looking at their bottled water, which is super cheap in bulk. You can get the 48-bottle packs for 2.99, which is a killer price. They had a pallet of water bottles wrapped in a green shrink-wrap. I inspected it and saw the bottles were flavored water. The label read: Sparkling ICE, Essence of Lemon Lime. I don't like flavored water so I moved on, and I saw a blue shrink-wrapped pallet at the end of the aisle. 'What flavor is blue?' I thought to myself. 'Blueberry?' I had never seen blueberry water.

It wasn't blueberry, friends. The blue label read: Sparkling ICE, Essence of Water. Water flavored water. And no, Water Day isn't fury at the product, although it did enrage me at the time. I was so incensed that I bought a pallet of each, just so I could take them home and preach to anyone who would listen about the gross idiocy that is water flavored water.

I bought too much at Costco that day, just like every other time I go and spent nearly fifteen minutes unloading the car. Brian, our oldest son, was splayed on the couch the entire time I was huffing and puffing. He doesn't even live with us any longer, but still finds ways to come over and make me feel like shit. He just sat and watched me carry in load after load. He didn't even try to feign interest in something else, like 'Oh I may have a splinter and that's why I'm staring at my hand.' He just watched me. On my second-to-last trip back from the car he says without getting up, "Was that your last trip?"

Too little, too late, I thought.

"Naw, I fly out to Singapore tonight, first class."

I delivered the line with cheery gusto, while my face painted a picture of disgust.

Brian dipped his head. Finally. A reaction of some sort. And then I brought in two more loads. All solo. I hate to be a Roger apologist here. You all know I accepted responsibility for Fire Day. But, wouldn't this upset you? Your twenty-year-old son, comes back home to lounge and to eat some free food, and while he's there he sees you carry in box-load after box-load of an epic Costco haul. And just sits there and watches? I know I am sounding like my mother, but that's rude.

I need to be clear. I don't hate it when the kids are rude to me. I said lots of shit when I was a kid. Whatever, you know? What I hate is being forced to react when kids cross the line. It's a proxy confrontation. Kid is rude. You ignore it. Kid is rude. You let it be. Kid crosses the line? Now, you have a goddamn task list. If you don't perform the appropriate countermove, you are screwed. You were trying to have five minutes of peace on the sofa but your kid was rude and crossed the line and now you have to do something extra. I'm not usually mad at what they said, I'm just pissed they gave me a honey-do list.

Brian came into the kitchen and sat at the bar, while I put away the groceries. I never stayed irritated for long with the kids. I handed him both a blue and a green bottle of water.

"Check these out. Hilarious."

He looked bored. "I don't get it."

"Water flavored water!"

He stayed bored and shrugged. "Yeah, I don't get it."

I was irritated again. "I'm saying it's stupid to market water flavored water."

"What's stupid about it?"

"What I'm saying, Brian, is that there is no such thing as water flavor."

"Yes, there is."

"OK. What's the flavor of water?" I asked. I know I shouldn't have said anything. Hell, I should have danced out of the conversation back at his first "I don't get it." I should have said, right on, and gone back to stocking my Costco haul. But I didn't. Water Day doesn't happen because you do the right thing. Water Day happens because your life is Wiley Coyote hovering before the fall.

I've thought about this a lot since. I suppose, while marketing water flavored water is stupid to me, that doesn't necessarily mean there is no flavor to water. I was juvenile on multiple levels for taking issue with this. But I did and I brought on the wave. The wave that led me to the Sinai.

Brian still looked bored, which frustrated me. "Dad, what if you aren't always right?"

I still had it together. I hadn't lost it yet.

"Well, I am always right," I said curtly. "Why would you think otherwise?"

He blinked and said, "Because, what if?"

And that is where I snapped. A wave of fury and

rage swept through me. Soaked in my own kitchen. Somehow, and when I say somehow, what I mean is that my arm instantly and unexpectedly flung the blue bottle of water in a fury to the left of me. It was a strange rage-induced involuntary reaction, and that reaction flung the blue bottle to my left. I want to stress that the bottle went to the left, because I wasn't aiming it at anyone and even in my unblinking rage, my body still knew better than to throw anything at anyone.

In the few times that I'm feeling generous, I consider the real and true possibility that a kid saying "Because, what if?" is the exact DNA code button for instantly flinging shit to the left.

The bottle flew to my left where it crashed into my wife's brand-new Starfire Rimless 80-gallon fish tank.

Just a quick sketch: Abby loves aquariums. She loves them so much that we have a beautiful rimless tank that's 32 inches long and stands at 24 inches tall. It has a center overflow built-in with pre-drilled drain and return holes in the overflow box. The simplicity and readiness for a sump tank means you can create whatever aquascape you want without being disturbed by artificial technology in your water. You see?

Waves of horror overtook me.

Horror Number One: Oh my God! I threw something.

Horror Number Two: Oh my God! I broke Abby's tank.

Horror Number Three: Oh my God! There is water everywhere.

Horror Number Four: Oh my God! I broke Abby's tank.

Horror Number Five: Oh my God! There are fish flopping around dying right now all over my living room.

Horror Number Six: Oh my God! I broke Abby's tank.

Horror Number Seven: Oh my God! Brian just saw me lose it.

Horror Number Eight: Oh my God! What the fuck do I do?

At Horror Number Eight, I think it was Eight, they were cascading down on me relentlessly, Abby walked in. Followed closely by Charlie and his girlfriend. I'm guessing they walked in ten seconds after the glass crashed. Abby may even have heard it when she was getting out of her car. She saw the dripping water and the flopping fish in all their raw glory. Her head turned to us where she saw Brian pointing at me.

The horrified look on her face turned to anger.

"Roger! What the hell, Roger?"

I stammered, but Brian bulldozed over me.

"Dad was being a dick, and then he got mad and threw a bottle of water at me. He missed and it busted the aquarium."

And that's when Water Day, bored with launching mere horror, started launching waves of fury.

Fury Number One: What the fuck did he say? I threw it at him?

Fury Number Two: Fucking 'because, what if?'

Fury Number Three: Roger you are an idiot.

Fury Number Four: Because, what if?

These continued and alternated with waves of horror as I took pictures of each dead fish with my cell phone so I could buy replacements at the store. They continued as I cleaned up the broken glass and sucked the 80 gallons of fish tank water from our carpets using a Rug-Doctor I rented from the corner store. They continued when Brian didn't want to hug me goodbye. They continued when Abby burst into tears later that night when I tried to explain the whole 'fling to the left' thing.

That's when Abby demanded that I get help. She even mentioned the drugs. She'd never mentioned the drugs before. She'd said that maybe I should consider cutting back or maybe even quit altogether. Her biggest point was that I had to make a change. And that I had to do something big to get back on track. I couldn't lose my temper over a water bottle with my son, or throw shit. We'd been getting fliers at the house for the last few weeks about some new age healing center. She suggested I check it out.

Fine. I needed help. I admit that. I was at the point where any other professional, white collar, middle-class American, would need to get some sort of psychological therapy. Why are you so uptight Roger? Because I do a shit ton of drugs and I killed someone and I'm not feeling myself. I wasn't ready to have that kind of conversation about my drug use, and I didn't want to go to prison so I wasn't ready to have that type of conversation about the killing.

I didn't want to pay to play games with a therapist: No, I'm not a drug-addict. No, I'm not guilt-ridden. I just display those types of behavior, ok? Now, let's get to the root of my problems so I can feel better! Therapy was out. I considered going clean for a bit. I thought, 'Hey maybe I could do Alcoholics Anonymous and at least clear that shit up. Maybe that would be enough to get me balanced. Maybe then I could shake what I'd done. But Christ, those people. They are just the biggest sheep. I cannot stand labels. I don't want to be a member of any club. And any time someone displays one of those AA chips and everyone cheers it makes me want to puke. Hurrah, you showed self-restraint for X days. Whatever.

No. I had zero interest in quitting any of the drugs. Even though I could feel my sanity eroding. What do I mean by that? I mean, I have been unable to control my thoughts. Unable to control my emotions. I've been worrying. Worrying myself incessantly. Every goddamn time I wake up, whether it's in the morning or after a nap, it's with a start. From the moment I open my eyes, the crazy, scary worry begins to roar in my head.

This is unusual for me. I'm a solid guy. I've been solid for the last fifty-five years. I'm a long-time, dependable city engineer. I even consider myself somewhat of a mental warrior, for facing intense psychedelics and coming out unscathed every time. If you've never done any hallucinogens you may think it has something to do with watching pink dolphins dance. But they aren't like that. They can be harsh, introspective and interminable journeys, where time stands still and the universe rubs your face in your shit, endlessly.

I'm pretty good at controlling my trip. When I take hallucinogens (the only ones I've tried are mushrooms, acid, salvia, mescaline, and some research chemicals like 4-ACO-DMT, 4-HO-MIPT, 4-HO-MET, 25i), I never have a freak out. I always control myself. I've learned to shut down intense introspection while tripping. I lock that shit down. A critical thought? Not right now buddy. Right now, focus on rainbows. That's always worked for me.

These days I'm a worrier who can't stop wringing his hands over the next five seconds. I worry about everything. My mind is a carousel of doom. What if this happens? What if she dies and that's the last thing you said to her? What if they get to talking about me and decide they don't like me? Or catch me in a lie? And other neat things like: What if the cops arrest me for murder? What if I get arrested for all of my thefts? No, I don't steal anything anymore. Honest.

I was tired of the cycle of fear and worry. It was bad. I would fixate on an issue. Sometimes it wasn't even a real issue, but I'd build it into something huge. The moment I resolved the issue, my mind would instantly replace the broken worry record. It would update it and add a new, different worry. Now things aren't okay because of this. You fixed this? Oh yeah? And you are relaxing? What about this new horrible thing? And the worry wheel goes round and round.

Sometimes I would try and resolve the issue. Find out if she still believes in me. Find out if my boss is angry that I came in late every day this week. Find out if Brian feels loved enough. I was pretty hard on him the other day. What if he's in trouble and doesn't feel like he can talk to me? I better go talk to him.

That was an exhausting path, trying to please and soothe these endless phantoms. The other method I'd try to control these thoughts was to shut them out. Kind of like when I shut out bad thoughts when I trip. Shut them out. Slam down a gate. Unplug the ride. But that way worked less and less after the killing. Now I have a brand-new trick. Rather than shut the thoughts out, I decided to simply label and observe.

I named my inside voice Wally. And every time he'd throw out something to worry about, I'd say, "Ah hello Wally. Working hard today as usual." I know this sounds silly, but that is what I've been doing and it's been helping. A little.

A couple of months ago, as the worry-go-round was winding up, I had my first bad trip. My first bad trip out of hundreds. It was brutal and I was totally unprepared.

I took six grams of a mushroom strain called Golden Teacher. That is a lot of shrooms. A standard strong dose is between 2-3.5 grams. Like I said, I'm a warrior. When I ingest shrooms I grind them in a coffee grinder and mix the powder with orange juice. I shake that up and let it sit for about thirty minutes. The acid breaks down the cells and releases the psilocybin, converting some of it into psilocin. The trip hits you much faster. Instead of trip onset after 45 minutes of ingestion, you start to feel it in about fifteen minutes. It also gives you a shorter trip, lasting only about 3-4 hours.

I did it to myself. I ate the magic mushrooms and thought: This time I won't shut down the introspection. This time I will face my fears. Big mistake.

When you are wracked with guilt and shame, mushrooms can be a frightening thing. I tripped on the fact that I was a drug addict and a murderer and a lousy husband and a lousy father. And by the time I realized I was in danger of freaking out, it was too late to put any of the intense emotions and thoughts back in their place. I was overwhelmed with what a loser I was. It was some dark shit. It was a hella bad trip. Four hours of Wally screaming and me crying.

The awful feeling stayed with me, the way a bad dream sometimes does, only it didn't go away for weeks. I was so paralyzed with self-loathing that I had a hard time going into work for a few days. I just laid in bed and cried. Abby would try to comfort me but I couldn't tell her what I had done. That I'd drugged her. That I'd told creepo he could fuck her and then killed him in our garage. That I'd shot and buried him. That I was a horrible liar. A horrible father and a horrible husband.

After a week or so of this, Abby took me for a drive. She told me she wanted to get me out of the house. I was sitting in the passenger seat, tears streaming down my face, going on and on about how I'm shit. She pulled off the road and looked at me.

"Sometimes you think about what a piece of shit you are. Then you stop and get on with life. If you don't, you're weird."

And that was that. It wasn't Buddha wisdom, but it was practical enough. If everyone sat around feeling all day, nothing would get done. I coupled that moment with this next thought.

People say that you do drugs to numb yourself. That you do drugs to avoid. That getting high is running away. But I did the mushrooms to face my demons and issues, not run away from them. And the more I faced them, the more they became like quicksand. Dragging me down with a circular gravity. Facing your problems is like looking at yourself in the mirror. It can be informative, but you gotta limit that shit or you will starve. And it's weird to stare at yourself for long. And the length of time spent looking doesn't increase the value of what you see. Hey, you are a shitty dad. Well, good to know. What's for dinner?

I wasn't going to stop the drugs, but I knew I had to do something. I had a bad trip! Only unstable people have bad trips. I felt frayed. I'm not the type of man who breaks down. Ever. I was going to have to be preemptive. No therapy. No crazy exercise regimen. Abby wouldn't buy that. I needed to do something substantial to help me calm down. I needed to stop being so uptight. So judgmental. So paranoid. Maybe then I wouldn't snap at Brian. It was a figure of speech, Dad. Maybe I would stop having Days. No Fire Day. No Water Day.

I was observing Wally trot this shit out one day while I was driving home from work and I saw a sign inside a dingy strip mall unit. It said: HHH Says, Be Well Now. Heal your Body, Mind and Soul. Higgins Holistic Healing. Licensed Pharmacy. This was the new office we'd been getting fliers for.

Be Well Now. I liked the way that sounded. And a

pharmacy? Some cool drugs, maybe?

I turned around, parked and entered the office. I was greeted by a bored-looking receptionist.

"Do you have an appointment?" she asked, not even looking up from her desk.

I don't know what I was expecting, but Holistic Healing has a hinky, mystical sound. And bored, nail-filing receptionist didn't fit the image I'd had in my mind.

I told her that I didn't but that I'd seen the sign.

"Well you can't just come in and see the doctor. You need to make an appointment. Do you want to make an appointment?"

"Sure," I said. "How much does a session cost?"

She laughed.

"You don't pay by the session here; you pay for a treatment plan."

"How much is a treatment plan?"

She laughed again.

"If you have to ask, then don't make the appointment. Getting well isn't a budget affair."

I was intrigued more than irritated. "Sign me up."

She gave me a little appointment card on which she'd written the time and date of my appointment. It was for the upcoming Friday at three p.m. The card made a reference to the window slogan and said in bubbly letters over the time and date: Be Well Then.

Friday came and I arrived at my appointment with Dr. Higgins promptly. The receptionist directed me to the waiting area that had the standard waiting room magazines. People, US Weekly, Good Housekeeping, Cosmopolitan. The magazine selection discouraged me a bit. They seemed mundane. I wondered what kind of pharmacist makes appointments to determine treatment plans.

A door opened and a short man with a paunch and a double chin bobbed out. He was balding, wore wire-rimmed glasses and his chins dripped down into his neck. He wore a pale blue, three-piece suit, jacket casually unbuttoned.

"Roger? Pleased to meet you. Come on in."

I entered his office and sat in a chair opposite the desk he moved behind. It was a fairly austere office. There were clinical magazines stacked on the floor and books stacked along the window sills. The room was rimmed with cardboard boxes of various sizes. His desk had a few blank sheets of paper, a pencil and some sort of crystal sitting in a Petri dish.

"You like crystals?" he asked, following my gaze.

"Uh. Crystals?"

"Yeah, you know, crystal power?" And he exaggerated the question. Like "you don't believe in the crystal hokum, do ya?" but there was one on his desk in a dish. And I was at just the type of place that might have a new age type crystal thing going on. I wasn't sure how to answer him, so I just nodded.

He picked up his pencil and asked me a few basic questions.

"How old are you?"

"55."

"What months were your parents born in?"

"My mom and my dad were born in November."

He pushed out a knowing laugh and his chins shook.

"That must have been ridiculous growing up? Both of your parents born in November eh?"

I was even more curious now that I was there. "Is this an astrology thing?"

"Ah, Astrology. You like it?" And again, he asked the question with sarcasm. This time he might have said, "you don't believe in chem trails, do ya?"

"I don't know much about it. If you mean, do I read my horoscope, I don't."

"Ah no. Of course not. Hogwash for the loons. Now tell me the first letter of your first serious girlfriend's name."

Ok, this was weird. But I went with it. The guy was confusing, but seemed nice. His voice was soothing.

"B."

"B, huh? That lasted what, three, three and a half years?"

"Yes, how did you know?"

"Well, you combine the B with both of your parents being born in November and you get a first-love star that burns bright and then out. Usually between three and four years."

He went on for a while, asking me seemingly random questions. He nodded at each answer, as if knowing how old I was when I first used a lawn mower could tell deep truths about my soul. (I was 22, okay? My parents always had a gardener and I didn't mow a lawn until I had one of my own, what can I say? Is that why I keep snapping at Brian? Come on!)

After about 20 minutes of questions he set his pencil down and collected his notes into a neat stack.

"Well, I think I have everything I need to craft your

treatment plan."

I was feeling stupid. Very stupid. I don't go for crystals and new-age mumbo-jumbo. I don't know what I had expected from a place that advertised holistic healing, but between horoscopes and crystals, I was ready to decline the treatment plan from Mr. Chins, The multi-color flyer king.

"Now that I've gotten to know you a little bit, I want to share a little about me." Higgins shifted in his chair and raised his hands up like a conductor. "Let's begin! I am a third-generation pharmacist. My grandfather and my father are both pharmacists. My mother is as well. As are my two brothers, my sister and my son. My family owned the pharmacy downtown next to the old bank for forty years before we closed up."

He balled his hands into fists and brought them down to his desk deliberately.

"Do you know why we closed? Because the game is rigged. We've been handing out the same drugs for years and nobody ever gets well. The drug game is designed to sell drugs, not heal people. Once I fully realized that as pharmacists, we were more drug pusher than medical professional, I couldn't hand out another bottle of Coumadin for someone with high blood pressure. That wasn't going to fix anything. I wanted to fix the high blood pressure issue proper, not band-aid the symptoms. Am I being too conspiratorial for you, Roger? Are you following me?"

I nodded. He was bringing some practical thoughts to our meeting and you know how I feel about shooting the shit straight.

"My father and my siblings came to the same realization about our profession at about the same time. Dad decided to retire. My sister went back to school for her MD. My oldest brother sold his share of the business and bought a boat. Left to see the world. My younger brother moved east to University of Minnesota to study hypnotherapy. I didn't bounce back like they did."

He shook his eggy head and his chins jiggled all the way down to his collar.

"No, that was a dark time for me. I was devastated when I realized the true state of medicine. As a pharmacist you hear conspiracy stories about how Big Pharma is actually an arm of Bigger Petroleum, but you shake all that off. You are important. You help prevent harmful drug interactions; you don't just dole out drugs. Once you've seen through the ruse, it's impossible to come back. You prevented harmful drug interactions for sure, which you had to do because you were doling out so many. And what's with the way Big Pharma rewards script-happy doctors with cash and vacations and gifts? And what parts have you played in this game as a pharmacist?"

He stared down at his desk as if he was afraid to meet my eyes during this part of the narrative.

"It was a very dark time. My first marriage had just imploded due to an affair I was having with an employee. I loved the girl, but she took off the minute we closed the store and I never saw her again. Her disappearance was further devastating because we had plans to move in together after my divorce. Instead, she left me alone to deal with the fallout.

During the cheaty rush I'd bought a stupidly expensive car- a Rolls Royce Wraith. It was 275 thousand dollars! Can you believe that? I spent a quarter of a million dollars because I thought it would be fun to drive my mistress around in a hot shit car."

"No marriage. No hot girl at work. No work, with the store closed. And no meaningful career. My family legacy of providing medical care was a sham. And with no work, of course, no money. The stupid monthly car payment? My auto insurance monthly? This was ten years ago and I was paying two thousand dollars a month. For insurance. And the resale on those cars is less than ideal. People with enough money to afford a car like that would never buy used. I had to make monthly payments on the damn thing for eight months until I found another pretender like me to sell the thing to. After the failure of my marriage and my affair, I was low and I started to drink. A lot."

"But then I met someone." And his eyes lifted up from his desk and met mine again. He smiled broadly.

"That person changed my life. I will tell you about him another time. That said, it is because of him and his discoveries that I found a new way to serve."

He stood and leaned his hands on his desk, head and chins bent down towards me.

"The non-bullshit line is: I have studied homeopathy, acupuncture, acupressure, herbal remedies. I combine that with my deep experience with western medicines and hit you with a combination of techniques- I am only one of five Master Homeopaths in the world. The bullshit line is:

I discovered I have a healing gift. I can visualize you as healthy- with some luck and some time, you will be well."

"Before you decide if you want to follow treatment with me, let's make sure we are on the same page. You are deeply insecure. Don't be offended. Everyone is. You are obsessed with how you look to your family. You see your family as a job, a duty. Since your nature resents any imposition into your bubble, you do not see your family for what they are. You see them as a burden. You love them, but what you love more is your self-image as a family man. And now that you've stepped out of the humdrum and into the world of criminality, your self-image is beyond repair. No matter what victories you may have had as a husband and father, they are hollow. Because even if your family does see you the way you want them to see you, it's a lie. You are not a good father, Roger. You are not a good husband either."

His words stung. Okay, stung is an understatement. His words felt like shotgun blasts to the gut. I felt actual physical discomfort, looking up at him and his cutting judgement. I had never been splayed out so completely before. I stood up in a wounded fog.

"I'm gonna," I mumbled weakly. I intended to go. He couldn't talk to me like that!

"Roger Clines," the doctor said softly and walked around the desk. He grabbed my hand. "I am not judging you, sir. I am accurately diagnosing the problems and offering you a path to wellness. Would you be interested in giving my therapy a shot?"

My faux-resentment left as quickly as it had risen

and I nodded. I was sold.

"Yes, I'd like that."

The hand hold became a shake as he pumped my hand.

"Glad to hear it Roger! Glad to hear it! I think we can fix things. Hmm? If you go out to the waiting room, the receptionist will have your medicine ready and will go over your treatment plan."

I stumbled back to the magazines and sat there. How had he known? Everything? How had he nailed me so perfectly? Maybe it's obvious and I'm an easy mark. I was looking for something, anything. He accurately summed me up. In a way even straight-shooting Roger couldn't. And maybe what he'd give me would help! Maybe?

Back to the treatment plan. What that meant was I owed 1,500 dollars for our initial meeting (all medicines prescribed included). Then one thousand dollars every month thereafter until plan conclusion. I asked the receptionist about our conclusion and she said at this point it was too soon to tell. I had to use a credit card to pay for the visit, but I knew Abby would be alright with it. That's a shit ton of money to pay anyone, let alone a quack. And I wasn't convinced he was a quack as he'd been so insightful. Seeing a doctor was a significant move. The kind of substantial step that would satisfy her.

The receptionist handed me three glass vials that contained tiny, round lactose tablets with instructions to take my first dose immediately.

I got into my car and ate eight tablets from each vial. I was shaken. The guy was weird. The meeting was weird. His questions were ridiculous. And yet, he knew me. He said criminality. How had he known? From my favorite breakfast cereal? No, he didn't ask me that question, but he may as well have. I didn't see any connections between his questions, my answers and any psychological insights. And holy shit that meeting cost fifteen hundred dollars.

Abby had been excited when I told her about it.

"You never know, Roger! What if it works? Do you feel any different since you took those pills?"

I don't think I felt anything from the pills. I definitely felt a slight internal shift, but I was chalking that up to my new sense of hope. Something about my meeting with Dr. Higgins left me hopeful. Bewildered and ashamed and skeptical, but still hopeful.

"A little," I said. Abby hugged me. I could tell she was hopeful too.

The next month was fairly smooth, and I felt like I was finally calming down. I was sleeping the entire night through, and in an overall better mood. The night before my second appointment, I was thinking about all of the silly things that had happened at my first meeting and decided to do some research. I looked into a few quack things online and was able to determine that yes, there was most likely a conspiracy with Big Pharma and Big Oil. I am not quick to jump on conspiratorial wagons, but I do subscribe to logic. Higgins story made sense in that regard. I read about the chem-trail conspiracy which was stupid. I read a bit about crystals and their energy fields and that was stupid too. But then, I'm not sure if he was pro-either.

I learned about homeopathy and that didn't look

legit. The dictionary says: the treatment of disease by minute doses of natural substances that in a healthy person would produce symptoms of disease. What this means is, hey if your joints hurt, let's give you a bit of this bark or flower that makes joints hurt in a healthy person and this will trigger your body to fix the problem. There are no clinical trials that prove efficacy. It's bullshit. I took the pills anyway, as I'd paid dearly for them.

I had never used the internet to look up conspiracies and got lost in a tunnel of crazy ideas. Each theory crazier than the next, but every once in a while, I would read something and think, sure I bet that's a thing. Like MK-Ultra, where our government secretly dosed people with LSD. That turned out to be real. I learned about the Drac. A vampiric, alien reptilian race that supposedly has infiltrated world governments at the highest levels. That was a good one. Some people believe that nearly all media video footage is manufactured by the same set of government actors. They've got photo after photo to prove it. See how Sam Donaldson's left earlobe is so large? See the same man in an old Folgers commercial and once again in the Bobby Kennedy assassination photo?

There was one thing I came across while researching conspiracy theories that stood out. I learned about a man named Roy Stacks. In the late seventies Roy was a wealthy, third-generation beet farmer in Montana. Summarizing miles of jazz, Roy discovers a white powdery substance that disappears when heated to a specific temperature and then reappears when it cools. He funds a bunch of research on the powder and scientists cannot say what it is, regardless of test. They could hold the white powder, touch the white powder, yet all scientific tests and instruments would report it as nothing. Roy surmises this to be manna, as referenced in the book of Exodus. When the Israelites were wandering in the desert after their escape from Egypt, God made it rain some white, light bread flakes called manna.

Roy was giving this white powder to several people and they reported gaining supernatural abilities.

I found a transcript of a speech Roy gave in Dallas.

Roy Stacks, Dallas February 1985:

"It's been called The Philosopher's Stone and the semen of God. When you mix the white powder of gold with water, it thickens up a bit like when you add powdered fiber. I can tell you it looks a lot like semen. Well, all, I'm a farmer. I see lots of it on the farm, with cattle. Yes, semen is an accurate way to describe it."

His speech was full of scientific methods and temperatures, all meaningless to me. By the time Roy finished the lecture he had explained how he descended from the Messianic line of King David from the Bible and is related to Jesus. And how he is becoming a superhuman from ingesting the white powder.

I dug a little more and saw that Roy was giving a lot of lectures during this time- trying to drum up additional funds for his research. I found a transcript of a speech in Denver.

Roy Stacks, Denver March 1985:

"They were talking about the white powder of gold in the hieroglyphs. The spit, the semen of God. The semen that spits from God. And I would know what I'm talking about, because I'm a farmer. We used a lot of semen on the farm."

I loved that he qualified knowledge of semen from being a farmer. After reading dumb shit on the internet, I got discouraged. I felt foolish. What part of me had thought that some mystical bullshit could work? None. I went to Higgins Holistic Healing so I could say I went. Not because I'd thought I could get fixed. And the price! What was I thinking? Ugh, that was telling because all I had been thinking was: what can I do to prove to Abby that I want to change? Better make it look good! Pathetic, huh?

But. But. The good Dr. Higgins knew things about me! He knew I'd broken the law. He knew how I felt. He knew intimate things about me that I hadn't even identified. Had I been conned? Maybe everyone breaks laws in some ways. Was this the same thing that happens to the poor sap who wants Jonathan Edwards to tell them what their dead mother is thinking? Did I have obvious tells? Was I standard? Did he give the same speech to everyone?

By the time I showed for my appointment the next day I had decided it was a con. That I had been vulnerable. That Dr. Higgins was ridiculous. That he definitely thought crystals are magical and then acted like he didn't when he read my disappointment. That my slight improvement had been coincidental. That I was going to get my money back. He could have his random fun facts and his horoscopes and his homeopathy and he could shove them up his ass. Fifteen hundred dollars would buy a lot of drugs. Self-therapy versus quack therapy. I liked the odds.

I stepped into the office and Higgins was standing at his office door.

"Welcome back, Roger."

He ushered me into his office and closed the door. I had been steamed for hours, but the anger inexplicably drained from me. I sat down, confused.

"You've been feeling better," he said, flatly.

"Yeah, but-," I faltered. I felt like my agenda kept getting reset. When I wasn't looking at the guy I could hold my own, but something about him in person calmed me. I struggled to decide how I wanted to express myself and I noticed the crystal was no longer on his desk. A-ha! I felt a small blip of rage from earlier. He was putting on a show.

"Where is your crystal?" I asked.

"Pish. I only keep that out for the nut-jobs. It makes them feel better."

"You determined I'm not a nut-job then?"

He laughed.

"You just aren't that kind of nut job."

I found a bit of my earlier courage.

"I read about homeopathy online. Why aren't there any clinical trials that prove it works? I'm a skeptic and the logic of it doesn't seem sound to me. I don't want to be impudent, I'm in your office. But at a thousand bucks a visit I am hoping to get some questions answered."

He leaned back in his chair and steepled his fingers

over his belly.

"You read about it online?"

"I did. I also read a bit about chem-trails and crystals. And vampire aliens."

"Ah yes, a bunch of whack doodles. I'm going to level with you. There is nothing in those pills I gave you. Purely milk sugar. Homeopathy is baloney, crystals are baloney, and horoscopes are baloney. The bottom line here is that I have an unexplained gift that allows me to look into people's minds and then to help them simply by visualizing their wellness."

He stood up, put his hands behind his back and paced a short spot, as if lecturing a class.

"Nobody wants to hear that. Sounds too much like magic. Sounds too much like a snow job. Therefore, I wrap it up in whatever the person wants to see. A patient believes in iridology? Well, I tell them I want to look in their eyes. They are Catholic? I tell them I want to pray. They like crystals? Then I set one out to help align their energy. You are right to be skeptical, but that's what we have. I heal you. You attribute it to whatever you want."

"What do you attribute it to?" I asked, looking up at him from my chair.

He shrugged. "You won't like my answer. The Light. I attribute it to The Light. But back to Mr. Clines. You are the reason for today."

He started to pace again; hands still clasped behind his back.

"You are skeptical. What some people see as magic, others see as science. Take the light switch, for example. You know that when you flip it a bulb will light. While a person from the Middle Ages would be crossing themselves. Magic! Your old thought patterns do not want you to evolve. But Roger, I ask you. If you could stand anywhere at any time, why would you stand in fire? I think something you are taking is hindering my work. Maybe cut out the kratom until next visit and we see how things go?"

I was first dumbfounded and then reflexively skeptic. Maybe he just guessed a commonly abused drug. Right.

"I really hope you will continue our treatment. I want to remove any barriers to your well-being. You will not be judged here, Roger. I simply want to do my job. It's amazing that I can do this but for some reason I've practically got to beg people to let me help."

I knew the answer to that one.

"One thousand dollars a visit."

He stood up and smiled.

"Hey, a man has got to eat. Premium price for a premium service. Why be shy? Stick with this another month and then see how you are feeling. Okay?"

I stood up to face him. I was taller and it was interesting to see a neck that tapers in reverse from my height.

"Stick with what? The sugar pills?"

"Yes. Let's stick with the treatment plan. Cut out the kratom for the next month. And stay away from conspiracy sites. Those people are bat-shit."

I smiled and said sarcastically, "Except for the Roy Stacks stuff, right? That stuff definitely is legit."

The Doctor opened his office door and gestured me

out, completely nonplussed. "Roy, yes. He's the person I met who changed my life. I referenced him at our last visit. I will have to introduce you when he comes out here next. Your life will change too. See you next time."

And you all must know that at this point I had decided to check my logic. I respected the answer he had given me about his gift, but I didn't buy that he actually had one. But wait. Had he just popped off about Roy "White Gold" Stacks as if he were credible? Was he being sarcastic to counter me? I didn't think he was. I wondered how long the treatment plan would be as I paid for the visit that I swore I wouldn't have. Then I scheduled a follow up appointment. You know why?

Because, what if?

I've made it back to the Nightingale Market and I'm pretty sure that's Tarek up ahead. Yes, he's waving at me, that's him.

We are behind schedule and are supposed to be up at Mount Horeb tonight. It's already dark and the mountain is about 45 miles east. I'll explain more when I can, if I can. Hopefully, I don't get killed out here.

I hate getting into cars with people I don't know, but it's something I do now. Wish me luck.

THE MYSTERIES OF MOSES

We are camped out on the south face of a sandstone plateau known as Serabit el Khadim (the Prominence of the Khadim). It's not an especially tall mountain-its summit is about 2,600 feet. Our specific location is 29°02'05.3"N 33°27'31.9"E.

Tarek had waited for me to grab a phone adapter at the Nightingale Market. The store was stacked with goods from floor to ceiling. The variety of items was astonishing. M and M's to iPhones, dolls to chips. Their chip selection was massive. There was an entire wall display of multiple chip flavors. The logo and bags looked a little like Lays. They were called Chipsy. Tarek translated for me: Salt, Tomato, Chili & Lemon, Cheese, Spiced Cheese, French Cheese, Black Pepper, Tomato & Thyme, Mixed Cheddars. I had always thought the wall of choice was an American thing.

And the chocolate was refrigerated. There were the

standard mini-mart cold drink racks, half full of Twix and Snickers. I asked Tarek about it. He shrugged and said, "No AC." There is no AC or beer, but by God, you get your choice of chip flavor. I thought briefly about the consequences of stealing something from the Nightingale Market versus an Albertson's in the States. God Bless America! It's easier to steal!

I did have a friend who just came back from Washington DC and he told me that the number one criterion for vetting a place to live was this: Do they have armed guards at grocery stores? He was there for a week, and he said there were armed guards at every grocery store he went to. There were no armed guards at the Nightingale. A bag of chips is never worth your hand.

Tarek was a good travelling companion. His English had slight British edges and he knew the area. He was full of jokes. Terrible ones. Here are the ones I remember:

Where do Pharaohs like to eat? Pizza Tut.

Why didn't Cleopatra go to the psychiatrist? She's Queen of Denial.

What kind of music do mummies listen to? Wrap.

We headed north east from Abu Zenima, and I was surprised at the quality of the highway. We were in the most desolate of desolates out here and the road was freshly paved. Fun fact: even though a third of the country can hardly afford food, the western access road through the Sinai mountain range is smooth sailing. The nearest good-sized city is Sharm El-Sheikh- it's on the eastern coast, about three hundred miles away. If that city sounds familiar it could be because ISIS dropped a plane there in 2015 killing 224 people. Or maybe you remember the Islamist Bedouin attack in 2005 where 88 people, mostly tourists, were blown up. I'm foregoing my usual American snark on this issue. Roger Clines is completely aware that you could be anywhere at any time and get blown up. Like in the United States, at the zoo. Ugh.

The circular guilt reminds me of why I'm here. I need to catch you up before Roy arrives. When he does, we are going under the mountain through an old cave system to a little known, underground pharaonic forge. At the top of the mountain is an ancient Egyptian temple, dedicated to the goddess Hathor. It was built by pharaoh Sneferu in about 2600 BC and appears to have been in operation for about 1200 years. The temple proper was discovered by Sir W.M. Flinders Petrie in 1904, but according to Dr. Higgins, only a select few know about the hidden furnace. I don't know if I am going to survive the night and while Tarek was hilarious and easy-going, he wore a shoulder holster on the outside of his t-shirt. There was a big handgun in that holster. I wonder if Tarek is going to kill me if things go south, or if Roy is going to do it himself.

Why am I speaking of my death so casually? And what the fuck? My new age egghead pharmacist.

After I'd been shaken during our second visit I followed the treatment plan. I quit the kratom, and yes it did make me sick, mildly. I can check unpleasant kratom withdrawal off my bucket list now. I had raging insomnia for a couple of weeks and restless legs at night. What a torture that is, eh? Any of you ever experienced any withdrawals and got the restless legs? It's a little thing, like a paper cut, that has huge impacts. You can't sleep and you can't stop moving your legs. They keep twitching and have a dull ache that only movement can soothe. Awful. Mild, flu-like symptoms, irritable, couldn't sleep, constant runny nose. After about two weeks the symptoms cleared up and I felt the best I'd felt in years. I knew it wasn't the milk tablets, though I was still taking those as instructed. I attributed my gains to the fact that I wasn't dosing kratom.

I revisited the white powder stuff online, but it still looked like baloney. I hadn't gone New Age. Roy Stacks appeared unhinged. He sounded like Randy Quaid. He drank the semen of God, traced his lineage back to Jesus of Nazareth and then goes out and tries to raise money? He'd been denied the permits he needed for a test facility and his patents mysteriously expired when he refused to share his mono-atomic gold research with the government. Super humans don't need money or patents, Roy.

By my third visit, my life was going better. My relationships at home and at work were going well. I'd been keeping my temper. Abby remarked that I was much more pleasant to be around. She said I was calmer. And I was. I was sleeping through the night again. My kids still said stupid things, but I was never phased. Higgins knew already.

"Things going quite well, eh Roger?" he smiled as he ushered me into his office.

"Yes, they are. I think stopping the kratom was

really good for me. How did you know, by the way?"

He waved me to sit in front of his desk.

"You spent all of your formative years living on an east/west street. You told me so the first day we met."

I laughed and sat down. I was feeling good. I made a basic connection at that moment. When you didn't totally hate yourself, people's craziness doesn't irritate you. It's just funny. I went with it.

"Right on, doctor. I've been sleeping every night. I've been more patient. More productive."

He nodded and walked around to the front of his desk, where he sat on the corner, one leg dangling. "Yes. Yes, this is very good. Now. I have two very serious things I need to say to you today. I need you to hear me. Are you hearing me right now?"

I nodded and he leaned down towards me, staring me in the eyes. He had watery blue eyes with puffy pink-rimmed lids.

"First, I don't care how many laws you've broken. I'm your doctor, not a cop. Do you understand?"

My good feeling evaporated. I felt the room yawning. My face was fire-flushed and I wanted to look away, but his eyes kept me focused. I wondered what he knew and how he knew it.

"I understand."

"The second thing. The people who died because of you are all in a better place. You've got to know, Roger."

Ninety trillion emotions flooded me and my brain overloaded. Relief, fear, exhaustion, anger, doubt, shame, guilt, understanding, forgiveness. They all came speeding in like an air squadron. The next thing

I knew I was standing, sobbing and the doctor was holding me. I stood there hugging the good Dr. Higgins and cried like a baby for nearly half an hour. He was silent the entire time, patting my back now and then.

And that's what happened at our third visit. I had cried a lot since the zoo, but never that deeply. After I came out of it, I apologized and stepped back.

"No need, Roger. I'm proud of you."

He beamed at me as he opened the door of his office and ushered me out, red-faced.

"You are on your way to wellness now, Mr. Clines. Until next time, enjoy."

I felt ridiculous as I paid another grand, wiping my nose with a tissue. The receptionist acted as if weeping patients were standard and typically curt.

I did not go straight home afterwards. I found myself driving up The Wheel, winding to the east side where the punk was buried. I knew I shouldn't go there. Ever, ever. And yet I was compelled. As I drove, I thought about what Higgins had said. What kind of powers did the guy have? My bet was that he had zero magic healing powers, but plus ten when it came to human behavior. He also had a soothing and deep charisma. I'd gone into the last two visits with the intention of telling him to take a hike, and yet each time all I did was nod, agree, feel good and schedule a follow up. He just gets how people work, I thought. And I was an open book, full of angst. An easy read. I turned at the side road off the spoke, and about a hundred feet down the trail I was blocked by a yellow band of police tape.

What the fuck?!

I backed up quickly onto the road. I blazed down the slope to town. What the hell was going on? Had they found him? Did they connect the bomb to him? If so, I was in trouble for sure. I had been so careless. Have you ever seen forensic crime documentaries where the cops link a fiber with a DNA test and a hair and catch murderers? It is nearly impossible to not leave some sort of forensic trail behind. I could have left a hair. There were probably fibers from my car trunk. I had applied the barest of minimum, underwhelming effort to cover my crime.

I stopped at a McDonald's to wash my face before I went home. My eyes were swollen and red. My heart was jack hammering. I washed my hands- they were trembling uncontrollably. I wondered if I should even go back home. I didn't know if the cops were on to me or not. I was assuming, and not wildly, that the tape meant they'd found the body. Maybe a hiker stumbled across it, or a dog dug it up? I knew they would find some sort of link. Cell phone records to Roger's phone? Ugh. GPS cell coordinates? Forensic evidence in my trunk? Or in the garage? Surveillance footage at the grocery store, or maybe at the Japanese Car Wash?

I went home. There were no police waiting. I made up a story about how I accidentally pepper sprayed myself looking at a colleague's defense kit. The family loved that one. They love stories where Dad is an idiot.

After I told this lie, Abby joined me in the shower and washed my entire body. She shampooed my hair.

She had me lie face down on the bed afterwards and she massaged my neck and shoulders and back. She was so good to me. She said it was 'Because you do so much for us, you go through so much for us, I love you so much.' She rushed out of the room and down the hall. She returned at full speed with both hands behind her back.

"Pick a hand," she said excitedly.

I laughed and chose her left.

She whipped out a Cherry Hi-C juice box. I'd grown fond of them. I know that's disturbing. I have no excuse.

"Cherry Hi-C," she said. "But that's not all. Pick another hand."

I pointed at her right.

She produced another Cherry Hi-C juice box.

"Another Cherry Hi-C. Because one is never enough. Right?"

She was quoting me. I had started drinking Cherry Hi-C. Lots of it. I'd become demonstrative about it. "I love Cherry Hi-C. I love two Cherry Hi-C's. Because one is never enough." My family just thought that was random old Roger, being a nut. Instead it was me being gross. But that's not my point. My point here, is my darling Abby. She worked overtime to comfort and please her lying, sleazy husband.

That is just one way a lie I told has hurt me. There were countless times I'd done something stupid, or too many drugs, only to go lie to Abby and be rewarded with her sympathy. Abby deserved better than me, and things were about to get worse.

The police finally did show up. They came to the

house about ten in the morning on a Friday. I was only at home because I had an eleven o'clock appointment with Higgins that day and hadn't planned on going into the office until after lunch. I was lucky I was there- everyone else was gone. Kids at school, wife at work.

It was terrifying. They'd found his body. He'd been dead for months. They wanted to know how I knew him. Detective Larry Schmidt, a giant man and the lead detective, had been consulting with Detective Vega on an unrelated case. They were going over traffic cam footage at Loughton Avenue and Twelfth, and miracle upon miracles, Schmidt recognized his victim sitting in the passenger seat of a car. Heading to The Wheel. Around his approximate time of death. So, naturally they ran the license plates and that led them to me. How did I know him? (I bought pot from him from time to time.) When was the last time I saw him or heard from him? (Several months ago.) What we were you doing heading out of the valley that evening? (He took me to a road off The Wheel where we met with a dealer. One of those, hey I can get it for you, but I need a ride, sort of things.)

Horrible questions and horrible answers but I did my cornered best. This was not unexpected. I'd been sloppy. I hadn't considered things. I hadn't been deliberate or stealthy at all. There must be closed-circuit footage of me yet to be discovered. Maybe me heading up Loughton Avenue in the middle of the night? So many loose ends. The cops left, but I could tell they were suspicious. They knew something wasn't right. They had saved the worst for the very last and Detective Schmidt casually said: It's no big deal if we request a DNA sample, right? You'd be up for that?

I told them of course, no problem. They left without incident. But the thoughts that sprung from the button he pushed when he asked for DNA took over and I had to sit down. Every thought I had was prison. The house was quiet and I was already feeling nostalgic. Looking at the rust colored rug Abby picked out for the living room. Sitting on the soft couch that I only payed three hundred dollars for ten years ago. It's still nice and soft. I looked around as if I were on my way to the big house and would never see it again. That strange, almost dreamlike condition lasted for about ten minutes and then my cellphone got a text alert that shook me out of it.

"Be Well Soon... See you at 11:00 a.m. -HHH"

Clever. It pulled me back from the brink. My pragmatism kicked into gear and I started thinking about lawyers. I was going to need one. Even if they never did come back and ask for my DNA, there were so many other loose ends I was certain they'd eventually make it to me. Then they would get the DNA. Then I'd be done. Toast. Imprisoned, humiliated, cast out of society. Ugh. I hated my options. Step one, get a lawyer. Oh no, folks. Step one was to go cancel my HHH appointment so I would have the money to get a lawyer.

I made it to their office right at eleven and Higgins was waiting for me at his door.

"Come in! Come in! I have exciting news, Roger."

I was on a mission but the moment I stepped into

Higgins' office I fell under his spell. I found myself sitting down in my usual seat.

"Excellent news, Roger! But first, a story."

The Story Dr. Higgins Told Me About Moses:

Amenhotep was born to an influential royal concubine circa 1394 BC and was educated at the Heliopolis by the Egyptian priests of Ra. Due to his mother's prominence, he was married to the royal princess, Nefertiti, who was also his half-sister, to reign as co-regent while their father fell ill. When their father died, he succeeded as Amenhotep IV.

Amenhotep IV did not like the power religious leaders had. He declared all of their gods to be pagan and shut down their temples. To fill the void, he developed the idea of an all-encompassing deity, Aten. He then changes his name to Akhenaten (Glorious Spirit of the Aten).

Akhenaten and Nefertiti are recorded to have had six daughters. There were plots against his life and threats designed to eliminate his hard line on the old gods. In 1361 BC he was banished from Egypt. He was replaced first by his cousin Smenkhkare, and then succeeded by his son, Tutankhaten, son of his deputy Queen, Kiya.

When Tutankhaten took over the kingdom at age eleven, he had to change his name to Tutankhamun. A move to symbolize a disavowal of Aten and back to the old god Amen. A move to undo his father's legacy. Meanwhile exiled Akhenaten fled to Sinai, to a rarely used temple atop Mount Horeb. Today this place is known as Serabit el Khadim.

Akhenaten's story continues, but not as

Akhenaten. At home, after Tut's short reign and a few minor hand-offs, the next significant pharaoh, Horemheb, forbade the mention of Akhenaten's name and removed the Amarna Kings from the signature King List. He then destroyed many monuments from the era, which explains why the discovery of Tutankhamun's tomb wasn't found until 1922. The Aten's were erased.

But outside of Egypt, Akhenaten fires up the secret forges of the Temple at Serabit and cooks some white powder of gold. He ingests this and becomes superhuman. He decides to go back home and use his powers to take his throne back, but he doesn't have any supporters left. The only people who rally behind him as the rightful leader of Egypt are the Israelite slaves. He decides to take these people and leave, and start a new kingdom but Egypt isn't keen on losing almost half a million slaves. He uses the power the white powder of gold gave him, performs many miracles (the plagues of Egypt) and then splits the sea (the Red Sea), leading his new people out.

He marches them straight to Serabit el Khadim. When he leaves the people at the bottom of the mountain, they can hear a great rumbling. They assume it means he was talking to God to get the Ten Commandments. The fact is that the rumbling was the forge working up, so their leader could get some more magic manna.

Their leader's name became Moses. In Hebrew it is a verb that means "to draw out/pull out [of water]." It is incorrectly applied to give weight to the baby in the reeds on the river story. It is the name that was given to him when he pulled the Israelites through the sea.

"Now that you have the prologue Roger, the news! Roy has agreed to meet with you and help you create some white powder of gold yourself. Roy doesn't believe the powder should be made for others, and that if it were distributed it would be hoarded and fought over. If you want some, you need to fire it yourself. That takes a special forge. One that is capable of heating the gold to incredibly high temperatures. If you can move quickly, Roy plans to use a secret forge, hidden underneath Serabit el Khadim at the end of the month. The temple was discovered in the early 1900's, but even today the existence of the underground chambers is shared by only a few."

"Needless to say, whether you go or not, we expect the utmost discretion regarding any of this."

I nodded. I couldn't help it. Higgins really was an okay cat. I even liked the Moses-was-really-a-deposed-pharaoh story. That would explain a lot. But I wasn't buying any of it for a single second. He was extremely persuasive, but I knew crazy. Higgins was crazy. Roy Stacks was crazy.

"There is a slight hitch you need to be aware of. If you have evil intent, or darkness in your soul, like a murder or something, then the powder comes out black, not white. It works the same, but it belies the evil in the creator's heart. This is another reason Roy doesn't believe in making it for people. He doesn't want this stuff in the wrong people's hands. It's for people like you. People who want to ascend."

I wanted to ascend away from the police, but I'd already witnessed one ascension and I never want to have my own. Punk ascended/descended into a dirt hole. Which got discovered. And the police were aware of my existence. Ugh. I was about ready to get up, jolly fun speech and all.

"In any case Roger, you must know that if it comes out black, they will kill you on the spot. We cannot have this powder falling into the wrong hands."

I laughed. I was definitely the wrong hands. Double-time to go, right? Roy Stacks will shoot me when I fire white powder of gold under Serabit if it is black? Even if I'd been bored enough (I was not) to follow the trail, death when something you burn turns black is a non-starter.

Higgins continued.

"But you don't need to worry about that. I'm sure you're fine, Roger. You have a good heart. The past is the past. And this stuff is really something, Roger. This is what enables me to heal you, and more! You can better yourself, and discover your purpose more easily. You're gonna love it. The manna does everything. I mean, it even changes your DNA. It literally alters your DNA! You will evolve!"

Wait. A. Second. It alters your DNA? I happened to be in immediate need of new DNA. I know it's ridiculous, but short of lawyering up and confessing, or getting arrested when they match my DNA, is there any other possible shot? Real life or fairy tale? Maybe I'd rather die than go to prison, I reasoned.

I was in. All in. I required that DNA. I didn't care how long the shot was. I purchased a ticket from LAX to Cairo the next day. Figured I'd just buy a ticket back when I was done. If I survived. I told Abby I had an emergency work assignment for disaster relief in Dallas. There had been tragic flooding in that area and it wasn't uncommon for engineers like me to pitch in at catastrophe recovery. Another lie gone well, folks. Got my shots. Snuck my passport out from the small fireproof safe Abby keeps it in. Got the meet date and time confirmed from Higgins, along with Tarek's contact information. Got my Egyptian Tourist VISA. It only took four days. And here I am.

Due to our camp site elevation you can see for miles. I can see a few headlights in the distance winding their way across the horizon toward us. I assume that's Roy.

I'm not crazy. And I'm not on any drugs. Couldn't bring any on the plane. So, you know I'm sober. I'm afraid the cops will make their way back to me. I left too much evidence behind. My only shot is to beat the DNA test. And my only shot at doing that, either within the scope of possibility or impossibility, is to make white powder of gold, pray it doesn't turn black, drink it, pray it alters DNA, jet back home, pray the cops haven't come around looking for me yet, and pass the test quietly when and if they ask for a sample. Lots of prayers to I don't know who.

Watching Roy's procession wind up, I feel ashamed that I ever blamed this on Brian. I'm not here because of Water Day. I'm here because Fire Day fucked me up. It was Charlie's fault. Okay, Okay. I'm here because I fucked up, and I don't want to pay the price. I want to cheat.

I could die out here, in the Sinai Peninsula. Abby would have no idea where I was. At some point, they would find flight records to Egypt, but would they ever find my body? Abby and the kids wouldn't know whether Dad was alive or dead. Thinking I'd committed whatever horrible crimes and then abandoned them. Charlie was almost done with high school, but the junior high kids would be heartless to Benji. His dad would be the boogeyman. Awful. And Abby. Her reward for supporting me. For believing in me. To be lied to and tricked by her murderous, thieving, drug-addled husband. And finally, abandoned when he fled to Egypt.

What I am about to do is the culmination of an avalanche of poor choices, and the most selfish move to date. I intend to make it out. If I do not survive tonight, that's where you guys come in.

I've told you a lot about me. You are at an advantage. You know my story, warts and all, but I will never know any of you. What I'm getting at, is that I have to assume a lot when I talk to you guys. And I assume I have opened myself up way too much. I'm too real. I'm the Conner family from Roseanne with none of the forced charm. But Abby. She is just sunshine and light. She deserves so much better. If you don't hear from me in the next month or so, will you tell her what happened?

Use the internet or something. It's Clines, with a "C."

THE FORGE UNDER THE MOUNTAIN

Currently at 35,000 feet, heading west. I'm going home! We had one stop in London, and we left a short time ago- I should hit LAX in about ten hours. I'd phoned Abby from Heathrow, but pretended to be in Dallas. She was happy to hear from me and didn't sound like she suspected anything. It's a goddamn miracle I made it out of Egypt alive. It's a long flight. I will tell you everything.

Roy and his entourage arrived at the campsite around 11:00 p.m. He had a driver, which I thought was disappointing. Wouldn't an enlightened being want to drive themselves? He stepped out from the back of a Jeep and waved at Tarek and me.

"Roger. You made it," he smiled as he walked towards me, arms outstretched.

He hugged me, clapping my back hard.

"Good to see you. Good to see you. Tarek take good care of you?"

"He was hilarious."

As Roy's driver approached me, I experienced a surreal moment. His driver looked exactly like Tarek. My head swiveled to the left and then right.

Tarek laughed. "My twin brother, Mido."

Two white Toyota pickups followed and four Bedouins joined us. I think they were Bedouins. Tarek and Mido were both dressed like me, with jeans, t-shirt and tennis shoes. But the four Bedouins wore filthy, ragged robes and head coverings. They looked like they slept outside in the dirt every night of their lives. Rough. They each had long curved blades strapped to their belts, while Mido was armed with a revolver in a shoulder holster, just like Tarek.

One of the desert natives lit a torch and led the way while another stayed behind to keep watch. We walked up the mountain a short bit then dropped down into a slight, unseen gully. Behind some scrawny, stemmy shrubs was a cave.

The seven of us made our way down into the mountain, a Bedouin with a torch at our front and at the rear.

"We have an army," I said to Roy as we walked through a series of downward sloping tunnels. The halls were squared and the walls were precise. They looked as if they were cut by machines.

"Can't be too careful," he said. He gestured back at the Bedouins in the rear. "They are absolute protection. You are in good hands with us Roger. Are you excited? You should be. One way or another, after tonight your life changes forever."

I shuddered. This was the second time someone

had casually mentioned killing me in the last year. I had decided I did not like Roy Stacks. Not one bit.

We had gone down zigzagging, sloped halls for about fifteen minutes when the passage narrowed considerably and ended at a slim doorway. There was an ancient wooden door, braced with iron and an orange glow emanated from the cracks. The lead Bedouin stopped at the door and backed up so Roy could enter first.

Roy paused and looked back at me.

"You are about to set eyes on a holy, secret place that few have seen. Higgins explained the consequences of burning black?"

I nodded. Burning black? What the hell was I doing here again?

"Are you ready Mr. Clines?"

"Ready," I said, trying to sound brave. I was terrified. My Wally voice was running around frantically in circles, banging a loud pot.

"Danger! Red Alert! Defcon and such!" Wally cried. "Turn around. Don't be stupid!"

But Wally was the boy who cried wolf at this point. He'd screamed from the heavens at every step of every day. White Noise Wally.

Roy pulled on the heavy door and it swung open with a groan. Bright, orange light flooded the chamber along with the sounds of fire. We filed into the room. It was a long, low space, with a glowing, stone forge at the far end. I guessed the room was about a hundred feet long and you could feel a thick wall of heat just from stepping in. I thought that if it were so hot this far away from the fire, there would be no way you could get close to the forge to operate it. How did they stoke it?

About halfway into the room there was a wide pit cut into the floor. Two men wearing nothing but shorts, bodies glistening with sweat, crawled out.

"It's ready," one panted. The two guys shakily made their way to the entrance where our lead Bedouin had two canteens ready for them. I think they were canteens because they each drank from them. They looked like bloated and cured animal organs. Do they make canteens from camel stomachs?

"It's beautiful, isn't it, Roger?" Roy asked. He was staring at the glowing forge.

"It's hot," I responded.

He began removing his clothes. I stepped back. What the fuck? When he was down to his boxers he knelt down beside his backpack and pulled out a leather apron. It looked like a classic blacksmith's apron from a medieval movie. Something happened to the dude's eyes when he put on the apron. His eyes got wider, like an anime character. I do not believe in magic, though I'm cautiously optimistic there are things still to be discovered. But I don't think that was in my head. His eyes widened and he got a fevered look.

"Blacksmiths, Roger. Blacksmithing is a royal skill, handed down from great king to great king. Many of the ancient Pharaohs were blacksmiths. Moses was a blacksmith. Moses' brother Aaron was a blacksmith. King Solomon the Wise was a blacksmith. They had it wrong about Jesus. He wasn't a woodworker; he was a blacksmith extraordinaire.

These metal workers have all done spectacular things, from the Pyramids to the parting of the Red Sea to raising the dead and walking on water!"

He was getting worked up, sounding like a villain in a campy movie.

"Do you know how the Egyptians made iron tools, Roger? Ever stopped to think about how they did it? First, they would collect some iron bearing dirt, like a dark soil from a river bed. Then they crafted a stone chimney. They would build a roaring fire inside and pour in loads of the soil and charcoal, then repeat for a few days. Pour in some more dirt. Shovel in some more charcoal. Repeat. After it cooled, they would break up the chimney and at the bottom there would be a chunk of iron mixed with slagg. The chunk is called a bloom."

"Then they would bring the bloom to a forge, just like this one, only less grand of course. Finally, the bloom is placed into the forge until it is red hot, where it is gently hammered, first on one side, then the other. Each flip resulted in more metal, less slagg, until what is left is pure iron. The piece that is left is called the billet. And that is what you then hammer into shape for a weapon or a tool. Amazing, isn't it?"

"But today, we aren't talking about common metal work. We are going to fire gold into a mono-atomic state where it becomes a powder. The powder contains all the powers in the universe. Power over gravity, thus over time. The Pharaohs used this powder to render the pyramid blocks weightless. Moses used this powder to rain plagues upon Egypt and even to feed the Israelites. The Druids used it to build Stonehenge. Jesus used this powder to heal the sick. What will you use it for Roger?"

Shit. I hadn't expected a test. I wasn't sure how close Higgins and Stacks were, but part of me felt like the thousands of dollars I paid Higgins were installments towards a guarantee.

"I want to change. I want to change for the better. I want to be a better husband and father."

And I wanted to hope against hope and bet against reality. I wanted this fairy-tale, clandestine shit to work. I wanted it to re-code my DNA. Ha! I didn't care about super powers, I just wanted to stay out of jail. And alive, if you please.

Stacks liked my answer and nodded.

"It's time."

He motioned to Tarek. It looked like the when-this-guy-burns-shit-black-shoot-him look to me. I liked Tarek too. Tarek lifted some sort of cudgel? A rod about four feet long, with a metal spoon on the end. What were they going to do to me? Spoon spear me? I had just assumed I was going to be shot, not killed by an ancient torture device. We walked down the room towards the forge, stepped around the rectangular pit and got as close to the forge as we could.

At about five feet away both the roar of the furnace and the heat were nearly unbearable. I was a sweaty, drenched mess. My t-shirt stuck to my middle-aged physique like on a girl at a wet –shirt contest. Roy's entire body glistened in the shimmering heat. Tarek looked as comfortable as I did, lifting his shirt and mopping his face with the hem.

"Ok, Roger. Here's what you need to do. Take this gold and place it in the bowl here."

He handed me a fist-sized gold nugget. It seemed hefty to me. I tried to calculate the weight. About five pounds? I don't know the precise value of gold, but in my mind when I think of stock reports I hear "the price of gold has gone up again. It's now something dollars an ounce." Five pounds, eighty ounces of gold? I didn't think it was actually gold. Roy Stacks, who gave speeches about being in the Jesus Messianic bloodline to get donations, certainly wasn't burning a hundred grand of gold for me as a favor to Higgins.

Tarek handed me the not-cudgel and I placed the chunk in the metal spoon.

"Now, extend the crucible into the furnace. Be careful to keep it level. It's going to liquefy before it granulates. Don't want to spill this."

I stretched the rod out into the glow, sweat pouring into my eyes.

"How long do I keep it in there?" I asked.

"Not long. I will tell you when. It will take about three minutes or so. Just focus on keeping it level. Breathe."

I breathed and focused. My eyes were stinging with sweat and I couldn't see. My arms ached from being extended. I know. Only three minutes. But it was hell in there. And while I was reassured that I wasn't going to be stuck to death, the gun was still looming over my head. I prayed. Please don't turn black. Please don't turn black.

After what felt like a solid hour, Roy spoke.

"Pull it back now Roger. Gently. Keep it level and

bring it back."

Tarek pulled something that looked like a stone mortar from his bag.

"Pour it here. Carefully. Careful don't burn me!" he said.

I squinted through the burn and managed to aim the spoon into the bowl and dump. I quickly wiped my face with a wet arm and peered in. It was white! The powder was white folks! No gun in Roger's back tonight, I thought. I was so relieved I started to laugh. I got a bit of confidence back, and used it to get out of there. The heat of the room was suffocating me and once I knew I wasn't going to die I wanted out.

"Cool. Let's talk outside the furnace," I said and headed through the wooden door into the outer chamber. There must have been a drop of fifty degrees. You could still feel arms of heat reaching out here and there. I peeled off my sopping shirt. Roy and the rest filed out after. Tarek had the stone bowl with my powder. The Bedouins grabbed their torches and headed up the tunnels.

The millionth odd thing about the night- that's it? All this hubbub to meet little old Roger and burn him a hundred k of gold? Tarek dumped the powder into a Ziploc baggie and handed it to me.

"Now that's about 48 grams of powder there for you, Roger," said Roy. He handed me a towel from his pack and took one for himself. We dried off while he talked. His eyes looked normal to me and I wondered if it was the heat that caused some illusion that gave him cartoon eyes by the fire.

"I'm not a doctor. I didn't come across this powder

to try and save mankind. I do not know exactly what this stuff will do to you. We've done some experiments. The first person we tested this on was Will French. The ancient Egyptians had a belief that you have both a physical body and a light body. And that you have to nourish your light body, just like a physical body. This is the stuff they fed their light body. They would drink 500 mg of the powder a day, for 30 days. This was the royal rite of passage. That is what Will took. 500 mg a day, for 30 days."

"On the fourth day Will says he begins to hear a perpetual high frequency sound. Each day it gets progressively louder. By the tenth day he said the sound was like loudspeakers in his brain, constantly roaring. This sound is roaring in Will's head. It's roaring day and night. It's roaring when he's falling asleep or at work. It sounds horrible right? I ask him about it and he says, 'No. It's nourishing. I would be sad without it.'"

"At the end of the 30 days he figured the sound would die away, but it didn't. It grows louder every day, and still is he says. Sixty days after finishing the powder he began to have dreams, then revelations, then visions. On the 97th day after taking the powder he calls me breathless and says, 'you aren't going to believe this. I was visited by light beings last night! They taught me things! They explained things! They didn't use words, there were no sounds, but they spoke to me telepathically.' Of course, Roger, believe what you will, but know I'm telling you the truth here."

"After a few months, Will started to have orgasms.

No erection, no emission, but still, he's having orgasms. I asked him what it was like. He said 'It's just like an actual orgasm.' He has about twenty to thirty a day. He has no control over them. He only sleeps thirty minutes a night now, and can tell you what you will have for lunch tomorrow, or why you called him on the phone before you can get it out."

"At month ten, Will became capable of levitating and bio-locating. This means he can snap his fingers here and reappear anywhere on the globe at whim. I know this sounds insane, but here's some science. When Will's light body grew to encompass his physical body, he became a superconductor. Have you heard of a scientist named Sakharov? He says that gravity is not a gravitational field. That gravity is actually the inter-reaction of matter- protons, neutrons, electrons with vacuum energy. He calculates that when matter is resonance connected in two dimensions, the third-dimension drops. Then matter retains only 56 percent of original weight, which is why your powder weighs less than the chunk we threw in. Resonance connected material that resonates in two dimensions as a quantum oscillator, is the actual definition of a superconductor."

"This will activate your 'junk' DNA. Only called junk because scientists have no idea what it's for. Ever wondered about the unused ninety percent of your brain they are always talking about? It's for ascendance."

Of course, I don't believe in mumbo jumbo. But for a man in the market for clean DNA, Roy's science-speak seemed legit to me. I sat, deep under a mountain, holding my wet shirt and listened to Roy raptly. Admittedly, I have no understanding of space-time, or of the science behind gravity. The one thing I do understand is chemistry. And I don't mean I understand how one mole plus one mole can equal just one mole. I understand chemistry from the standpoint of a daily drug user. And by that, I mean I know chemistry decides. Chemistry is the final arbiter. You can want to stay awake when you take a Xanny bar, but you can't beat chemistry. You out.

A man like me doesn't need to be convinced to try a drug. The research chemicals I ordered online were proof of that. Several Chinese laboratories created analog versions of several drugs in the early 2000's. Analog here simply means a compound that has similar properties to an illegal drug. Synthetic chemicals that push the same buttons as their counterparts. Chemical-analog THC, chemical-analog meth, chemical-analog hallucinogens and such. Before the government locked that down, you could order limitless amounts of these fully legal compounds that fucked you up, indistinguishable from the real thing. I smoked, snorted, and ate volumes of those until the government cracked down with the Federal Analogues Act. This act says that any substance that is chemically similar and generates the same effects as a banned drug is just as bad as the real thing.

Not that this powder was a drug. It was a mineral. Like an iron pill. But Stacks described Mr. Will French as being perpetually high. And that sounded appealing. I turned the plastic bag of powder over in my hands while he talked. I was starting to look at the powder in a different light. Because Roy wasn't sounding like a mad man to me. He was starting to sound genuine. Before you judge me too harshly for softening my stance, please consider my great need for this to be real. This had to work. You know they are coming for me. I know they are coming for me. This had to work. And I had gone this far. And was under Serabit El-Khadim. With some manna in my lap. I combined my pressing need with the story Higgins told me about Amenhotep IV/Akhenaten/Moses. I combined that with the sounds-like-he-knows-what-he's-talking-about science jazz. Maybe this will actually work, I thought. Maybe Brian was right. Because, what if?

"Would you really have killed me if it had come out black?" I asked, feeling safe for the first time since I arrived in Egypt.

Stacks and Tarek both laughed.

"Of course not. I'm no killer, I'm a seeker. I tell people that so I can gauge their intent. We've had two people turn away at the door when I asked them if they were ready. They both paused and I could see they were considering whether to go in or not. As if they were calculating their sins and then weighing them against the risk of burning black powder. I'm glad they didn't get any. Who knows what those dark souls would want to use their powers for?"

"What happens when it does burn black?" I asked, confused. "Nothing?"

"It doesn't turn black Roger. It's science, not magic. We just use it as a screener. A most efficacious screener. You had no hesitation earlier. None. You were ready to go. Can you imagine how a murderer would squirm standing at this hot door? Not knowing if he was about to fire something in a forge and then get his head blown off?"

I could imagine how a murderer would squirm standing at the ancient door. I could imagine it very well. It's a miracle that Roger, the man with no poker face, pulled off a smooth entry.

We were interrupted by the Bedouins. They burst into the chamber, breathless, brandishing their wicked blades. When Roy saw that the Bedouin who was standing guard had come down, he stood up alarmed.

"Who is keeping watch?" he asked with a frown on his face.

The natives all had blanched faces. Mido just pointed dumbly from where they had come, his revolver out. A group of heavily armed men burst in, automatic weapons drawn, shouting. I don't know how many there were. More than five.

"Down on the ground! Get down on the ground!" they shouted.

Tarek and Mido each dropped to one knee and had their guns trained in a second, but it was an empty gesture. The strangers were wearing body armor. A handful of red sighting lights crawled over the twins' chests. It was futile.

"Don't think about it. Drop your little guns."

'Think' sounded like tink.

The speaker pulled his mask up casually and lit a cigarette. Blonde hair, blue eyes, square jaw and giant. He was the tallest man on Earth.

"You must see," he said between drags, in a ragged, cartoony German-American accent. No W's, just V's. "We have you outnumbered. It would be stupid for any of you to fight back."

The mercenary gestured to the polished stone floor.

"Knives go here. Guns go here. Get to the ground."

Tarek looked at Roy and slowly placed his gun on the ground then lay face down. Mido followed reluctantly. The intruders moved their sights to the Bedouins who were tightly grouped by the forge door.

"Stupid knives. Shoot them."

There was a brief silence, punctuated by the sound of me dropping my bag of powder. It plopped to the ground between my feet. I swayed on my feet as I realized that I would never get a chance to try this miraculous sounding substance. I was going to die. In Sinai.

The armed men opened fire and cut the Bedouins down in an instant. Their blades clanged to the ground and they fell dead in a heap of bloody, dirty robes.

When they died, Roy cried out. "No no no!" He leapt to his feet.

I grabbed him and yanked down hard. "Get down Roy! Get goddamn down!"

We both lay face-down. Roy started to cry; his nose pressed into the stone next to me. As frightened as I was, I felt bad for him. Sure, he'd sounded like a nut at first. But after spending a bit of time with him, he seemed genuine, passionate, and bright.

The big Nazi started barking orders.

"Search the sand niggers. Get the weapons. Hood

and hog the doctor and his associates."

Hood and hog. New to me. As they hog tied each one of us and then tied coarse, burlap sacks on our heads, I realized what a neat time saver 'hood and hog' was. I heard a thump and a groan. Followed by another thump and groan. Followed by another. I had three thoughts in my head at that moment that all jockeyed to be first.

They're going to hit me.

Mercenaries have their own jargon?

Has anyone ever tried to snort the white powder of gold?

And then I felt a burst of light from the back of my head and I blacked out.

When I came to, the only thing I was aware of was pain. Throbbing, wet pain at the back of my head. I had no idea where I was. I couldn't see. My eyes were open but it was pitch black. Then everything rushed back at once and I remembered. We had been tied up and knocked unconscious. I was in some sort of vehicle, the bag still on my head, ankles still tied to my wrists. I was lying on my back, smashing my arms and legs which were folded underneath me. They were screaming with a fierce, red pain. I lifted my head and rolled onto my side, lifting my weight from my cramped extremities.

You see, friends, I had been kidnapped. Kidnapped for the second time in less than a year.

I was living like Liam Neeson in Taken, only I had no specific set of skills. At best, I had anti-skills. I couldn't tell how long I'd been out. I'd never lost consciousness from a violent blow before. I didn't know if it had been minutes or hours. I wondered if I was still in Sinai. Was I even in Egypt anymore? I tried to picture the geography. Israel was the closest country to Serabit. But it had to be nearly 500 miles to Israel. I calculated from the pain in my arms and legs that I hadn't been out that long, thinking that if I had maybe they would be more numb than angry.

I heard a low moan followed by a cough from my left. I wasn't alone!

"Who's there?" I asked timidly.

"Roger. I'm so sorry."

Roy's voice sounded thin and defeated.

"Who are those guys?" I asked.

Roy sighed. "This is all my fault."

"Do you know where they are taking us?" I asked.

The vehicle lurched to a stop and Roy and I tumbled into each other. Roy called out for the twins, but they were either unconscious, dead, or not with us. We heard doors open and voices. They sounded American. Someone cut the rope between my ankles and pulled me to my feet. My legs weren't working and I was dragged between two guys for about a minute, then forced roughly into a chair. My arms were still bound behind my back; my fingers slammed into the wood of the chair. I heard Roy shoved down next to me. Then, still bound and hooded blind, I heard a familiar voice. I couldn't identify the voice, but it was definitely ringing bells for me. Which was odd, considering I was in Egypt, far from anyone I knew.

"Nasty business. Just a very nasty business, eh?"

I couldn't place it. I could hear the sound of waves

and I assumed we were somewhere in or near Abu Zenima, on the Gulf.

"Gentlemen. I know right now neither of you will believe me when I tell you that today hurts me more than it hurts you. So many senseless deaths lately."

"Where's Tarek and Mido?" Roy interrupted.

"Part of the senseless deaths, I'm afraid. Let's get those nasty hoods off, shall we?"

The hood was ripped from my head and it took me a few moments to see clearly. We were seated on a brightly lit patio-balcony overlooking the Suez. It was a fancy patio, with a plush, maroon rug under our seats. Our chairs were low wooden folding-type chairs with soft, white cushions. The railing had a repetitive temple design. Through the gaps I could see white blurs lining the incoming waves. I craned my head to see our captor. He was coming around from behind Roy on his left. I felt reality yawn around me when I realized who it was. Higgins!

"You killed them," Roy snarled.

"Well, I didn't kill them, Roy. Larry and Gunther killed them."

"Higgins?" I asked, incredulously.

Higgins' egghead swiveled towards me.

"And you. You were supposed to be dead right now. I wanted you to be dead right now!" he snapped.

It was chilling to hear the change in Higgins' voice.

"I will get to you," he glowered at me. He stepped to face Stacks.

"Many questions," Higgins spit out. "Off the top of your head, oh holy metallurgist, do you know the amount of money you stole from me?

"You shouldn't have killed them."

"Six million dollars is the answer, Roy. You stole six million dollars from me. How is it that Roger is still alive? His hands are dripping blood, Roy. He's a fucking killer! How did he fire white?"

Roy laughed. "It never fires black. Science is fairly predictable, as you should know. I told you that this wasn't magic."

Higgins shook his head violently. "You lied to me. You ripped me off. Massively, Roy."

"My work needed more money. You got your powder."

"That wasn't gold, you jackass! When I realized you were a shyster, I had the powder tested. I should have had it tested right off. Of course, it wasn't gold. It tested as rhodium and iridium. Both rare metals. Expensive metals. What the Devil are you up to, Roy?"

"It works the same! Orme-rhodium works the same as orme-gold. You still got the white powder. In fact, you got much more than six million dollars' worth of rhodium and iridium. Closer to twelve million. No one needed to die."

"I'm not stupid like the zealots you surround yourself with these days. Rhodium is found in platinum. Iridium is rare on Earth, but common in meteorites. Do you have a meteorite farm, Roy? Is that what you spent my money on?"

"Look, we analyzed brain tissue from a pig and a cow. First, we destroyed the organic matter then we did a metals analysis. Over five percent of the brain tissue by dry matter weight is rhodium and iridium.

It's just orbitally rearranged and no one knows it because it can't be directly measured. When we did a 300 second spectroscopic analysis the results were clear. Rearranged rhodium, rearranged iridium. These elements are flowing the light of life in the body. The elements are the light. It doesn't matter if it's rearranged gold, or platinum, or palladium."

"Hmmm. A 300 second spectroscopic analysis, eh? You overtly sold me powdered gold, and covertly sold me powdered animal brains," mused Higgins. He caught his hands behind his back and began to do the little pacing lecture I'd seen him do before, back in America. "How many animal brains does it take, to make twelve million dollars of rhodium and iridium? Can one un-rearrange the atoms of the powder? Could this be converted back to a measurable state?"

"I don't work with killers, Dr. Higgins," answered Roy bravely.

"And yet you had no problems working with this idiot over here?" Higgins pointed at me. "He's a goddamned murderer. Responsible for so much pain, aren't you Roger? Eight children, 23 adults? I'm missing one, aren't I? There's another adult. Isn't there Roger?"

I gasped. How the fuck did Higgins know this about me? I wracked my brain, going over our sessions. I hadn't told him anything. Our meetings were always brief and he did all the talking. I was terrified and confused.

Roy looked just as confused. Professor Higgins began the hand behind his back speech again.

"I want to elucidate. I intend to keep both of you in

my employ and it serves me to explain. Roy, when you cut me off, I was furious. I even ruined my favorite crystal. You know the rare Stellar Beam Calcite? I threw it in a rage. You can say you didn't cut me off, but telling me that going forward I had to fire it myself, and that if I had a heart of darkness it would fire black, was cutting me off. You scared me off with a ghost story, and I turned tail like a hokum. It wasn't an easy time for me. I got hit with a lot of strife at once, compounded by my dear, altruistic friend Roy Stacks' betrayal. Punctuated bitterly with my first great loss. The death of my nephew."

Higgins stopped in front of me and looked as if he was fighting mightily to keep his hands behind his back and away from my throat. What was he going on about?

"Sure, he was a lost cause, but he was still family! A bright boy at that! Roger. You. You killed him. My brother's son! And you buried him up on- "

His voice cut off and he turned and stared out at the sea, away from us, clenching his knuckles white. The punk was related to Dr. Higgins? My mind spun. He knew I'd killed the punk creep all along? He manipulated me into coming to Serabit in hopes that I'd die? I got Pied Piper'ed by some rainbow flyers all the way to Egypt?

Higgins spun around dramatically. "The Wheel. You buried him up on The Wheel, Roger. I almost killed you the day I found out what had happened, but while I was consoling his father, the bomb detonated at the zoo. And I instantly knew that he'd set it. That was his style. Strike out at families. Scare kids, that sort of thing. Jasper's last bomb. He had a brilliant mind, but he was, twisted. Twisted all up."

Higgins alternated between looking like he was going to kill me and then wistfully remembering his miscreant Jasper. So, the kid's name was Jasper. The person I'd killed was named Jasper Higgins. Knowing his name didn't change anything. I was still glad he was dead. But the news floored me. It smashed all of the hope right out of me. I was in a foreign country, no white powder of gold, and in deeper shit then I'd ever been. Yes, I knew there would be consequences to murder. I believe that even when self-defense is legitimate, there are consequences to killing. Murder or not. But I'd hoped.

Brian was certainly my son. I passed the "believe in magic" gene. What if, y'all? I had just hoped that things would turn out differently. That I could avoid the accompanying shit sandwich when I killed the punk kid. And escape, unscathed. Naive. Short-sighted. Juvenile. My hope had made me this way. I'd veered away from my priority value of pragmatism and just put my head in the sand. Hadn't covered my tracks. Didn't do anything clever. Hell, didn't do anything. Just went about my business.

"And I knew that someone had helped him. My immediate suspect, of course, was the person who killed him. I know he visited you at your home, I found your address in his notes. I know you were involved in sick sex games with him. You people never think things are going to go south when you play with fire, do you?"

Higgins laughed at my scowl and head shake. "I

saw the pictures of your perfect wife. Abby? Vulgar pictures. Pictures he took. I don't want to know what you and he were up to. Base. Animals. Actually, Roger. I have decided that I cannot look at your face."

Higgins walked behind me and bent down. He came back up with the dirty hood and tied it loosely back around my neck.

"Better," he said. "I'll continue. The bomb did two things. First, it made me remember my nephew. To think of him for what he did rather than how he was. Such a smart boy. He made an impact, as have you. Their deaths are on your head, Roger. You were the adult in this scenario for Christ's sake. Secondly, it helped me see how you could be useful before your death. I could send you to Roy. He would fall over himself to help my dear friend Roger who just wanted to be a better father. He would deny me, steal from me, lie to me. But he'd give it freely to any other sap with a sob story. Well, Roger, add sap to your growing rap sheet. Mass murderer. Drug addict. Piece of shit. Sap. It was easy to corral you, and you took the bait cleanly. I knew you wouldn't be able to resist the ultimate drug."

Higgins was still pacing. I could tell because his voice would get closer and louder, then dampen as he turned around. I didn't need to see. The pompous fucker was pacing, hands probably clasped behind his back.

"Everything worked perfectly, except for the fact that you are still alive. I had been working under the presumption that Roy told the truth. That when your murderous soul burned the gold, you'd be shot to death. It pleased me to think about your family back home never knowing what happened to you. No matter."

Higgins ripped my hood off again and stepped back to look at me.

"Here is what comes next. You are going to smuggle that powder back home for me. It's weighed. You are to use none. Listen to me. If any weight is missing when you bring it home, I will kill one person in your family per gram stolen. This powder is mine now. It's mine. Now you figure out how to get it through customs and on the plane. I may have you perform a few more odious services for me, perhaps not. Regardless, I most certainly will kill you when either you've outlived your usefulness or my rage and grief compel me to wipe you out sooner. From here on out, your final game decides whether your family lives. Not whether you do."

"Roger Clines. I declare your life forfeit. Larry will get you back to Cairo. I want you out of Egypt tomorrow! I'm assuming you will make this happen. Abby's life depends on it."

Another blond American stepped onto the balcony and called for Higgins.

"Hey Boss."

Why was he so familiar to me? Even though I was facing certain death, I was inordinately curious about the big guy. I could swear I'd seen him before. Back home somewhere. He and Higgins stepped inside and I heard their voices fade as the glass door slid shut.

"They were already dead, you know," Roy said sullenly. "The pigs. The cows. We didn't kill them."

I didn't respond. What could I say? I had decided I liked Roy Stacks. He was a good man. Crazy. But good. Although, I must admit that my litmus test for judging people has changed. The bar is lowered to "do you want to kill me or not." Say you don't and I place you in the good camp.

The guy Higgins called Larry came out onto the porch and untied me. Handed me the baggy of powder which had "48.7 g" written on it with a Sharpie, and gave me my backpack and cell phone back. He led me out to a car and drove me back to the Cairo Airport. We didn't speak the entire trip. I wanted to hide in the back seat, but I forced myself to sit in the passenger seat next to him and not shrink away.

The drive took about three and a half hours on the marvelously paved Ras Sedr Highway.

I thought about a lot of things on that drive. I thought about my imminent, guaranteed death. I thought about keeping my family alive. I thought about avoiding the cops. I debated which was worse, getting killed by Higgins versus turning myself in. Going to prison was decidedly worse. I'd rather my family never know what happened to me than for them to know the truth. I definitely did not want to die, but how could I protect my family from Higgins if I were locked up? How could I protect my family from Higgins if I were dead?

I thought about Roy Stacks and the stark contrasts between the first time I saw him and the last. Earlier in the night he'd been luminous and large, but when I turned back to look at him as I left the balcony he was deflated. Trapped in a madman's grasp. Tied up in a chair. Friends dead. And through it all wanting me to know he didn't kill millions of pigs and cows to burn their brains for the trace metals. They were already dead. I briefly pictured Roy and Tarek directing truckloads of animal carcasses into massive industrial forges. Raking through the ashes for whatever. Sad.

As we pulled into the airport, I realized there was one, tiny silver lining in the horrible events. While Higgins is a clear and present danger, so are the police. And I'd been scattered trying to formulate action on more than one front. Overwhelmed. How would I fight the police and Higgins at the same time? I don't think I'm going to have to worry about the police. I figured out why Larry looked familiar. He was one of the 'cops' that had come to my house. The one who asked for the DNA. Detective Schmidt. I don't think the real cops have connected me at all. Maybe they will.

I smiled at the shred of good news as I got out of the car.

"See ya, Officer Schmidt," I called cheerily as I shut the door.

I gave as much thought to smuggling the powder as I did to concealing the killing. I intended to take a few bottles of vitamin capsules and replace the contents. Well, yes, I'd done this more than few times, with a multitude of substances. Roger is expert level at emptying capsules. You gotta twist them between your fingertips just right. Filling them up sucks. Believe it or not, there are several product choices to fill capsules yourself. They have sweet names like the CAP-M-QWIK (sucks), and The Capsule Machine (sucks). The "machine" is a tray that you have to populate one by one with the larger half of the capsule. The empty capsules you buy come as complete capsules. This means that you have to separate each capsule, setting the top half aside carefully. Then you dump powder onto the tray, scraping it across the top, distributing the powder into the painstakingly positioned capsule-halves. Then you have to painstakingly populate the top tray with short capsule pieces and then fit the top tray with the bottom tray and push, connecting and snapping the pieces. It's just as much of a pain to do it one by one by hand, and it doesn't take a complicated machine with multiple pieces. In the end, I don't mess with capsules any more, other than to empty them. They just don't digest/dissolve evenly and you can't predict how much you are getting.

As soon as Larry's car was out of my sight I hailed a cab. It was about eight in the morning, and other than the time I'd nodded off on the flight from LAX to Cairo (about three hours) and the time I'd been unconscious (probably about 45 minutes) I hadn't slept in fifty hours. Imminent death gives you a bit of a rush and I wasn't tired. I asked for the driver to take me to the closest vitamin store. I had no idea what vitamins meant to an Egyptian, but the driver spoke English and I told him I wanted items like Calcium and Vitamin-B. He nodded and said "yes, yes" and took me to a place called Protein We Vitamin in Nasr. He said he'd wait for me.

The store was less crowded than some of the other shops I'd seen in Egypt, but it was laden with bottles of supplements. Big, colorful, plastic tubs of creatine and whey powder. No vitamins. Just NITRO TECH WHEY GOLD (strawberry, French vanilla creme, chocolate banana split), RUSSIAN BEAR 10000 XTREME, GAINER CODE, and MAS FREAK. Things were looking up. Why bother with capsules? I thought. I bought a plastic tub of something called Flavored BCAA POWDER 10,000, vanilla flavor. I hopped in a taxi, dumped the tub out in an airport bathroom stall, and poured in the baggy. I put the tub in my backpack, then used my phone to coordinate return flight and call Abby.

Airport security in Cairo is a joke. No screening at all, just file past bored guards. I boarded the plane without incident and that was that.

And yes, things are still looking up. I get to see Abby and the kids in just a few hours! My god I miss them. I get to die at home, in America and yes, that matters. I don't get any DNA changing powder, but maybe I don't need it. Perhaps the only genuine link between me and Jasper Higgins' death is his uncle. There's precedent now. I know what has to happen next. I'm invoking the Stand Your Ground Law or something.

Higgins was going to have to die. Just like his nephew. How hard could it be? Get through some henchman? Larry and Gunther the Giant Nazi? And a perhaps a handful more?

BENJI GETS BENJI

I want to get straight to it. Directly to the shit sandwich. I lost my job! For the first time in my long and lovely marriage, things are not going well with Abby. As in, they are going poorly. I believe she is close to leaving. So many bad things have happened. Higgins sent Abby copies of The Photos in a manila envelope. Benji got a dog that he named goddamned Benji and he whines all night and shits all over the house in secret spots. And Earth Day happened. Yes, there was another fucking meltdown with another kid. Another sweeping moment of searing pain and trauma. I'm aware that there are only so many elemental disasters possible, but that doesn't make the most recent one suck any less. I've only been back from Egypt for a month. That's all it has taken for my life to implode. One month. And Higgins dances while the Clines burn.

It is currently 12:15 a.m. and I am sitting in a little

blue rental in the parking lot of the Frozen Feline's Lounge. It is a charming little strip club in Rochester, Minnesota. I have never been here before. It looks beautiful, but it's too dark to tell. I don't like strip clubs.

From Egypt to Minnesota in only thirty days.

The jackass I'm meeting here shows up in about half an hour. I can't believe I got here early. Google Maps said it would take me an hour and twenty-three minutes to get to Rochester from St. Paul, but I made it in about an hour. I left Benji in the hotel room with the dog. Yes, that's bad.

We flew to Saint Paul International and drove a rental car south to Rochester. Benji wants to visit a cave called The Mystery Cave and after Earth Day I felt like I had to do something to try to salvage our relationship. Want to know how bad Earth Day was? Earth Day was so bad that I told Benji he could even bring the dog with us. On the plane! And in the rental! And in the hotel room! Anyway, they were both asleep, worn out by 11:00 p.m. and I snuck out and bee-lined here. I'm taking a huge risk. Benji is only eleven. Abby would kill me if she found out I've left him alone. I'm just praying he and/or the dog don't wake up until I've made it back. I'm meeting a guy named Thick Rick for Higgins. I'm picking up a 'small package' from Thick Rick at the Frozen Feline's Lounge in Rochester, Minnesota. I'm getting ahead of myself again.

Let's start with the white powder of gold. Larry had told me to sit on the powder until Higgins returned to the states. He said they would contact me.

I'd been back from Egypt for about a week when I got a text with specifics on the delivery. It was 9:27 a.m. and I was at the office.

UNKNOWN NUMBER: HHH in 60 minutes. Don't dawdle. You have a lovely family.

I was in the middle of an internal presentation for the design of a new library downtown. My co-worker Jacques, had worked very hard on it. He'd been thoughtful and deliberate, adding touches you don't normally see in a stuffy, government building. I had worked with him on frame and facing, and was particularly proud of the results. It was a high-visibility project with casual public recognition. It was the type of project that was very good for my career. Critical, even.

And the goddam, cartoon-villain text came right in the middle of this. Horrible. I'm 56 years old. I'm tired on a standard day. I'm getting old. But there I was juggling my career with a madman. A dead man walking, trying to advance his career while running errands for his executioner. For the executioner who threatened to kill his family. And to make things worse, I was high. Mega-high. I'm back on the kratom again, and that's not all. My 'recovery' was expensive baloney from my ultimate and immediate nemesis. I was going to be doing the opposite of all he ever advised. All drugs were back on.

I had gotten my hands on a powerful research chemical called A-PHP. That is short for a-pyrrolidsomethingverylong. It's pretty fucking amazing, quite similar to cocaine. And it's legal so I ordered some online. It was a fine white powder that looked exactly liked the white powder of gold or iridium or whatever I'd fired with Roy. I had been snorting a line before I left for work, one in the parking lot when I got to work, one in the car at lunch, one when I left work, and then between ten and twenty more lines each night once I'd gotten home.

I'd been using a lot. It had been helping me deal with all the drama in my screwed-up, clock-ticking life. A line gave me extreme clarity and thought acceleration for about 30 minutes. It gives you a short boost of fuck yeah! The rush was followed by a pretty steep crash, but it was nothing like a coke comedown. It was manageable. All of that said, the constant use was tearing me apart. My mind was a tangle of zealous dead-ends. My short-term memory shot. I'm sure I looked like an idiot when I was high on the stuff, but I get so aggressive that people part for me like the Red Sea did for Moses. And I got this white powder online. No forge. No cave. No burning bushes.

So, there I was, "coked" out of my head presenting our library, when I got the text. A-PHP gives you a ridiculous boost of confidence. It's the kind of confidence that pushes you to do ridiculous things you would never consider sober. I was speaking about how we'd came up with the idea for the front walkway railing when I got the text. Sober Roger would have finished his presentation then checked his phone. A-PHP Roger said, "Give me a minute gentleman" and just strolled on out. The text scared the shit out of me. Apparently, there is not enough A-PHP in the world to nullify the fear that comes when your family is threatened.

I ran straight to the restroom and snorted two lines. They didn't help. They made things harder. My heart was already racing too fast. There were a couple of minutes where I sat in the bathroom stall on the toilet, hearing my heart pound. BOOM, BOOM, BOOM, BOOM, BOOM! If you've ever done coke or meth you know what I mean. Sometimes your heart pounds so hard and loud you just assume everyone else hears it too. How couldn't they? I stepped out of the stall feeling stretched but confident, when I began to wretch. I darted back into the stall, slamming the door behind me. I vomited a strange orange foam. After the purge I stayed hunkered on the ground.

"I'm okay, I'm okay, I'm okay," I said to myself, puke on my lips, body still trembling. A-PHP is some strong shit. Undaunted, I cleaned myself up and moved on to my exit from the office.

No, I hadn't murdered my nemesis, but I had thought about what I would do if Higgins demanded the white powder of gold while I was at work. I was an expert at escaping the office. Think of the standard exits. My kid got hurt. My wife was in a car crash. My dad had a heart attack. My mom has fallen in the shower. I never liked any of those. They weren't clean and were obvious unless you carried on afterwards. These things require endless follow-up stories and it can get hard maintaining all the lies. My plan involved me being sent home. Strikingly different than leaving work due to an emergency. Getting sent home eliminates the worry about your lie's effectiveness.

I had done some research and saw that higher doses

of Niacin (vitamin B3) could cause temporary red, angry welts. A Niacin flush happens when the vitamin flushes and expands capillaries. Google said it can look and feel like a sunburn, but it typically lasts about an hour. The flush is harmless but can be mildly uncomfortable, which is why most vendors make a flush-free Niacin. I had to go to three different stores before I found the straight shit. The pills I bought were 1000 mg oblong white tablets.

I had taken four and put them into a plastic baggy. Then I mashed the pills using a can of fruit cocktail until they were a smooth, white powder. I kept this in my lower desk drawer next to a baggy of pepper. I figured anyone who looked would assume it was salt. After breathing for a bit and calming down as much as the drugs would allow, I grabbed the Niacin from my desk and poured the baggy into some orange juice. It was bitter as hell but I was a literal veteran of drinking nasty shit in OJ.

I shouldn't have bothered with the Niacin baloney; I should have just left. But I wasn't thinking clearly. Somehow in my stressed-out, obtuse, drug-addled head it seemed smarter to go back into the meeting, wait for the "hives" to appear from nowhere, and get sent home.

But I was tore up even before the Niacin took hold and there was no hiding it.

"Are you alright, man?" Jacques asked in a hushed voice when I re-entered the meeting.

"Never better," I replied loudly. I dutifully shifted my attention from speaker to speaker and managed to contain myself. About five minutes in, I started feeling fiery pricks of pain over my face and arms. Every pore felt like it was screaming. Smashing the tablets and mixing with orange juice no longer seemed like such a good idea. My boss, who was seated across from me, looked at me with concern.

"Roger. Holy Lord! Are you okay?" he asked.

"I feel hot," I said as I looked at my arms in horror. They were covered with fiercely raised welts. I had more welt skin than normal skin. Jacques actually got up from his chair and stepped back from the table, as if I could be contagious.

"Oh my God, Roger! You need to get to the doctor man!"

"Go to the doctor," my boss echoed. "We've got your designs; Jacques will represent you. Are you okay to drive? Do you need a ride?"

I shook my head, excused myself and held it together until I reached my car. My eyes felt like they were bleeding. My skin felt hot; miles hotter than any remembered fever. I checked my cellphone. I had twenty minutes to get to HHH. I should have just split when I awkwardly left the meeting the first time. I could have pulled out one of the established lies and already been there. Instead, I decided to do two more lines, eat 4000 mg of Niacin and then go back into the meeting.

That was the moment I realized that drugs are the luxury of the secure. And I was not secure. Not in the slightest. I was the opposite of secure. I was wholly un-secure. There was only one thing I could say to myself as I started the car. I made eye contact with myself in the rear-view mirror and declared myself sober. Forever Sober. I was literally too high to do my job or keep myself and family alive.

I have had nothing since. That was twelve days ago and there were no problems putting them down, save for a moment or two of doubt. You don't need a twelve-step program when you have a gun to your head. I needed my wits. I needed to keep my family alive long enough to kill Higgins.

I made it to HHH a minute early. I walked into the office with the powder and handed it to Larry, who was standing in the waiting area. He stepped back from me, curling his lip.

"The fuck's wrong with you?"

I shrugged. "I dunno but it hurts real bad. With my luck it's smallpox."

"Okay. Yeah. Take off. The boss will be in touch." He waved me away.

I could hear Higgins in his office on speaker phone. He was talking to Roy. My heart jumped when I heard his voice. I was thrilled to hear he was still alive. He didn't sound happy. All I heard before I left was: "You gotta get these guns away from me. They are in my house, Higgins!"

It didn't sound like things were going well for Roy Stacks, the manna man. It sounded like Higgins was using him the same way he was using me. "At least he's still alive," I thought.

Once I pulled out of the parking lot and sped around the corner, I got to face what the niacin had done to me. It felt like an extreme sunburn. You know the kind where your eyes are hot and you are shivering and even blankets hurt your skin? The symptoms did not let up for almost three hours. There was a brief period where I seriously considered going to the emergency room. That was a funny thing. After all the drugs I'd taken, it took a vitamin to scare me enough to consider going to the hospital.

It was about 2:00 p.m. by the time the fire had worn away. My body was exhausted. I decided to lie down and go to sleep. I texted Abby that I hadn't been feeling well and had come home early. I passed out hard, my body stretched.

A few hours later I was jolted awake by the slam of our bedroom door. I shot up out of bed, tangling my sweaty sheets around my legs and fell down to the floor. Abby was standing in front of the door, holding a large manila envelope and goddammit, she was crying. I hate it when Abby cries. She handed me the envelope.

"Honey, what's going on?"

"Like you don't know!" Abby snapped.

I undid the clasp and dumped out the contents. There were several 8 x 10 glossy photographs. Holy shit, they were The Photographs. I stood still, frozen in terror. There was no return address but it was from Higgins, without a doubt. For a brief moment I thought I might pass out. Total doom yawned wide in front of me. What the hell was I going to say? What could I say?

"What did you do, Roger?" she screamed at me. "What the fuck did you do?!"

Her tears had smeared her makeup. She had black streaks under each eye. She looked beautiful. Abby was always beautiful. Even her cry face managed to come across as a delicious tease.

"I'm looking at you, Roger. I'm searching your face for something. A clue. A hint that you aren't behind this, but you are, aren't you?"

I shook my head. "No, no. I'm not behind this. I don't know how this happened."

Abby sighed a very long sigh and sat down on the edge of the bed, her head in her hands. She sat with her face buried for a long while, and when she looked up her face was different. Hardened a bit. Edged. She was starting to get some raised, red splotches on her face and neck.

"Who sent these to me and how did they get them?" she asked in a new voice. It wasn't the sweet, soft voice of an angel. It was different. It was cold. She sounded like a stranger.

That was the first time I didn't have an easy lie. The first time I couldn't glibly explain. I wanted to tell her everything. But, how could I? There were so many unsavory details. I would describe Abby as a reasonable woman. She is fair and open-minded. She never loses her cool or leaves the track of logic. There is one exception to this. There is one thing Abby is simply not logical about. Her modesty. She told me she only had one partner other than myself, and I believed her. She takes extreme pride in her modesty. I'm not saying that this is unreasonable. It's a disproportionate response. It's ape-shit. I need to explain.

She never wears anything that could be construed as risque or immodest. Single piece bathing suits. Light makeup, not that she needed any. She dresses like a Sunday school teacher by default. I don't think she ever comes across as stuffy, but Abby doesn't swear in public. (I do not count as public and she swears just fine when she chooses to do so.) She would never put a photo of herself on Facebook.

Indiscreet, nude pictures of Abby engaged in sexual activity, regardless of how amazing she looked, are literally the only thing in the world that could derail her. Kryptonite. Her unraveling was swift.

While I stood holding the pictures, trying to think of some lie, some excuse to diffuse, she began to pace. She walked to the far wall and began marching around the edges of the room, dragging one hand along the wall. She would follow three edges of the room, stop at our bed and reverse course. The whole time she was staring at me, expectantly. She looked like she was getting ready to blow. She began to walk like she was strutting a runway.

After she had cat-walked around the room a few times, she stopped abruptly. She cocked her head at me a few times like a mama bird, never breaking eye contact.

"Who sent them?" she asked coldly. Her face matched her voice. Hard and unrecognizable. Her head jerked up and to the left. She was a bird, looking at me from this strange sideways angle, and then suddenly from another extreme.

"Who sent them? And why? You gave these to a friend and now he wants in on the action? Or? Am I being blackmailed?!"

Her head bird-cocked again and she balled her

fists.

"What the fuck, Roger?" she screamed at full volume, immediately warlike. "What the fucking fuck, Roger? What? The? Fuck? Roger?"

There was a knock on our bedroom door, followed by a concerned, "Mom? Dad? Are you guys ok?"

Abby and I looked at each other. Her face was a mess. The raised hive situation on her face and neck had gotten worse. She looked like she had taken too much niacin. But I knew better. She had too much Roger. Roger poisoning.

"Everything's fine honey," Abby called through the door. "Your dad and I are just working through a few things. Give us a few minutes to finish."

"Okay Mom," called Benji. "I have something to show you guys when you have time."

Abby turned to me and snarled, "I'm taking a shower and cleaning up. Don't bother trying to make up some sort of lie. I don't want to talk to you right now."

She went to our bathroom and closed the door. I heard her lock it. That hurt. We never locked the master bathroom door. She wanted me out. She didn't trust me.

I couldn't blame her. I wasn't trustworthy. My mind was spinning. There were so many things going on. When the boys were overwhelmed with tasks I always would say, "You eat an elephant one bite at a time." Not this elephant.

I have potential drama with the police for the murder of Jasper. Potential drama with the police for the zoo bombing. An impending death sentence from

Higgins. A nude picture fiasco could be the kiss of death for my marriage, which would be moot if I were killed. And Benji heard the drama in our room. My folks fought non-stop when I was growing up and divorced when I was twelve. It crushed me. I swore to myself that my kids would never have to go through one. But that was before I fucked everything up.

I sat on the edge of our bed for nearly thirty minutes trying to pull my thoughts together. To make a plan. The only thought I could focus on was: Kill Higgins. But he'd already messed up my marriage. I couldn't think of a single way to salvage things. How could Abby ever trust me again? What could be going through her head to explain the photos? Whatever she was thinking was certainly not as bad as reality. I could hear Abby crying in the shower and I wanted to go in and comfort her.

I knocked on the bathroom door.

"Abby?"

The sounds of crying stopped but she didn't respond.

"Abby?" I called again.

No response. I washed my face in the sink and went to find out what was going on with Benji. He was probably terrified. I don't know what things sounded like from his point of view, but he couldn't be feeling great about it. Mom screaming about nude pictures isn't a happy sound.

I found him in the living room. His laptop was casually underneath one arm. He adores that thing; carries it with him everywhere. The kid loves to make PowerPoint presentations. It's an unusual thing.

While his friends were making YouTube videos of themselves talking or riding their bikes, he was making informative slide shows. Why Does the Sky Look Blue? by Benji Clines. What is Dirt Made Of? by Benji Clines. He looked away from the television and smiled at me. He was so beautiful, so innocent. I loved him very much, but what kind of world was I building for him?

"Everything cool, Dad?" he asked with concern.

"It sure is, bud," I said and smiled back at him. "What did you want to show us?"

"I wanna wait for mom. Is she okay?"

"She's fine. She's tired, but she's fine. She's in the shower."

I pointed to the laptop.

"What do you have to show us today?"

"Today. Today is the ultimate." He stood straight and used his snooty announcer voice. "The History of Movie Dogs (and Why I Need One) by Benji Clines."

He was so sweet. I actually felt a twinge of pain in my chest. I saw one tiny ray of sunshine. I could make my boy happy, we could get a dog, I decided. Easy. One good thing, one slam dunk. We had a family cat, but never a dog. Neither Brian nor Charlie had wanted to take care of one. Abby and I valued the scintilla of free time after working and taking care of kids too much to have wanted one ourselves.

Benji and I had breakfast cereal for dinner. Abby didn't come out all night. I spent the evening alternating between shame and anger. I wanted to storm into our room and ask her to go reassure our son, but I was too afraid to face her. I put on my most cheerful face, explained that Mom was not feeling well, and we watched cartoons together for a few hours. The Huckleberry Hound Show was on and Benji had never seen it. Do you remember that show? I loved it as a child. The first cartoon of the show was always a Huckleberry Hound piece. The next two segments were Yogi Bear and Boo-Boo, followed by Pixie and Dixie and Mr. Jinx. Benji had also never seen Yogi Bear before. Can you imagine not knowing who Yogi Bear is? He's so young. Or we're so old, or whatever.

Charlie came home around eleven and headed straight to his room. Total time spent inside the house, but outside his room, about eight seconds.

I had just put Benji to bed. I promised we'd watch his slide show the next day when Mom was feeling better. I stood in front of Charlie's door, listening. I could hear a muted conversation. I wondered who he was talking to. I wondered why he bee-lined for his room. Had he been drinking? Maybe doing other things? I wanted to open the door and check his eyes. Make sure he was okay. I know that seems hypocritical. I don't care. Wally, who'd been locked in a closet all night, burst free and started to shout. What if he needs your help? What if he's a druggie like you? I heard Charlie laugh. It was a good laugh. An innocent laugh that panged me slightly. The kids seemed so pure when compared to their begrimed, yucky daddy. I convinced myself he was fine and walked down the hall, past Benji's slightly opened door, to our bedroom.

I pressed my forehead against the door and

listened. Silence. There were no lights on. I thought she probably had fallen asleep. Maybe she had exhausted herself with the distrust and fear and betrayal. But there was no precedent for this. We'd never had any problems. Over twenty years and we've never had a row.

I need to re-frame this. My drug use was tearing my family apart. That's it. We were a statistic. Casualties of the Drug War. This is your brain on drugs. Any questions?

The short-cut. The easy way out. The pipe-dream. I've always had this problem. I just could never outrun it. I can remember reading the story of the Grasshopper and the Ants when I was young. Maybe nine, ten. I remember this because it was the first time that I had ever spotted a lesson in entertainment outside a Bible story.

I resented it. I had been enjoying the tale, eating up the sentiments hook, line and sinker and then seen the lesson. It cheapened it. As if making something educational negated all the fun. So, I sidestepped the didact and thought: Maybe the Grasshopper is the smart one. He didn't work all summer and he still got the warmth and the food he needed. And his work was hardly slave labor. Play some music and dance a jig? A cautionary tale? Please. I'd carried that smugness along with me my entire life. And somehow, I had stayed afloat. But then. A bit of a wobble, right folks? First a bit of a wobble, then a landslide of debris, then a car crash.

Maybe there is no short cut. Maybe there is no hack. Maybe there is no defying gravity. Even the

Catch Me If You Can guy got caught. Roger was no mastermind, just a pompous drug addict who thought that the rules didn't apply. And now people were dead. And now a hardworking, loyal, beautiful woman cries herself to sleep. Betrayed in untold and unknown ways. I suddenly thought of the pictures and straightened. Where had I left them? I mentally retraced my steps. Abby had been in the shower. I had collected the shambles of my thoughts on the bed, eager to get out and soothe Benji. Where had I left the pictures? Just sitting on the bed, left out in her face? Had I hidden them at least? Slid them under a pillow?

I took a deep breath and opened the door. The room was pitch dark. The light that spilled in from the hallway cut a bright swath across the chaos that was our room. Family pictures knocked to the floor; glass cracked. Frames split. Clothes strewn about. I looked to the bed, but it was empty. I flipped on the overhead light. She wasn't there! She wasn't in the bathroom. I ran to the garage. Her car was gone. She must have taken off at some point while I was with Benji.

I looked at my watch. It was 11:55 p.m. I had stood in front of my empty bedroom, afraid to go in for nearly an hour. Ladies and gentlemen, introducing Roger Clines, literal poster child. Make sure you take the shot from the opposite end of the hallway. That way you can see him silhouetted, fearful of entering an empty bedroom on a Tuesday night. Messed up on fear, adrenaline, and drugs. Hopped up weeknight bliss, eh?

She didn't come home that night. I cleaned up our room as best I could. It was trashed. The pretty lamps

I bought her when we stayed at the Biltmore for a weekend getaway? They were shattered and the glass was ground into the carpet from where she had done the stilted marching. The cool cuckoo clock her grandfather had made for her by hand was busted into pieces, springs and gears strewn through the glass shards. It took me nearly three hours to clean things up to a passable level. I hoped she'd return, but we were in uncharted territory. That's when I decided to tell her. 3:45 a.m., Wednesday morning.

I am going to tell her everything. She deserves the truth, as awful as it is. In the end, I was able to reason past it all, except for her humiliation. How do you spin intimate shame? I know the naughty pictures we took in private are circulating god knows where, but... But nothing. The game was over, and if I hadn't lost her completely at that moment, I knew the final shoe drop was pending.

I collapsed in my bed, alone and exhausted. When I woke up the next morning, my heart felt dead. Abby and I had never fought. We had always worked everything out. We would just sit down and talk- it had been easy to connect. We had never exchanged harsh words. I had never experienced a divide like this. I cried in the shower that morning, like a teenager who had just gotten dumped. I had forced myself to refrain from calling or texting the night before, but I started texting her the moment I woke. No response. I even phoned her a few times, but calls railed to voice mail.

My life actually was a Lifetime Television Movie. Banal dysfunction, mute communication, and shattered family photos.

The loneliness and gloom I felt from Abby's disappearance had me questioning my resolve regarding the drugs. I kept them in an end table that had a hidden compartment. It was a square, pressboard cupboard, with a sliding top piece. I removed the broken lamp, slid open the top and surveyed my stock. Looking at it made me burst into tears. I flashed back to Abby and I putting the stock together. We'd had a great time figuring out the perfect way to keep our stash. At first, we considered a nice gun safe, but they were too obvious. Next, we considered a wall safe, but wall safes are too shallow to keep much. We settled on a night stand with a sliding top. The top slid backwards to reveal a hidden compartment. It was about eleven inches deep and eighteen inches wide. Abby had liked mine so much she got one for her side of the bed too.

We had bought some smaller mason jars. Abby had a stroke of genius and she painted the jars with chalkboard paint. It was brilliant. It gave us a way to label the jars and contents while keeping the insides nice and dark. Light is the enemy of hallucinogens, breaks down potency. On the face of each jar I used chalk to show what was in it and the potency. For example, the MDMA jar face said "MDMA, 100 points." The top lid of the jar had the note for how much. It said "40." When I took some, I'd wipe the lid and chalk on the new total.

I had four jars of different magic mushrooms: Golden Caps – 28 grams, Golden Teacher – 16 grams, Penis Envy – 72 grams, and the highly visual

Mazatapecs – 13 grams. There was a large jar of Phenibut capsules, 200 mg. I had five different strains of 250-gram pillow packs of ground kratom: Baik Bali, Green Vein Borneo, Red Vein Thai, White Bali, and Green Vein Maeng Da. There were fifty tabs of 170 micro-gram LSD blotter tabs (the blotter design was the cover of John Lennon's Imagine album.) Three grams of JWH-018 (a marijuana synthetic), seven grams of 5-IAI (a synthetic MDMA), and seven little blue mescaline pills. There were forty points of MDMA, broken down into one-point capsules. There were two unopened 25-gram packs of A-PHP. My eyes stopped on the A-PHP for the longest. It did give a swift boost of happy. But by then, the damage drugs had done to my life was clear to me and I further resolved to be done with them. I had to sober up. Try to save my marriage. Eliminate Higgins before he could do any further damage to me or my family.

That's when I thought about my friend Albert. Well, he's my drug dealer. Or was my drug dealer. Albert is cool. A very unique individual. Smart as hell, but dumb at the same time, like a horny teenager. He is an electrical engineer for IBM. And a drug dealer. It's strange to think of an intellectual professional who goes home after work and sells drugs. But Albert does.

He is the ultimate dealer. Not sketchy. Bright. Has some of everything, nearly always. He can get anything you want. I would scour the internet looking for new or interesting drugs, hallucinogens mostly, then he would source. I asked him once where he gets everything and he just shrugged and said the 'Dark

Web.' He buys some Bitcoins, then uses the TOR web browser (a secure and anonymous sub-web browser), and simply orders whatever he's looking for online.

When I first met him he only sold pot. At the time I was looking around for shrooms and couldn't find them anywhere. I asked him if he could get some and he called me a few weeks later. He had ordered several strains for me to choose from. I had no experience with shrooms back then and my mind was blown by the fact that different strains could give different effects. I bought them all. Next, I asked him if he could get LSD. A couple weeks later he had blotter and gel tabs. He has come through on every request I threw at him, even when I was looking for designer drugs like JWH-018. Looking at my stash and preparing to destroy it I thought, "I guess I will never see Albert again." It was strange because up until then I'd never thought about him as anything more than a dealer. Certainly not as a friend I would miss.

I flushed everything. It took less than five minutes to destroy my elaborate stock. Years to collect, trashed in moments. I called in sick to work. I needed to find Abby and talk to her. I missed my best friend.

I must have texted Abby a hundred times that day. No response. She had never cut me out like that. I felt like someone had turned off the Sun. I realized how much I had been using her. I'd used her to make myself feel good. I loved the way she saw me. Her view of me as a great husband wasn't accurate, but it was preferable to the truth. The thought of her seeing unvarnished, fucked up Roger was humiliating, embarrassing and scary. She was not going to want a guy like me around. Not around her. Not around the kids. She was going to want nothing to do with me after I divulged.

Abby may have been blind to my failures, but she isn't a weak woman. There were plenty of non-drug addicted, trustworthy men with good jobs that would love to be with her. I realize that I haven't told you how beautiful she is. Stunning. She's always been incredibly fit with a flat tummy, an hour-glass figure and the face of an angel. But her physical attributes were never her strongest feature. The greatest thing about Abby is her smile. Her smile feels like everything wonderful: a warm blanket, a hot fudge sundae, a first-place trophy, young love, summer sun showers. I'm tempted to include a picture here for you. Your jaws would drop when you saw her. How did a murderous addict like me score a woman like Abby? Trickery and lies, that's how.

I spent the day obsessing over my phone and its silence. Abby hadn't replied. After I replaced the glass from the shattered photos and rehung the pictures, I decided to call her office. I used a *67 and disguised my voice. My call to the front desk was sent to her office voicemail. I called back and asked if she was in. She was not in. They told me to try back tomorrow. I was in such bad shape, that I took that as a bit of hope. Abby had only called out for the day. Not forever. They didn't say she's moved out of state. "Try back tomorrow."

By the time Benji got home from school, I was starting to panic. I had no idea where to even look for her. Benji was all smiles, holding his ubiquitous laptop.

"Think you and Mom will be able to check out my slideshow today?" he asked as he crawled onto the bar stool and sat on his knees.

"Yep," I lied.

I maintained the rest of the day and had to stifle a yell when I saw her come down the hallway a couple of hours later. She looked beautiful and sad. Benji ran to her and hugged her.

"You guys gonna watch my slideshow now?" he beamed.

The rest of that evening was a borrowed-time quiet. I know I can be seen as a bit of an over-sharer, but I'm keeping the contents of that evening private, minus a few things. I told her nothing. There was no reveal. We didn't talk about anything. I didn't ask her where she'd been and she didn't offer. I held my breath the whole night, afraid that the slightest misstep might drive her away. We watched Benji's presentation together, as if it were any other day. We pulled it together. I'm going to tell you about that part of our night because it's both sweet and germane. It's also the third most devastating moment in my life to date. Earth Day.

Technically Earth Day began before Benji's presentation. Abby and I gathered around Benji's laptop, but it wouldn't power on. Benji was chomping at the bit to show us so I handed him my work laptop. He emailed the presentation to my work mail and opened it on my machine. It only took him a minute and he was back on track.

The presentation opened with a dark blue slide with a title in bright yellow font: The History of Movie Dogs and Why I Need One by Benji Clines. He tapped the space bar and the slide progressed.

"Fade transition," he called out. "Next slide."

Yes, the kid calls out his transitions. Before Benji's PowerPoint obsession I didn't even know there were variants, let alone names. The next slide was titled: The Top 15 Best Movie Dogs – Countdown.

"Wipe transition. Next slide."

He gave each dog its own slide:

15. Baxter from "Anchorman"
14. Petey from "The Little Rascals"
13. Hercules from "The Sandlot"
12. Lassie from "Lassie"
11. Otis from "The Adventures of Milo and Otis"
10. Slink from "Toy Story"
9. Hooch from "Turner and Hooch"
8. Jerry Lee from "K-9"
7. Milo from "The Mask"
6. Toto from "The Wizard of Oz"
5. Marley from "Marley and Me"
4. Buddy from "Air Bud"
3. Beethoven from "Beethoven"
2. Old Yeller from "Old Yeller"

Old Yeller was followed by a spacer slide with a picture of a drum. An embedded wave file played a drum roll sound.

"Drum roll please," Benji announced. "And the greatest movie dog of all time is-"

He paused melodramatically and hit the slide button with a flair.

"Dissolve transition! Benji!"

This slide showed a picture of Benji. My son advanced the show to next slide. A picture of him faded into the slide next to the dog.

"Fade Transition. Obviously, the best dog, Benji. Was I named after him?"

Abby laughed. It sounded beautiful. "Nope."

Benji advanced to the next slide. A red heart floated across the screen.

"A Benji dog is actually a Border Terrier, mixed with some mutt. He is believed to be part Miniature Poodle, Cocker Spaniel and Schnauzer. Border Terriers are smart dogs – they are listed as the 30th smartest breed according to the America Kennel Association."

Benji hit the next slide. This slide showed a picture of a boy crying on a front porch.

"Flash transition. And why do I need one?" he asked. "Because Charlie never plays with me anymore. That's why."

The final slide struck a chord with me. Charlie was home less and less lately. I needed to spend some time with him. I flashed back to myself hovering at his door the night before. I should have gone in, talked to him. It was normal for older brothers to distance themselves from younger siblings. They get a peer group and lock on. I tried to pinpoint the moment I spoke with him last. I couldn't remember. The drugs, the drama- they had got in the way. Distracted me. I made a mental note to check in on Charlie.

Abby hugged Benji. "I think we can make that happen. But you would have to take care of him. He'd be your dog. You would need to feed him and bathe him and walk him."

Benji jumped for joy. "I want to take care of him, Mom! I want to!"

We jetted off to a few shelters and found a Benji-looking dog at the third one we checked.

"I'm going to name him Benji," laughed Benji.

He was a bedraggled little thing, guessed to be approximately two years old. Seeing Benji holding his new friend in the backseat was bittersweet. Abby and I were cautious with each other, neither wanting the peace to end. Her hand had found mine on the way back from the pound. I resolved to tell her, just not yet. I wanted one more night of together, one more night of family.

We were exhausted from all the drama and collapsed in bed. Together! As I fell asleep holding her, I thought, "Maybe it doesn't have to end. Maybe she'll understand." My inside voice had a million counters to this, but I shut them out and fell asleep.

That was where the next part of Earth Day occurred. While we were sleeping.

Do you recall that I'd given my work laptop to Benji (the kid, not the dog?). Well, after Abby and I collapsed, exhausted and consumed with our own dramas, our lovely son Benji decided to do his old man a solid.

He was so grateful for Benji (the dog.) I can't keep doing this. I'm going to have to do something about their names and I refuse to use Benji 1 and Benji 2. This is something horrible that Benji lobbied hard for. It may seem heartless, but from here on out I'm calling it 'the dog.' Benji was so grateful for the dog, that he did me a favor.

I realize the conceit of Roger being wounded by his children on various elemental days no longer holds up. We've worked through that. I've grown from there to accept my own responsibility. But. Benji made an Earth Day slide presentation and he used my company laptop to send it to everyone in my contact list.

Subject: Happy Earth Day!!

When I asked him why he sent the email from my work email account later he said, "I know you don't have time for things like Earth Day and such, but it matters to a lot people. I was just trying to help out. I want everyone to know what a great Dad you are. Great Dads care about the Earth."

So, while Abby and I were collapsed in our disintegrating marriage bed, Benji, bubbling over with enthusiasm and being grateful for the dog, decided to use the laptop I'd literally handed to him earlier, and send an Earth Day slideshow that he authored to my work contacts. To show them what a great guy I was.

Jacques had looked strange when I greeted him that morning and shook his head. "Man. That email you sent."

"What email?"

He frowned. "It looks bad. Coming after the strange meeting the other day. Weird."

He looked serious and I dashed to look at my laptop. I found it in the Sent items. "Happy Earth Day!!"

Benji had created the presentation from a good place, with good intentions. Well, minus the rebuke of having your son wanting to work on your image.

I knew I was in trouble at slide one. Benji had used a beautiful pot leaf in the lower left-hand corner. Slide two had it. Slide three had it. Goddamn every slide had a little pot leaf and "Happy Earth Day!!" in the lower left-hand corner. I watched the presentation over and over, dumbstruck. Dissolve. Fade Blocks. Tile Drop. PowerPoint transitions sounded off in my head. Wally was crying in the corner. And that's when my boss called me.

"Roger. Got your email."

"Yes, I apologize for that. My son got his hands on the laptop."

I didn't know what to say. I decided to play it cool. Avoid the pot leaf. Keep it light.

"Roger, I don't know how to say this. I'm just going to level. There's some chatter from HR that you may have a drug problem."

"My kid didn't know that was a pot leaf. He's eleven."

"I get it. But you haven't been yourself lately. And Christ! What happened at the meeting the other day? What were those, hives? Did you go to the doctor?"

My forehead was crawling like it does when I have too many pancakes or Twinkies.

"Yeah, just hives. I'm feeling recovered today. Not sure where they came from. That's never happened to me before."

No, because I'd never smashed up four non-time release Niacin tablets and drank them in an OJ smoothie before. I was in trouble.

"Well, I know you Roger. I know you aren't into drugs. I know it. But things look bad. I've decided to do a preemptive strike. Let's send you through to drug-testing and we can head any nasty rumors off at the pass. Can you hit them up today for me?"

Let's distill this last bit of information.

My drug use was out of control, and it was finally going to cost me my job. Because I'd been high at work and acted like a fool, and because Benji sent out a death warrant, I was going to lose my job. My job was the one thing I always had going for me. My career was the proof that I could handle my drugs. My job was my confirmation of value.

I made my way down to HR, dead man walking. I avoided eye contact with people along the way, but I could feel everyone's eyes on me. I could sense their whispers. I thought to myself, "Please don't be Kyle. Please don't be Kyle." Kyle works in HR and I have hated him for 22 years. I could not bear the smug look he would have given me, the superiority he would have felt while administering my doom. I didn't know the lady who gave me the pee cup, that was some solace. Thank goodness it wasn't Kyle who tested me. Fuck Kyle.

The proctor told me they would have results in by the end of the day.

She smiled at me and said, "You look nervous. Relax. I'm certain you have nothing to worry about."

But she didn't know Jack, did she? I wondered hopelessly what types of drugs they would test me for. I Googled standard drug-test and saw that a "five-panel" was the basic default for employment tests. I was screwed.

I stumbled through the rest of my day, dumb with shock. Thoughts about telling Abby anything disappeared. My co-workers avoided me and I avoided them. I continually fought the urge to hang my head, but also avoided any eye-contact. I thought of the creepy poem The Ballad of Reading Gaol by Oscar Wilde. It's a poem about a lot of things, framed by prisoners waiting on death row.

"Yet each man kills the thing he loves…"

And that was how my career ended. I was fired that day at 2:37 p.m. That's when I got the phone call. At 2:42 p.m. Krazec, the security guard I'd said hello to every workday morning for the last twenty-two years, came to my office with a box. I packed the few personal things I had. A picture of my kids. A picture of Abby. A fake nylon-leafed potted tree. My Nike sports bottle. That was the bottle I always shook my kratom in. Most recently I'd made the Niacin smoothie- I hadn't washed it, I'd been in such a hurry and it smelled sour. That was it. And Roger left the building.

I sat in the car and looked at my termination paperwork, dumbfounded. It had all happened so fast. One minute I am a proud City Engineer. The next, fired in disgrace for illicit drug use.

I'd failed the five panel, no need to send to lab for further testing.

THC: Dirty. I hadn't smoked since the Great Quit two days earlier, but I probably had enough pot in my system to test dirty for months. Opiates: Dirty. I had taken two 10 mg Vicodin three days prior and one small, blue 15 mg morphine pill the day before. That pill didn't even get me high as it was an extended release, but it made my test look like I'd shot up heroin first thing that morning. Cocaine: Dirty. Well, now we know a-PHP can throw a false positive. I hadn't had any cocaine in a year or so. Amphetamines: Dirty. Another false positive from the a-PHP. PCP: Clean!

I failed four out of five panels on my drug test.

I drove out of the parking lot to a nearby park to endure the final part of Earth Day. I stayed in the car and bawled my eyes out. 56-year-old man. Unemployed. Drug addict. Shoplifter. Murderer. Crying in his car at a park in the early afternoon. It doesn't get any creepier than that for bystanders. Once the major sobs subsided, I sort of 'came to' from the haze of grief and saw several kids pointing at me. One of them ran off and I thought maybe he was going to call the cops on the creepy old man at the park. I knew I had to get out of there, but where would I go? Home? There was no way I could face the kids at that time. I certainly wasn't ready to look Abby in the eye.

Thoughts of coming clean were pushed to the back of my mind in the face of the new immediate crisis. Confessing all to Abby was one thing, but confessing all on the heels of losing my job was another. She already thought I was a creepy piece of shit. A lecherous, nude-wife-photo swapping drug addict. She didn't know about the cherry on top. Her husband's unemployment.

I drove away from the park, red-faced. I had to get

away. I had to think. I was beginning to panic. I could feel the knit of reality loosening around me. I drove up to The Wheel. I went east instead of my normal west and drove to the edge of the valley. It was a hot day, and the vista was glazed with shimmering heat. The city looked peaceful from that vantage. Note that I say it looked peaceful. I knew better.

Approximately 2.5 miles to the immediate east was Jasper's grave. Behind his "shed." Blue Blade Cemetery was about six miles due south. All 22 of the bombing victims were buried there. Approximately sixteen miles southwest was Dr. Higgins' House of Evil. I imagined launching a guided missile from the hood of my car. The world would be better off without a Higgins. Every once in a while, I felt the world would be better off without a me.

I sat up there for hours. I actively considered suicide scenarios. I was losing Abby and had lost my job. The kids were certainly next. I will be honest and tell you that every time I have come across a suicide story, I've rolled my eyes and thought: hogwash, poppycock, bullshit cowards. But now I understand. I'm betting embarrassment and shame are the most common reasons for offing yourself.

I have never felt such a crushing shame. I couldn't even look at myself in the rear-view mirror. I felt like I couldn't let anyone see me. Like everyone would see me as the most loathsome creature. Like I'd be offending anyone who had to bleach their eyes after looking at me. I entertained running off. I could just head on north, out of the valley. Start over somewhere. I'd have more luck as an out of luck drifter than unemployed, drug-addicted, divorced middle-aged man. No job? Ugh. Everything else I could have spun.

Around 9:30 p.m. that night I got a text from Abby.

Abby: Where are you?

I thought for a minute before responding. I wasn't in a good head space.

Me: Up at The Wheel.

Abby: What's happening, Roger?

Me: I don't know. I'm barely keeping afloat. I have some stuff I need to tell you.

Abby: When are you coming home?

There it was. My heart leapt! She wanted me to come home. I felt immediate relief at her question. The relief fled about two seconds after it came. I'd lost my job. She wasn't going to want me to come home when she found that out. I had nowhere else to go and I missed Abby so much. The single night we had spent apart hurt. I needed to see her. Our entire marriage had been a team effort. Until Jasper. That's when our team began to unravel. My secrets were tearing us apart. I decided again to hurry home, and tell her everything. Again! I couldn't bear the divide between us. I had to come clean.

Me: On my way.

Yes, I'd committed to this and backed out before, but this truly was the last stop. All trust was gone. My guilty demeanor and evasiveness were blowing us up like a bomb. The nude photos were the icing on the cake, the straw that broke the camel's back. I was not naive. I recognize that I should have told her immediately, the day I was kidnapped. The first time

I was kidnapped.

As I drove home, I tried to rehearse my confessions. Abby, I am so sorry. I screwed up so big. I love you so much. So many horrible things have happened, and I tried to hide them, but I'm just making everything worse. Etc, etc. Even though I am a fierce cling-to-hope kind of guy, it felt over to me. The previous two nights had been the worst in my entire life. Monday night I had slept alone. The next night, even though I felt lucky that she was with me, felt like bleak, beggared time. I had never felt a divide like this with my wife. We had become strangers. Twenty years of the closest bond, and overnight I was afraid to touch her. When I put myself in Abby's shoes, I would be running for the hills. Why didn't I just tell her when all the shit started to hit the fan? Or why didn't I tell her Monday when she got the photos? What kind of a fucking schmuck of a husband, friend, partner just sits there and says nothing? I can't tell you why you got these hot nudes in the mail. I won't even try.

My worry voice Wally said the only nice thing I've ever heard him say in response to that question. "You were so ashamed; you could not speak. But that was before you'd lost your job. Any human in your position would be even more ashamed now." Thanks, Wally. Thank God for self-humanization. What would I do without it?

As I pulled into my driveway, I steeled myself. I was finally ready to tell her everything. I was ready because I was being honest with myself. Telling Abby everything was the only shot I had at keeping our marriage together. I wasn't going to tell her from a position of coming clean, or morally honest. I was going to tell her every last detail as a tactic. I was deciding on honesty as a tool for personal gain.

But none of that happened. Because I sat in my car for about thirty seconds too long. Ok. None of that happened because I'm an idiot.

While I was breathing and quieting Wally in the car, pumping myself up for the Great Last-Ditch Clines Salvation, I got a text.

Higgins: Heard you had a rough day. Need some cash? I have an easy task, even a slug like you couldn't fuck up. Pays 20 K. Come by the office tomorrow a.m.

The first two thoughts I had were:

With some income I wouldn't have to tell Abby I got fired!

Fuck him. I'm no slug!

Cool first thoughts, huh? Not, what type of job? Or, I need to talk to Abby first. I didn't even wonder how he knew I'd lost my job.

I had half-convinced myself that the rock bottom job loss was going to be good for us. You always hear that things can't get better for addicts until they hit rock bottom, right? I still think that's true. But you see, I wasn't at rock bottom yet. There was further to fall.

Stupid and cowardly Roger Clines, faced with going in and telling his wife he'd lost his job and directly killed at least one person, indirectly killed a host of others, and lied about four hundred billion things, looked at the text like a lifeline. A get out of jail card. Like bringing in some money changed my desperate situation, or reversed my firing, or resolved things with my wife.

And that's when my synapses set me off on a new trajectory of destruction. I decided to take the gig. I decided to walk in and try some half-truths. Certainly, I could use some finesse in our talk. I didn't have to bury myself. Right?

Sure, Roger. Go play it off legit with Abby. It will work.

That's how I sauntered into the house that night. Buoyed with asinine thoughts like, never let them see you sweat or always bargain from a position of strength, I sealed Instrument of Death Number 476.

The house was quiet. Too quiet. Charlie wasn't home and when I looked in on Benji he was engrossed in his laptop. Abby was sitting on the bed in our room waiting for me. She had been crying, her eyes were red and she clutched a ball of tissue. Seeing her sitting there, in our broken room, felt like a gut punch. It actually pained me. She looked so small and alone.

I rushed to her like nothing had changed. Like our marriage wasn't a lifeless corpse sharing the passenger seat on a road trip.

"Honey, what's wrong?" I tried to brush her bangs back to see her eyes the same way I always have and she backed away with a jerk.

Like I was a poisonous stranger trying to cop a feel. Like she didn't know me.

She scrambled backwards across the bed using her hands and feet like an upside-down crab.

"I thought I wanted to talk to you," she said,

starting to cry again. "But now that I see you, I don't. I want to run away. I don't know what it is about you, but something about you scares me. You feel dangerous."

"Honey-" I tried to make a plea, but was interrupted as she backed away off the bed and then made her way around the bed to the door.

"You aren't safe," she continued. "I don't know what it is, Roger! I don't know who the hell you are."

I tried to reach out to her, and I threw out a lame duck "I need to talk to you and explain" knowing fully that Abby did not want to hear anything I had to say at that moment.

"Rhetorical statements Roger, and your dumb ass has no intentions of telling her anything," offered Wally.

"Don't you touch me!" Abby snapped. She backed out of the room, her eyes burning wildly. She threw one fevered stare at me and then bolted down the hallway. Seconds later I heard the garage door open, and she was gone. Shit was so fucking broken I didn't even text her that night. No 'I love you please let's talk'. No 'where are you' or 'are you ok?' I knew she wasn't ok. I had no idea where she had gone. She didn't have any serious friends. We had always been so close; we'd been each other's best friend for years. I felt like someone had died.

I hadn't realized how much I really counted on Abby until she wasn't there. She was the most positive, gentle, loving, sweet person I'd ever met. The best person I knew. She saw the best in everyone. She always found beauty in the mundane; she had a way of making the average magical. Years ago, when Brian was about three, we drove him to the beach for the first time. His little mind was blown when he saw the ocean.

"Where are we?" he asked, looking out at the expansive waters.

We had laughed and Abby answered, "We're at the beach." He was so impressed with the sand, the seashells we found, and the roaring of the waves that he kept asking "Where are we?"

When we got in the car and strapped him into his car seat he asked again.

"We're at the beach," Abby answered.

'We're at the beach' became an inside saying in the Clines home. It meant, things are beautiful, perfect, we're at the beach! One time when we got stuck in a terrible traffic jam on the notorious 405 Freeway in southern California, the kids had a meltdown. Brian had been torturing poor Charlie mercilessly in the back seat. We didn't have working air conditioning at the time, and it was 118 degrees Fahrenheit. The windows were down and everyone was cranky and sweaty and sticky and irritable. Brian had taken his shoes and socks off. He had to, you know, it was just so hot.

At some point he decided to drag one of his sweaty, dirty socks over little Charlie's face. Charlie punched out blindly and caught Brian in the eye. Brian hollered and then slapped Charlie across the face, hard! And then they both burst out into tears. Fifteen-year-old Brian crying just like his little brother.

"He hit me!" they both cried.

I tried not to turn around, to focus on getting home. But the cacophony and the crying and the shaking and the violence in the back seat, combined with the excessive heat pushed me to a mental limit.

Abby noticed my hands gripping the wheel tightly. She lightly placed a hand on mine and smiled at me.

"We're at the beach."

At first, I didn't understand and my blood continued to boil.

"We're at the beach, baby," she explained. "It might not feel like it right now, but we are in the most beautiful place in the world. Together."

We're a long way from the beach now.

I raged at myself the entire night. Even though I was exhausted I couldn't sleep. How could I? Take some Z's as my marriage's body decomposes in the corner and my best friend twists. I cried when I thought about her, alone in her car. Or sobbing at a kindly co-worker's house. Or maybe at a bar, looking stunning even in her grief. And all the while, as Wally pointed out, I stewed in the knowledge that I had done nothing to connect with Abby since the bomb.

I thought about her stroking my hair the night we heard about the zoo on the news. She had been so trusting and supportive. She had been so lovely. How the hell had I let this happen? Why did I abandon her?

Wally gave me the obvious and textbook answer: You have been traumatized by multiple kidnappings, a killing and the attachment to multiple fatalities at a family zoo. You haven't worked through any of these issues. Nothing's unpacked, Roger. Every single thing is stacked in moving boxes in your head. Where there used to be pathways for function, now there are blind alleys. All you can do until you face all these boxed horrors is shamble about, watching in mute horror as you destroy your life.

"Fuck me. I'm going crazy, huh Wally?" I asked, answering my own question. Shit! How long have I been going crazy? How long have I been talking to a separate personality in my head? I thought about a moment a few years earlier where Brian was having one of those teen aged moments of crisis. His girlfriend had left him for his best friend. What a mess that was. Brian was devastated on multiple fronts. He couldn't process the betrayal from what he framed as 'everyone I care about.' He was crying in his room and I had gone in there to try and give some advice. Or comfort. Or whatever. I fully realize all my parenting cred is zero.

But this was before the fall. And Brian was in pain.

"I'm never going back to school, Dad. Everyone knows."

My heart had gone out to him. He was a great person, and no one deserves a one-two punch like that. I tried the standard "this too shall pass" and other platitudes, but Brian grew more upset with each dumb thing I said.

He lifted his tear-stained face to me and anguished, "Dad, I think I'm losing it. I think I'm going crazy."

"You'll never get that lucky," I replied immediately, without thinking. "Crazy is a luxury we don't have access to."

In that context, maybe I was just wounded and needed to get fixed. I'd always rolled my eyes when people cried PTSD. Surely the events I'd been through qualified. Self-induced or not, I'd been through the wringer. No, folks. I wasn't losing it. Goddammit, I was just fucking up. I let the shit stack up and choke out my relationship with my wife. My marriage and my job. My family and my livelihood.

When I got up, alone in my broken room, I flashed back to the dumbest moment of the previous night: I don't need to be honest with my wife because I can make 20 K and avoid telling her that I lost my job. Stupid drug-addict thinking and I wasn't even high.

Charlie hadn't come home the night before. I was worried about him too. He had texted me late that he was staying the night with a friend, but I'd been feeling a growing distance from him for a while. I'd just been too engrossed in my own drama to worry about it. I was hoping everything was ok. Hoping it was standard teenage stuff.

I got Benji off to school. He asked where Abby was. I didn't put on the standard sitcom dad "hey kiddo" hair-ruffle act.

"I don't know."

When I was getting ready to head to Higgins office, he texted me, on cue, in his standard creepy way.

HIGGINS: Payment wired to your bank account from Los Noches Investments, LLC. Destination: Minnesota. Be there tonight. Don't fuck it up. Instructions emailed.

It was heartening to see crime integrating technology and I was glad to not have to go to that fucking office. I texted Abby a few times and tried phoning but got no answer. The receptionist at her office recognized my voice and froze me out. But when I drove past her work, Abby's car wasn't there. At some point in the morning I decided to just bring Benji with me. Grabbing him from school to take him on a trip to Minnesota sounded fun. I wanted to engage with him, do something to pull his attention away from the fact that his family was disintegrating. I pulled him out of school and he was absolutely thrilled. I shot Abby a text, not thinking of how threatening it might feel to her for me, Mr. Unsafe, to take Benji out of state.

ME: Have an unexpected meeting in Minneapolis. Bringing Benji with me. We will be home tomorrow night.

"But what about Benji, Dad?" he had asked. "I don't trust Charlie to take care of him. I don't even know where Charlie's been lately. He's not the same."

I made a mental note to get to the bottom of the Charlie business when we returned. After all, I was a new free-agent. I'd have all the time in the world to figure things out with him now that I wasn't encumbered with a day job. I was trying to focus on the positive.

"Okay, let's bring him along."

Benji was overjoyed. He cheered. The look on his face? That look of pure happiness and love? He looked too much like Abby for it not to hurt. Would I ever see Abby smile again? I wanted to make Benji so happy, that I didn't even blink at what a drag bringing the dog would be. We ended up getting lucky. The dog was small enough to fit in a carrier under the seat. It was easy. When I called, they asked me his breed. I

shrugged and said "I dunno. He's a little Benji dog."
The lady said they allow terriers under 25 pounds.
And that was it. They charged an extra 150 dollars and
we were off.

That's how I got here. Meeting Thick Rick at the
Frozen Feline Lounge in Rochester. My instructions
didn't tell me why I was here, only that I'm to contact
Thick Rick. My last text to Abby was: Actually,
taking both the Benji's with me. Have you heard from
Charlie?

She still hasn't replied. I finally heard from Charlie
about an hour ago: See you tomorrow Dad! God bless
him. At least there is that. Brian is okay. Charlie is
okay. Benji is okay. I mean, I think. I figure. I hope.
Shit is less than ideal. I admit this. But the kids are
okay for now. I just gotta clear this hurdle, get back
home, find a way to kill Higgins and…

No, I don't know what the fuck I'm doing. I don't
know what the fuck I'm going to do. How do I fix this
mess? Talk to Abby? Well, fucking goddammit! I
can't. I can't talk to her! It's too awful. I'm so
ashamed and embarrassed. I've never been like this
before. I've always been a good communicator.
Things are changing.

Roger's shutting down. Shit.

It's now 1:00 a.m. on the dot. I'm going to get out
of the car, walk into the Frozen Feline Lounge, and
casually ask to see Thick Rick. It's no big deal.

ROGER GOES TO MINNESOTA

We arrived at the Forrestville Mystery Cave National Park around ten this morning. Benji was hopped up on being eleven. Do you remember what that was like? Your future stretched out ahead of you full of every possibility? It is still cool to hang with your parents, and bad days can be fixed with a cold soda or some ice cream. Or in Benji's case a docent-led tour of a cave. The boy with the PowerPoint slide fetish also loves himself some docents. He won't shut up about them. If you didn't understand the words he was using, you'd think he was talking about his favorite NFL quarterback.

"Dad did you know that a quality docent can increase the amount you learn by up to one thousand percent?"

I'd like to point out, that even though my back was against the wall, and I was entirely at everyone's mercy, I still refused to acknowledge that one.

Ridiculous. My fingers tightened on the wheel.

"Did you know that a quality bowel movement can increase food capacity by a thousand percent?"

Yes, even while the ship is going down, Roger still fights fire with fire, folks. When your kid says stupid shit, you can't take that lying down. Right?

About 45 minutes from Rochester there was a split. We turned off onto a gravel road that wound into the woods a couple of miles. We spilled out from the rustic gravel trek into a clearing that looked like it was straight from the suburbs. Spacious, well-paved parking lot. Clean white parking line paint. The lot was nearly full, even at ten in the morning. I cringed, and tried to guess how many cars were there. Maybe a hundred? For a cave tour at ten in the morning?

"It's called field trips, Dad," said Benji rolling his eyes. "Did you really call ahead and get us a tour spot?"

"Sure did, kid," I lied.

The Benjis shot from the car the second I turned the engine off. This is a key moment, because this is the moment that I lost the thread. I was laser focused on getting to the ticket office without Benji finding out I had lied about reservations, and while I didn't see where they went, I did note that it was in the opposite direction I was headed. Not only was I focused on covering my lie, but we also didn't have much time. Our flight back was at 5 p.m., which only gave us a few hours before we had to make the two-hour drive to the airport.

A pristine, modern building sat at the foot of a wooded hill, standing out in contrast to the surrounding nature. The building had the words "VISITOR'S CENTER" in raised metal letters over the brick. It looked like a brand-new elementary school in the suburbs. In a small moment of foreshadowing I paused before entering the building. A mural on the side of the building made from black iron caught my eye. There was a dark tree, where half of the leaves looked like they were being blown away. The "leaves" on the other side were hanging bats, sleeping. Creepy. Fucking creepy bat stuff on a ridiculously expensive and fresh-looking Visitor's Center outside of the Mystery Cave in the woods in Minnesota.

The employee was very nice. She took one look at my California clothes, i.e. short sleeved T-Shirt and jeans, and told me that we would need jackets. The caves were a constant 47 degrees Fahrenheit. She fit us into a an "hour long walking tour, led by our most knowledgeable guide Terrance." Benji was going to be thrilled. "This is the longest cave in Minnesota at over 13 miles long," she intoned. "Full of twists and honeycomb maze turns, you are taking the scenic tour. It consists of an easy walk across a mostly modern walkway. This tour is guided, because getting lost in there is easy as pie."

She charged me nineteen dollars for our tickets and let me know in closing "of course, no pets are allowed in the cave." I should have assumed as much, but my head had been lost in the dust of deconstruction. I hadn't really been thinking of Benji all that much. He was here as a guilty convenience. Because his criminal father had to make a trip to Minnesota immediately after driving his mother away.

The meeting with Thick Rick had been ominous. I introduced myself. He scowled and grunted off through a doorway and came back with a small package, wrapped in butcher paper, taped neatly. I could feel something hard and round inside. He told me he had a message – asked me to write it down. So, there I was, transcribing for Thick Rick on a cocktail napkin.

"Cannot find your brother. No one has any idea. He left no clues. His students say he's been getting weirder since his boy got killed. Found what you wanted at his house. Was where you said it would be. PS. Who is this messenger clown? He's a pussy. Write that down."

I wrote every terrifying and insulting word down. Rick was an imposing figure. He was tall and stiff, like Frankenstein. He was dressed in a matching sweat suit, like a Russian gangster from a car-heist video game. Maybe Higgins had sent me across the country to face what I'd done. To see the destruction that I'd caused. In that case, he'd be disappointed. Beyond wondering if Thick Rick intended to kill me right there, which was scary, but didn't seem likely. I didn't care. I don't care that Jasper is dead any more. I'm glad he's dead. Good! I did wish that someone other than myself had done it. It had fucked me up fiercely. But good riddance. The trash had to be taken out. And I didn't care about Higgins' brother, twisting in grief somewhere. Maybe he'd gone out to the woods and shot himself out of shame for raising a piece of shit.

Thick Rick grabbed the napkin from my hand with

a meaty paw and gave it an approving glance before handing it back to me.

"Get the fuck out of my face," he said, waving his hands dismissively.

When I got back into the rental my bravado fled and I started doing the shaking, shivering thing that I recognized as some sort of shock. No big deal, that's just how you feel after you narrowly cheat death. And it's a sensation I'm becoming increasingly familiar with.

But that was last night. And while it's strange to look back at that insane moment as a better time than now, trust me. Mark last night as a preferred destination in the time machine. If I could roll back to last night, I may still be above water. If we could do today over, I may have had a chance. Maybe.

The second I stepped out with tickets in-hand I knew something was wrong. I expected to see Benji bounding about, but I didn't see him or the dog. I scanned the lot; I scanned the edge of the woods to the left. We were at the base of a smallish mountain and off to the right was a fairly steep embankment of scraggly brush and rock. It didn't look like they would be that way. I started to walk towards the woods, calling out. As I neared the wooded area, I saw a sign that read, "Mystery Caves, This Way."

I headed into the woods along a dirt path and was swallowed by greenery. I've never been anywhere so verdant. I'm from Southern California and my one trip out of the country was to Egypt. I've only known deserts. I'd never felt greenery that was so aggressive. Looking down the path I could see a small, squat building at the end. There was a slight metal railing that led to the building. The bushes and trees were engulfing everything- the rail looked like it was floating on leaves.

My heart sank as I looked around and didn't see my boy. We were out of state in the woods and I hadn't been watching. I was so preoccupied with covering my lie and being right, that I'd lost him.

Even though we were only a few miles from the highway, and only a few hundred feet from the frosted parking lot and shiny Visitor's Center, it felt like I was in the wild. As I hollered, "Benji! Benji" I futilely tried to identify any natural predators. Were there bears? Moose?

The door on the small building flung open and a ranger puffed out, his face red. I ran towards him.

"Ranger! My son is missing."

I could tell from the look on his face that he already knew something was up. His face turned even redder.

"The father. You're the father," he huffed.

"Yes, my son is missing. Have you seen him? His name is Benji."

"Your son is okay sir, but the dog is missing. Come on."

He turned back through the doorway and I followed, my knees weak from stress and adrenaline. The door opened into a sparse, square room that had nothing but some downward stairs in the corner. He bounded down the stairs.

"The entrance is down here. Come on," he said as he descended. The stairwell deposited us in the cave. It was a strange place. The building had been erected over the cave entrance, and the first chamber of the cave was a strange combination of nature and man. There were what looked like steel support beams that were driven into the rock, and smooth concrete walkways that twisted off into a moderately lit tunnel. There were accent lights in the upper corners and lighting the path. Weird.

My eyes caught Benji. He was wearing one of the ranger's green jackets, sitting cross-legged on the ground in a heap. His face was buried in his hands. He looked up, saw that I was there and then covered his face again.

"Sorry Dad," he said, his voice small and muffled.

"We found him running around in the lower chambers, looking for the dog," explained the ranger. "He said he ran in after it and got lost. Gene is in there right now. He'll find it."

That was a shitty moment. I was relieved at finding Benji, but I was ashamed for losing him. I hadn't even dressed him correctly. My mind flashed back to a sign in the Visitor's Center: The cave is constant 48 degrees. Bundle up! I was irritated at myself and embarrassed. I hadn't even packed Benji a change of clothes, let alone a jacket. I went and hunkered down next to him.

"The dog ran in? You ran in after?" I asked. "What were you doing in here? You brought the dog? In here?"

"I lost him Dad," Benji cried. "I lost him. I'm crummy at taking care of dogs. I'm a horrible guardian."

He threw his arms around my neck, pressing his

teary face against mine. There I was, kneeling down in a cave-building amalgam, fifty miles outside of Rochester, Minnesota, holding my grief-stricken boy. His words stung because, while they weren't true, they highlighted a truth. The truth that Roger Clines was a horrible guardian.

"Benji," I said, my voice cracking. "Benji this is my fault son, not yours."

Benji pulled his face back to look at me. "You are a great Dad. You are the best Dad. I'm so, so sorry. Do you think they will find him?"

Staring back, I cracked. Seeing his grief and pain, caused by my neglect, I broke down. Looking at him I thought: I'm a piece of shit. A complete piece of shit. That was followed by an overwhelming sensation of tumbling guilt. And I started to cry. At first my breath started to catch, then my chin started to tremble. I made several sounds I didn't recognize. A few faint combination squeak-scratch noises like a rat behind a wall, and then my grief caught an unstoppable momentum. And the dam burst. I cried big baby sobs, the kind of sobs where snot runs from your nose and you have to gulp for air. I was only faintly aware of the look on Benji's face as he stared down twin roads of desolation. His dog was lost. And his dad? What was wrong with his dad?

At some point, while I was weeping on the floor, Benji stood up and then over me, and hugged my head. I was vaguely aware of him holding me, trying to soothe me. At the back of my wailing grief there were two typical Roger thoughts: I'm so fucked up that my son is comforting me. I'm so fucking fucked up that my boy is the one comforting me, rather than the other way around. Okay, so shame was the first thought. Double shame was the second thought, as I wondered how ridiculous I must look to the ranger. I'd forgotten he was there. He was standing off to the side, looking like he wanted to disappear.

He saw me looking at him and politely offered, "Gene will find it. He's real familiar with the cave."

"Will Benji be okay, do you think?" Benji asked.

Just then we heard some sounds from the cave. Benji leapt up.

"That's him! They found him!"

A ranger, clothes muddied, emerged with the dog in his arms. Benji began to cheer, but the look on the ranger's face stopped him cold.

"He's been hurt, son," Gene said, and handed the dog to Benji.

The dog was a shivering, wet mess. Benji cooed and stroked him. I could see blood on Benji's clothes.

"What happened to him?" Benji asked, his voice small.

Gene looked around the room. First to his co-worker who just shrugged, then at me, red-faced on the ground, then to Benji.

"It was bats, son. A whole lot of bats. They didn't mean any harm, but he scared 'em. He ran into a roosting colony and they got frightened."

He put a hand on the dog's snout and lightly pushed the wet fur to the side. There were hundreds of fine, red lines crisscrossing the dog's nose.

"Bats are blind, sure. Even still they usually see better than we do. But when they are in their roosting caves, they turn off their sonar. When they get woken abruptly, they swarm around for a bit before they get their bearings. That's why we don't allow pets in the cave – they can mess with the bats patterns and hurt either the bats or themselves."

A single tear fell down Benji's face. "Will Benji be okay?"

Gene glanced at me, then back at my son. "Could be. Could be. I would take him to a vet right away, he's in shock."

Benji looked at his me, still collapsed on the ground, and said, "He's bleeding, Dad."

Somehow, I pushed myself up and staggered to him, trying to shake off my paralyzing grief and to do something right for the goddamn day. I laid a hand on his head and looked at the dog. He was a disheveled mass of wet fur and mud and blood. There were countless scarlet scratches all over his body. The dog was shivering. I ignored the fact that a moment ago I was snotting in the dirt and got my dad hat on.

"Let's go, son. We'll get him some help."

We pushed the door open and exited into the bright woods. My cellphone led us to the nearest veterinarian office, which was all the back in Rochester. The dog had bled all over the rental's interior and bloodied Benji's T-shirt. It shivered in a heap and whimpered faintly. I glanced at the time as we brought the dog in, Benji carrying him gravely. It was noon. We had four hours to get to the airport and catch our flight back home.

The vet was very kind, and examined the dog carefully. Benji watched, his face strained, explaining what had happened. The vet just nodded and listened. The vet told Benji that his assistant was going to take the dog in the back and get him cleaned up.

"Do you like puppies?" he asked my son.

"I sure do," answered Benji.

The vet put his arm on Benji's shoulder, and glancing at me with a knowing look, guided him to another room with a row of kennels. He knelt down and opened one of the cages. Three retriever puppies bounded out, yapping and licking. Benji dropped to his knees entranced. The vet gestured to the doorway and I followed.

He told me in a hushed voice that the dog would need to be put to sleep. He'd been bitten and scratched hundreds of times, and a percentage of bats carry rabies. The dog was undoubtedly infected- if he'd been bitten just once or twice the protocol would be to isolate the dog for a week or two and see if he displayed any symptoms. But with hundreds of wounds, the odds that he had the virus pointed to certainty. I kept my face flat. Looking at my son, happily playing with the puppies, I felt the overwhelming grief from earlier bubbling to the surface. I had to hold it together! I nodded and told the vet that I understood. Let's get it done.

I explained the situation to Benji. He asked if he could tell the dog goodbye, and a vet assistant took us to the back. The poor dog laid there trembling. He licked Benji's face and Benji whispered something to him. Then something even more painful happened. Benji straightened up, his back stiff.

He turned around without a backwards glance and

said "Okay Dad. Let's go."

It was the adult in his posture that hurt. The ramrod straight back, a stiff neck. He didn't look eleven in that moment. He looked like a man. Like a soldier at a friend's funeral. We drove to the airport in silence. I was numb. I had ruined my son. I had killed his new pet, killed his joy. He still had that stiff stance, his face impassive, showing nothing. Awful.

We were next in line at airport security, when I remembered the package I'd gotten from Thick Rick. Holy shit, I'd forgotten about it. It was forgotten at the bottom of my backpack. I teetered for a moment when the TSA agent gestured for us to come forward. What if Higgins was framing me? What if the package was a bomb or drugs and we were about to get popped in the X-Ray machine? Benji marched ahead and I followed, deciding it was too late. I craned my neck back to look at the screen over the conveyor belt. Nothing looked suspicious, I couldn't even detect the package. We made it through without incident.

I checked the paper wrapped package in the restroom and debated opening it. I shook it, but nothing rattled. It felt like a singular item about the size of a walnut. A polished stone maybe? I reassured myself that it probably wasn't going to explode and decided against opening it.

4:00 p.m. saw us sitting next to each other in airport chairs in silence. Every time I looked at Benji he was staring straight ahead, expressionless. I recognized that look. Benji was in shock. My son was in shock. The dog was dead. Dead because I suck. My son was in shock because I suck. My wife was reeling in shock somewhere in California because I suck. Wally noted that I was somewhat of a Federal hazard. I was so miserable that I was grateful he used the word 'somewhat.' That was kind.

At 4:35 p.m. things went from utter disaster to full, unadulterated DEFCON One. I got a text from Abby. Finally, I thought. My heart shot up, and then was shoved back down instantly. What was I going to tell her? She was going to kill me! She was going to explode! But the text wasn't good news. It was the worst news. The bottom of the barrel news. News that made Benji's dog loss pale. News that made my exploding marriage look like Saturday morning cartoons.

Abby: Charlie is hurt. He has overdosed on something. I'm following an ambulance to the hospital now. What time will you be back?????

Sitting there at the St. Paul Airport, my son an impassive rack of hurt next to me, I experienced an out of body moment. My vision swam and I rose up from body until I was looking down at us. We looked like any other father and son waiting for a flight. I couldn't see the horrors from that vantage point. We looked normal. For a quick moment my heart went out to poor, old Roger Clines. Would the hits ever stop coming? Would he ever know peace?

My vision swam again, and I plummeted back down into my body. Looking out from Roger's eyes, the feeling of empathy drained. There was no feeling sorry for Roger. He was the reason everyone was in so much pain. Roger's selfishness was the reason his family was in shambles. He just had to get high.

Gross.

I regained control and responded.

Me: Benji and I are in St Paul, our flight leaves at 5. We should be home around 9. What happened? Which hospital are you going to?

Abby: I came home about an hour ago. Charlie was in his room, lying on his bed, foaming at the mouth. He was having a seizure. I don't know what he took. We are at Winchester Medical. Just got here. Will know more soon.

Me: I love you Abby. I'm so sorry. We are on our way.

We boarded the plane and took to the skies, heading home in silence. I felt the most helpless rage. I tried to will the plane to fly faster. I contemplated what I should tell Benji regarding Charlie, and when. He fell asleep about 30 minutes into the flight, thank goodness.

We were at 30,000 feet when I got even worse news. I know, right?

Abby: Charlie is asleep. They say he will be fine. When you get back, I want you to take Benji home. I don't want him to see Charlie like this. And I don't want you here.

Me: Thank God. He will be fine? What did he take? I will be there soon.

Abby: No. You aren't allowed.

I assumed I knew why. I was a real piece of shit who couldn't be trusted. I couldn't even keep our kids or our pets safe. Or even alive. But Abby didn't know that then.

I wanted to see Charlie so badly at that moment I

didn't care. I needed to see my son. I needed to hold him. I needed to talk to him. To tell him I was sorry. To see that he was safe. Abby couldn't keep me away at a time like this. That was madness. Certainly, you all understand. A father needs to see his son when he OD's and almost dies. So, dumb ass, disgusting, piece of shit Roger texted something stupid.

Me: I have to see him. I should be there in a few hours.

Abby: He overdosed on 25I-NBOMe. He told the doctor he took an "N-bomb." Any idea where he got a hold of this deadly substance, Roger? The police are on their way here to talk to us. If you show up, I will give them my theory on how he acquired it.

Me: But I flushed all of the drugs. All of them! Days ago!

Abby: Take Benji home and stay there. I will talk to you when I come home.

Me: I swear I got rid of everything!

Abby: Stay the fuck away and wait.

That was a couple of hours ago. Benji just woke up, but he still has that heart-breaking wooden expression. I want to see my son when we land but I can't. I gotta take Benji home. Without his best friend. My God, he looked scarred. Did I permanently ruin my kid Benji today?

And Charlie? Overdosed and almost died a few hours ago. And I wasn't there and I can't be there. And what the fuck? What is Charlie doing fucking around with that shit? I know this sounds lame, but I'm nearly certain he didn't get it from me. My stuff was hidden pretty well. When I'd flushed the 25I, it looked untouched. It probably seems obvious to non-drug users that my kid got the rare drugs from me. But I truly was careful. Our room was always locked. The stuff was hidden. I'm not trying to shift responsibility or absolve myself. Obviously, I'm too far gone for any considerations at this point.

He didn't get it from me. And if he didn't get this ridiculously lethal and rare designer drug from me, where did he get it? How many dealers in our valley are pushing 25I-NBOMe? How many dealers anywhere, for that matter? Albert. It had to be Albert. For the first time in my life I sympathized with the anti-drug crowd. Fucking pusher, poisoning my kid, I thought lamely.

My mind is racing down blind alleys, fracturing at each dead end, desperate for a thread of good news. For a clear path forward. For anything that justifies my existence. Anything at all.

The captain just announced we will be making our descent. The engine is roaring and the seat belt sign is lit. There is a voice inside my head saying things I don't like. It's Wally. My constant pal Wally.

"How many drugs do you think you've brought to town over the years? What do you think Albert does with the drugs that he doesn't sell to you? It's your fault that there was any 25I for Charlie to get his hands on."

Okay, sure. But.

My God.

ROGER MANUFACTURES AN ILLICIT
SUBSTANCE

And that's how I lost my family. That's how I found myself alone in a home I could no longer afford. There are so many layers to my grief now. Abby packed Charlie and Benji up and left to 'clear her head' at her parent's house in New Jersey, over two thousand miles away.

Fortunately, Charlie recovered quickly and was released without any lingering complications. Unfortunately, I only got to see Charlie once after he got out of the hospital and he avoided me completely. That hurt so badly. I needed to talk to him. I needed to find out where his 25I had come from. Abby acted like Charlie had indicated he'd gotten it from me. Knowing him, he probably had determined that letting Abby think she was right was his best course of action. Mom's mad at Dad, so I will hint that it's Dad's fault.

I wanted to tell Charlie that I wasn't mad. That I didn't blame him. That we were cool. In the back of my mind, however, I wondered how cool we could possibly be. What if he had gotten the drugs from my stash? Was I any more or less culpable for his close call either way?

I was so desperate to prove that I wasn't the source of Charlie's drugs that I did something stupid. Abby and the kids had been gone for 22 days and I was going crazy. I guessed that Albert was the one who sold them to him. It wasn't a huge logic leap, but then I did a douche thing. I drove over to his house in a huff and pounded on his door. I accused him of pushing drugs on my son through his screen door.

"I never sold your son shit, yo!" he spit back at me. "Get the fuck outta here."

"You almost killed my son! You piece of shit!"

"Get the fuck outta here before I call the cops, Roger."

Albert snarled as he shut the door in my face. The slam of the door snapped me out of it.

"Oh Jesus. What the fuck am I doing?" I asked myself, standing on his porch.

"Cracking up," answered Wally. "You're cracking up."

That was the moment I decided to do something about it. I needed advice. I needed serious advice. If I had been in a fantasy kingdom, I would have decided to seek out the Oracle. But this is real life. And real life doesn't have any all-knowing Oracles.

I slunk back to my empty house. Embarrassed, ashamed and alone. Well, not completely alone.

Bryan still lived in town, and he had been surprisingly sympathetic. But he's only stopped by once and the empty house hurt him. He split in a hurry. I didn't blame him.

Later that night I found myself four beers in, alternating between helpless rage, shame and grief. The house felt barren. I was listlessly surfing the web and I found myself reading about hallucinogens.

I admit it. I miss them. I miss all the drugs. I know they are what got me in this spot, but hell, now I'm here. The damage is already done.

"Why stop now?" I thought. I missed getting out of my head. I missed the crisp, hyper-reality of LSD and the fuzzy love of mushrooms. That's the night I came across DMT. Have you heard of it? I've got to explain what I learned about this.

DMT, or N, N-Dimethyltryptamine is a tryptamine molecule that exists in many plants and animals. It has been called "the spirit molecule." DMT naturally occurs in rat brains, human cerebrospinal fluid and other tissues of humans, plants and mammals. Our bodies produce the stuff. In 1965, German scientists were able to isolate it in human blood and urine. Subsequent studies detected it in human blood, urine, feces, kidney tissue, lung tissue and spinal fluid. In 2014, a study showed that DMT aides the immune response in some cells through sigma-1 receptors and may play a role in tissue regeneration.

The super-magic theory accompanying DMT, is that it is generated in the pineal gland and that it is consumed when you die in order to facilitate your soul's exit. They say that users aren't hallucinating while under its influence. That maybe they are leaving their body and having a fully realized experience in another dimension. In 2013, scientists were able to isolate DMT from a rat pineal gland, but to date there is no proof that the human brain generates the molecule to facilitate spiritual breakthroughs. Some theorize that Jesus had a lot of naturally occurring DMT, and that is how he was able to speak to God. (Fuck you and your Manna-Jesus, Higgins. It's DMT-Jesus all the way.) Not quite an illicit drug, although it is illegal to have or use.

DMT is the active drug in the trippy potion, ayahuasca. That drink has been used for thousands of years in native ceremonies in South America. You know, the brew that makes you puke and see your spirit guide? That sounds edifying, but you puke and have diarrhea and it lasts for hours. No way. A smoked DMT trip only lasts about fifteen minutes. Most users who take enough of this stuff report meeting an entity. Users who smoke enough DMT (breakthrough dose listed as 30-50 milligrams) say they leave their body via a tunnel at high speeds, break through to other dimensions, and then meet someone or something that helps give advice and perspective.

A substance that takes most users to another world where they meet and interact with an entity? They also report a strong spiritual connection with a guide, a spirit creature, that helps give advice and perspective.

One user experience I came across was of a fifty-year-old neuroscientist. He said that after he took a large hit, he fell back on the bed and could no longer feel his body. His field of vision was first filled with morphing fractals and he was overcome with a loud sound. The sound carried him rapidly through a dark tunnel that appeared to be made from an onyx snakeskin. He popped out on the other side of the tunnel and was in a large canyon. He got the sense that he was an orb, a circular spirit creature. He could not see the top nor the bottom of the canyon, but as he hurtled along, the stone walls of the canyon morphed into large, roaring hyena heads made from stone. Ahead in the dark he saw a spirit orb coming towards him. He had a sense of familiarity he couldn't explain.

"It was as if this creature before I was a human, and he recognized me and I recognized him, and we had a joyous reunion. We spoke but we didn't use words. You could send a thought to someone and they would hear it in their head."

He claims to have zipped around for years in that wide canyon with his old friend. He explained things to him about how life works, what death is, his spiritual purpose. When he came out of it, only fifteen minutes of real life had passed. He said he was afraid as he woke up, thinking he'd been away for upwards of 50 years, that everyone he loved on Earth would have died while he was gone.

There was similar experience after similar experience. This person visited an emerald city. This one visited with his dead father. Another was taught the cure for cancer although he claims he is unable to articulate what he learned. What if this substance really did transport you to alternate dimensions? Could I discover some bit of precious knowledge that would allow me to rescue my desperate situation?

I know how kooky this probably looks, but consider my position. Remember friends, when you are up against a wall of doom, self-imposed or not, you are the beast with a bloodied paw in the trap. Your eyes cast about wildly, desperate for a life raft or flash of inspiration in the face of impending destruction.

Consider my logical and sane options with me. Let me set the stage:

I'm home alone. I'm unemployed. My wife and youngest children are in New Jersey, "visiting" my in-laws. Abby hinted that they may decide to stay out there. She believes me to be dangerous and flawed. The stupid aquarium sits there lifeless. Abby took the goddam fish with her too. I look like criminal dog shit to my kids. It's my fault that Charlie OD'd. It's my fault I lost my job. It's my fault I'm a murderer. It's my fault Jasper built and deployed a bomb. It's my fault the dog is dead. My only income is spotty deposits from a modern-day despot who hates me as a useful idiot. And has sworn to kill me for the murder of his nephew. His thugs could burst in and kill me at any time.

This is the objective stage, as set by facts. Agreed?

On to my logical and sane options. The baseline for "logical and sane options" will be options a rational human might consider. Forward movements that folks like you could endorse.

The most logical and sane option would be to turn myself into the police. Tell them everything. Accept the fate of justice. This would be the best logical and sane choice for the benefit of Abby and the children. Yes, Daddy is crap, but at least he accepted responsibility for his actions and owned them. At least there is that. He's in prison. He can't screw up our lives any more. I would escape the slow death by Street Justice Higgins.

I think that's it. That's the single logical and sane option before me. It's the most logical from a social standpoint, and the sanest from a survival standpoint.

However, as I sat there alone feeling despondent, another cog of my sanity ran off the track. I physically felt an unhinging occur that night. The interesting feature accompanying my loosening grip looks a lot like hope. When I came across the DMT I felt the same crazy sense of wonder and possibilities that I did when I considered manna. And while I know it's insane to entertain the thought that DMT may point me to the way out of my mess, it's directly sane to want a way out. Unless you are just a masochistic zealot who hates good times, you will always hope for a way out. My pragmatic survival drive used insanity and desperation as a tool to locate possible solutions.

I didn't want to go to the police. I didn't know about a bomb; I don't want to be tied to a bombing. I had to kill Jasper. I ruined my job myself. I can't genuinely blame Benji for that. I wanted my family back. I'd followed the ebb and flow of my guilt and each time when I pictured desired outcome it was to have everything I wanted.

The epic quality of what I'd read about DMT excited me so I decided to look on YouTube to see if I could find any more information. That was initially discouraging. A search of DMT gave me results like: Why I Will Never Do DMT Again, How DMT Made

Me Rich, Portal to the Spirit World, Your Third Eye and Your Pineal Gland, Joe Rogan's DMT Experience. The comments for these videos were general nuts, but I felt as though I found a thread within them.

Comments for YouTube Video 'DMT Entities':

Jodi Art – "Yup, the entities exist. They are like interface. The Bible talks about Jesus doing healings on people extracting the spirits. People don't realize that they hop from person to person around you. They act through you and other people and hop around you. I discovered I might be a shaman, walking in the woods every day. Then I realized it was Native American spirits wanting me to do stuff they wanted me to do. Then I realized, this is my body, my experience. I didn't feel like a shaman anymore. It's all our freewill and they play on our emotional injuries. So, if you want to feel special, they will make you feel special. But if we feel like we are all brothers and sisters equal, even the entities that passed on, they leave you alone."

Bear with me here folks, I'm getting to a point.

V A – "Do gentle parasite cleanses. The parasitic entities in the astral realms have their physical counterparts in the microcosm of our world, tiny amoeba, parasites, fungus and virus within us. They live off of commercial food and meats mainly. Every time I do a parasite cleanse, I feel the emotions and thoughts that go with them."

Jillian Schuster – "I astral project a lot and encounter shape shifting, trickster Draconian beings. Also, these little mischievous gremlin-like creatures.

They definitely attempt to act as gatekeepers to prevent us from getting to the higher dimensions. Super annoying!"

When I first read about DMT it sounded promising and fascinating. But when I dug deeper, I found the typical nutty center. Druggies, nut jobs, schizophrenics, out of touch dreamers. Zealots. And what seemed possible at first quickly degraded by the association of internet riff-raff. And then my desperate brain engineered a ray of hope. A link. I remembered something Aldous Huxley had posited. While George Orwell had predicted a world of information control, Huxley foresaw a world of hyper-information. He claimed there would be so much information and mis-information, that the facts would get lost in the mess. In a sea of data.

Maybe the truth looks so ridiculous that it lies in plain sight, I thought. I decided to try some. In the past, I would just call Albert and he'd find it, but those days are gone. I cringed looking back on all the drugs I brought into town while, simultaneously typing "how to make dmt" into the Google bar.

The top result was "The Super-Secret Way to Make DMT".

I found quite a few recipes that seemed legit. These recipes were called "teks". The simplest ones called for a DMT-containing plant to be ground into powder, and then for a DMT extraction via lye and naphtha. I was no chemist, but the steps looked fairly straightforward. Doable.

I learned of a plant called Mimosa hostilis, also referred to as Mimosa tenuiflora that contains between 1 to 1.7 percent DMT. It is a perennial tree native to northern South America that grows from Brazil all the way up into Mexico. It has fern like branches, and it supports cows, goats and sheep in the areas it grows. This is the root that is traditionally used to brew Ayahuasca for spirit quests.

I was able to find a company in the UK that shipped powdered Mimosa hostilis root bark to the United States, but the website looked shady. I Googled "customs mimosa hostilis" and found a few news articles about a handful of people who were arrested for having it shipped in from Spain. But they had ordered huge quantities. Pounds. I checked for legality and discovered that while the bark was legal in the United States, they had busted these folks for manufacturing. The Feds let the shipments through, then raided them about three weeks later. Gave them time to set up a lab and prove intent. But I didn't need pounds. I was able to find that the USDA has assigned a hardiness zone to the plant – "Mimosa hostilis requires USDA Zone 9 or higher." So, the plant itself isn't illegal.

I decided to risk it and get a small amount. There was a legitimate use for this bark. Apparently, it made a rich and vibrant purple dye. The root bark has been prized for hundreds of years for its vivid coloring qualities. I was going to tie-dye some shirts, I would say. I ordered a kilogram for 256 US dollars. According to the guides I had found online, a kilogram should produce approximately 5-10 grams of DMT. That seemed like a lot, but I was determined to experience the breakthrough tunnel everyone was talking about, and to hopefully meet the right cosmic cat, come back home and score my family.

The bark arrived seven days later. It was a light purplish-brown powder that smelled like dirt. Here is my list of supplies:

Eye dropper (the chemistry teks call this a 'pipette') or turkey baster

Rubber spatula

Coffee filters

Naphtha (VM&P)

Lye (granulated NaOH)

Safety goggles

Dust mask

One-gallon glass mixing jar

Collection jars – 4 wide mouth 8 oz jelly jars with lids

I was able to grab everything at Lowe's. And yes, I paid for it. There are some things you don't steal, like electronics from Wal-Mart or goods from a hardware store. They will catch you. They will prosecute and harass as far as they can push it. And, I don't do that shit anymore. Says the drug addict who doesn't do drugs any longer. Except for DMT. For a good cause. More sighs.

Just common items. The naphtha is a solvent used to thin oil-based paints and enamel. And the lye is a toxic chemical used to make soap. It was hard to believe that I could 'cook DMT', the single most hallucinogenic substance on earth, using fifty dollars of supplies and a kitchen. The simplicity of the tek, pour chemicals on the powdered root bark, agitate, pour off chemical and let evaporate, seemed too easy.

But you know me. Roger always is holding a torch for the underdog, for the long shot.

I gathered my items together, and got started. It was a Monday night, six weeks since I'd lost my job and four weeks since Abby had left.

First, I made my lye-water. Lye is legitimately used to make soap. Its scientific name is sodium hydroxide, also called caustic soda. It comes with a few risks. Permanent blindness is possible if it gets in your eyes. Severe exposure to the skin can result in deep burns with massive scarring. Making the lye-water is the most dangerous part of the process, and that's been done for a thousand years and people seem to do okay. Lye is also what is used in some pipe clog removers.

I know this because the bottle of lye I bought says: CRYSTAL DRAIN OPENER – Clears Clogs & Melts Grease. There are skulls and poison warnings all over the bottle. Yikes. The instructions in the recipe say to never add water to lye as it could explode and splash. One should add lye to water. They even included a helpful rhyme to make sure you don't fuck it up:"Add water to lye. You will die."

I measured out 750 ml of distilled water into a glass Pyrex 4-cup measuring cup. Then I weighed out 50 grams of the lye. It was in the form of beaded crystals and looked like large coarse salt granules. I slowly added the lye to the water and per the instructions began to stir. As I stirred, the water began to get hot. I stirred until the water turned clear and all the lye granules dissolved.

I won't bore you with the details I found easily via

Google, but when I had completed the process, I was left with a cloudy liquid that I emptied into a glass Pyrex 9 x 13 cake pan. I covered the pan, set it in the freezer and fell asleep. The next step involved emptying the contents into a glass Pyrex 9 x 13 cake pan. The solvent was no longer perfectly clear. It had a spotty, opaque whiteness to it. I covered the pan, set it in the freezer and fell asleep.

The next morning when I looked in the pan, I was surprised to see white, vague masses suspended in the liquid and clinging to the sides and edges. It looked like someone had jacked off into the liquid. I'm sorry for mocking Roy and his semen descriptor, because I have learned sometimes it's the most fitting. There were white strands ending in splits of thin milk-trailing tendrils. Gross. If I didn't live alone, I can guarantee you I would be on the hunt for the asshole that spunked in my pull. It looked just like that.

The final step was to pour off the solvent and let the pan air dry. The solvent took about 30 minutes to evaporate and there was a thin residue across the entire pan and I'll be damned, piles of white crystalline structures jutting up where the globs of "semen" had been. I took a razor blade and scraped the sides and bottom of the pan, pushing everything into a pile in the center. When I was done, I had a small mound of white crystalline powder. Holy shit!

My hands started to tremble as I leaned over the Pyrex. I saw myself objectively for a brief moment. A graying, paunchy white guy holding a razor blade, chopping up his crystal cook. The gravity of what I was doing finally hit me. Hit me in a rush. I was manufacturing an illicit substance. I lost my career, my wife, and my kids.

See Roger alone, manufacturing powerful hallucinogens in his empty house. Nothing good in his life whatsoever. It's just Roger and his poorly rationalized attempts of fantasy escapism.

It sucks to realize that's all my life has been for some time. Poorly rationalized fantasy escapism.

It is Tuesday night. It's six weeks and one day since I lost my job and five weeks and one day since Abby packed up our family and took them to New Jersey.

I'm looking at the DMT I made and trying to work up the courage to smoke it. The drug is referenced as "thousands of times stronger than LSD." If you've ever done LSD then you would understand my trepidation. LSD is the strongest, most world-obliterating substance in the world. The concept of things stronger than that is terrifying. The big selling point for me, other than the "leave your body and visit other dimensions and ask for wisdom" is that it only lasts 10-15 minutes. LSD lasts for hours and hours. 8-14 hours. That is a long time to be balls-to-the-wall discombobulated. And there is no turning back, no way to go to sleep, no way to limit. Once you've ingested the acid you just have to surrender.

I was just thinking about a DMT experience I had come across on YouTube. The user said that he was teleported to a five-dimensional realm where he was greeted by a group of alien figures. They welcomed him warmly, like he was long, lost family. They explained to him that he was one of them, and that for some crazy reason he had decided to take a journey to Earth and experience being a human. He said they were shaking their heads in disbelief.

"Why would you ever have wanted to leave here?" they asked him.

He couldn't remember why he left there, but he didn't want to come back to 'reality.' He was in a magical realm of light and love, and felt like he was home. They gathered around him and hugged him and told him that he had to go back to his human state.

"You will come back here when you are done. Don't worry, you'll be back home with us in a blink of an eye," they assured him.

He heard a loud cracking noise and realized his eyes were closed. When he opened them, he was on his bed in his apartment.

"I wanted to go back," he said, tearfully. "It's awful here. Bad things happen here. Bad things don't happen wherever I was. So, I grabbed the pipe and took another long hit and blammo! I was back. Everyone was surprised to see me back so soon and laughed when I told them that I wanted to stay. They told me no, I had to go. I heard the same cracking noise and when I opened my eyes I was back home again."

Whoa. The internet was full of stories like this. Nearly universal reports of being blasted to another realm, and of meeting God, or benevolent beings. The stories were modern day incarnations of native people's vision quests. I need some vision.

The DMT is on the bar in the kitchen. My naked kitchen. The old Clines homestead kitchen bar. The kids used to eat cereal at this bar. I had sex with Abby on this bar once.

"It's your home, Roger. And I'm your wife," she had said, gazing at me with her smoldering eyes. "Right here, right now."

And now I'm crying again. I miss them all so much with an unbearable shame. Juxtaposing the warmth that a family brings to a home, with the lifeless shell it has become, is too much. I'm going to have to get out of here soon. I've never been afraid of spirits, or scared in the dark. But this empty house is full of ghosts. The first couple of weeks alone, I would lay in bed and I swear I could hear the garage door open. I would bound from my bed and run out to the hallway. Each time I'd think, "They're back!" and my heart would jump. But when I opened the door to look in the garage, hoping against hope to see my family, there was nothing. The door was closed like a tomb. Each time I'd look up at the safety pull cord on the garage door, inspecting it for movement. Had they been here? Did I possibly just miss them?

Even though the house was empty I'd sometimes hear Charlie laughing in his room. Or Benji calling out, "Dissolve transition!" I had to move out of the master bedroom. The room still smells like Abby. Sometimes I go in there, close the door and sit alone for hours. That's where I look at the only pictures that I have of her. Yeah, The Pictures.

Pictures are something I never paid attention to, but that my wife cared about deeply. She was always taking pictures of the kids. She had pictures of us and the kids all over the walls, on desks and tables, lining the hallways. She would spend long nights carefully pasting together photo albums, making notes on the back of photos, adding dates and names. I never knew how powerful and important pictures were. How could I? Everyone I loved was always right in front of my face. I had no need for photos.

You may never have thought about this particular pain, but when a wife leaves her husband, she takes the pictures. And as we were packing up her things in silence I was too busy weeping and feeling sorry for myself to ask for any photos. "Hey, I know I'm a loser of epic proportions and you feel compelled to move our family across the country to escape the Roger millstone, but you're gonna leave me some of the family photos, right?"

Abby stripped the house bare when she left. And I don't mean that she took everything. She took hardly anything. But the things she did take hurt the most. She took the things that were hers. The plants she watered every day. Her fish. Her books. The pot holders that Charlie knit in third grade that were so well made, we still used them years later. The things that made our house a home. The things that made it feel alive, and gave me my drive.

I found the manila envelope containing the nudies when I was moving out our bed. I must have slid them under the mattress during the confrontation. I used to hate these pictures. They were the straw that broke the camel's back for Abby. The one creepy thing I couldn't explain away. For a while, I even thought that if it weren't for that horrible day my family would still be here.

But now? Now I thank god for them. They are all I have. I'm not some leering pervert, but goddammit. That's my wife. And that's all I have left of her. I never wanted to embarrass her or shame her. She was lovely, always lovely. I know she'd be happiest if I got rid of these, but I need them. I fucking need these pictures.

ROGER GETS A FRIEND

I couldn't do it. I tried, but I couldn't breakthrough on the DMT. Apparently, freebasing requires skills I don't possess. Contrary to popular belief Roger hasn't done every drug. I've never touched crack, never touched meth. Research amphetamines sure, but only some lines. I'd never freebased anything. I didn't even know what that meant prior to this. Or that ingesting the DMT would take so much effort.

I was familiar with marijuana smoking. Pipes, bongs. I wasn't experienced smoking crystals. I read that DMT should be smoked from a glass pipe, also known as an "oil burner." I went to a head shop and asked for one. The girl there looked at me sideways and said, "We sell glass rigs, not crack pipes." I hightailed it from their judgmental, shameful stares.

"You have no idea, little girl," I thought. "I've got the goddamn Philosopher's Stone at home piled up on a piece of binder paper, and I need something to smoke it from. You wouldn't understand."

When the head shops can't support your activity, you have to go underground. I made a light bulb pipe. I figured if meth heads can do it, I can do it. It was a messy, uncertain process and I broke two bulbs before I got one prepared properly. You pry the metal disc from the bottom of a non-polarized bulb. Then use a screwdriver to break the grey, ceramic seal and you bust out the insides and empty the bulb. Then you take a plastic pop bottle cap, poke a tube through the top of it. This fits snugly at the base of the bulb. You sprinkle the DMT into the hole at bottom of the assembly, allowing it to fall to the bottom of the glass bulb. Next, you heat the bottom of the bulb causing the DMT to melt into a liquid, then you heat up the glass just so causing the DMT to vaporize. You suck that up through the tube and blast off.

A breakthrough dose is listed between 20-50 mg. I must have sprinkled nearly a gram in that bulb, but it was messy, as the bulb was fragile, incredibly hot and everywhere the lighter's flame touched left a sticky soot behind. I scorched most of what I dropped in. I only got one actual hit the first night I tried it, and that hit scared me. You are supposed to take three hits for the trip, but I can't see how you could hit the bulb three times in a row and get the right amount of vapor. Let alone how you can push through the fear of the first hit, and on to the next.

The one full hit I did get overwhelmed me. The lights in the room were oscillating wildly before I had even exhaled. By the time I blew out the hit, the armoire in my room was dripping onto the carpet. The white shag carpet in my bedroom was comprised of wriggling, white Claymation worms with striking indigo segments. Taking another hit from my sooty, hot light bulb was the furthest thing from my mind.

"I got too much," I thought, as I could literally see my panic as pulsing, colorful waves. I set the bulb down, suddenly afraid of it. A small paisley swatch of air swirled larger and larger until it encompassed my entire field of vision. I heard the distant, constant tone of a horn. My room was gone. There was no armoire, no bed, no carpet, no ceiling fan, no ceiling. It was so intense. Yes, psychonaut Roger got scared. I saw the shadow of a female figure coalescing in front of my eyes and became gripped with a terrible fear. I don't know who she was, nor how I knew it was female as she was hooded.

Just as suddenly as it had overtaken me, the hallucinations drained away. I was alone on the bed in the master bedroom. I found the filthy light bulb on the carpet, which was no longer Claymation. My body shivered with fear. What the fuck had just happened to me? People take more than whatever I inhaled? Ever? It had been the single most intense moment of my life. I did not see how I would ever be able to push past the first hit. It made having a gun in your face an elementary school field day. I decided the problem was the light bulb method. It was ghetto and flawed. I was going to have to get the right kind of pipe if I wanted to leave my body.

I ordered an oil burner pipe from Amazon. It was 5.99. I spent the days waiting pacing, watching old Twilight Zone re-runs, and feeling majorly sorry for myself. I wrote Charlie and Benji letters and mailed them to their grandparent's house. I had agonized over every word, writing each one with the idea that someone else may be reading them first, screening. Ugh, how embarrassing. Gotta screen from Dad? From Roger?

When the new pipe came, I readied myself. I was surprised to feel genuine panic, staring at the bona fide crack-pipe. I was determined to push through. This was the red pill, right? A possible gateway between worlds. A goddamned Star Gate. Maybe. Possibly. I reasoned with myself, if it isn't an actual journey to alien lands, then at minimum it's a lucid dream. Right?

Suddenly, the drug seemed like the tallest mountain in the world. I tried to imagine some personal heroes finding themselves in my spot.

"Well, Mr. Einstein, if you smoke this, you could possibly be teleported to alternate dimensions. To a base reality. While there, you will be able to meet and discourse with resident entities. There is no possibility of any ill physical effects and the experience lasts about fifteen minutes. What do you say?"

"Well, Mr. Roy Stacks, if you smoke this, it is entirely possible you could have a quick fireside chat with God. What do you say?"

"Well, Mr. Roger Clines, if you smoke this, you could meet your spirit guide, heal the pain in your psyche, and learn how to win your family back. Learn how to regain Abby's love and trust. What do you say?"

All Seekers would jump at the chance. And here I

was, hemming and hawing. Okay, that's not completely true. I tried. I did try. I steeled myself and dropped thirty milligrams of my DMT into the glass bowl. I followed the guides. Don't touch the flame to the glass, keep the flame a small distance away, so that you don't burn the DMT. Well, I don't know what I did wrong, but I only got a faint, burnt plastic taste in my mouth, but no actual hit. I sprinkled another thirty milligrams in, tried again. I couldn't get a solid hit from the thing. By the time I gave up on the pipe, I figure I must have wasted nearly another half gram of the stuff. My never-ending supply was running low. All I was doing was wasting it. Burning it up.

That was the second time I tried. With each failure my anxiety grew. I even considered tossing the shit out a few times. I don't know exactly why I was so afraid. Okay. Yes, I do. I was afraid of the truth. Deadly, stone-cold afraid of the truth. Afraid to be faced with my true insignificance. Faced with my sins. I had visions of being the defendant in an intergalactic trial. I imagined alien judges sitting atop impossibly tall desks. Judges so far above me that I couldn't see them passing judgement. Afraid of being stripped bare. I was afraid of the red pill. Hell, Roger Clines is afraid of the mirror!

The next morning, I decided to test the drug at lower doses. Maybe I needed to acclimate myself.

The following is the diary I kept of that day:

Friday – 10:00 a.m.

I took one hit, put the pipe down and closed my eyes as I exhaled. I felt so strange; my body so heavy I couldn't push through to a second hit. A giant grid of fine green lines rose behind my eyelids. I moved my head and "looked" up, keeping my eyes closed, and I couldn't see the top of the lines. I turned my head behind me, still with my eyes closed and all I could see was endless black. Nothing. I turned my head forward and there was the green grid tower, rising to infinity. I opened my eyes and the world looked, I don't know, swirly. The blades of the ceiling fan were wilted, liquid petals, drooping downward.

I was in Benji's old room. It was completely empty, and though the room was small, it felt like I was sitting in a warehouse. I closed my eyes again and the grid was back. It had a feeling of permanence. Like a barrier of sorts. I was surprised when suddenly there was a movement behind the wall and part of the grid bulged out in the shape of a face. The face zoomed up to me, and my God, I felt like someone was looking at me. I opened my eyes expecting to see the face right in front of me, even with my eyes open. That's how vivid and real the face was. A wide face with a bulbous, oversized nose built from green grids. Like someone or something was pressing his face into a transparent membrane towards me.

It was unnerving. It didn't feel like a hallucination. It felt like I hit the pipe, saw a giant green wall made of lines and then something noticed me. It noticed me and it pressed into my world, stretching the wall, trying to get a closer look.

I bravely closed my eyes again, but everything was dark. Upon opening my eyes, the room appeared normal. The entire experience lasted about two minutes.

How does anyone smoke three of these hits? Do I even want to have an out of body experience? How does that help me repair the rifts between me and my family? Yikes.

Friday – 11:00 a.m.

From what I read there is a tolerance window with DMT. Since your body breaks it down ridiculously fast, you only get whatever you can intake within about a sixty second window. The tolerance fades after an hour and you can try again. Here we go.

The body load was so intense after one giant hit that I panicked and set down the pipe. The ceiling fan blades melted downward and the room tinted entirely blue by the time I exhaled the hit. Three hits?!?! Who? How? I'm a drug bad-ass. Specifically, a psychedelic drug bad-ass, but this shit is different. With LSD or mushrooms you see shadows, hints of things. Ripples on the wall, shimmers on the carpet. But this is a different order. For Christ's sake the first time I tried it, I literally saw a hole begin to yawn open into my reality. I saw the carpet come alive. Not hints. Not tricks of the light. And let me tell you how uniquely unsettling it is to actually hallucinate. To vividly see that which you know is not there. Ten of ten, friends. Ten of ten.

When I closed my eyes, I saw a world of magically dancing, multi-colored lights. Everywhere there was a character, doing something to get my attention. Some were flipping, others juggling, others spinning in mid-air. All appeared to be trying to get my attention. I can't tell you exactly what they looked like. They were like sparsely drawn, rainbow-colored circus sprites. All moving at hyper speed. Each one was looking at me, showing me something. I opened my eyes and the room looked like it had last time. Unsteady. I closed my eyes again and then the light dancers morphed into more substantive creatures. They became pastel Claymation creatures from a children's educational show.

They were on a stage and thousands of vaguely drawn light creatures were gathered around, watching intently. My vantage point was as if I were up in a box seat.

There was a lumpy, pink creature who was pointing at a wagon. I don't know how I knew, but I could tell they were re-enacting something. There was something wrong with the wagon and the pink creature was pantomiming tears. It looked like one of the wheels had broken.

Next, entered a purple Claymation creature who looked like a centipede, walking upright on his hind legs, staggering under the effort. Somehow, I realized this creature represented me. The purple worm bent down at the back corner of the wagon and then labored upright. The pink blob cheered. Purple me had fixed it. The crowd cheered. I felt amazing. It was incredible. After the cheers died down, everyone's colors faded to grey. It made me sad watching the colors fade. The now gray creatures began waving at me.

"Goodbye! Thank you! Goodbye!" they said.

I heard them in my head. They had tiny, high-pitched chipmunk voices.

"Goodbye! Goodbye!"

I opened my eyes and the room looked bleakly normal again. I closed them, hoping to get a final glimpse of these friendly lights, but the show was over. Wow. What a trip. I didn't blast off to another dimension, but whatever I just experienced felt ridiculously grand.

Friday – 12:00 p.m.

I took one big hit and leaned back. Sorry folks. Once again, I chickened out and stopped at one. Other than slight visual sharpening, the room appeared as it always does, but when I closed my eyes, I saw a vivid and frightening scene.

There was a void. This expanse spread out horizontally. I was at the very bottom of existence. I could see myself standing on an opaque surface. A group of shadows rose from the dark ground. They looked like they were about a mile away. I could see individual shapes, silhouettes and they started to march towards me. When they were about halfway to me, I was able to make them out more clearly. There were three of them. In front there was a rhinoceros creature that was walking upright, carrying a spear. Following were two chipmunks. My view was smoothly choreographed, with flourished zooms and melodramatic pans. As they got closer, I could see that they were each vividly, although realistically, colored. Rhino Man was the typical rhinoceros grey, but his scaly skin also had a starry sheen. The chipmunks were brown and grey, and they also had a faint shimmer.

Rhino Man stiffened and held a hand up. The chipmunks tumbled into each other in a heap. He had seen me! He turned his head and his eyes met mine. He dropped his hand and started to run to me at full speed, the rodent-slash-creatures bounding along on either side. I couldn't tell if they were friendly, but their speed didn't feel nice. My eyes popped open, everything looked sane. I realized I was breathing rapidly. I slowed my breath and closed my eyes again. I was in the same place but my view was elevated. I was looking down at the space I had been before, where the same three creatures were milling around, sniffing the ground and peering out in all directions.

I heard a flapping noise and a giant, winged creature rose from the darkness to hover above Rhino Man.

"He's over here," it announced in a gravelly voice I "heard" in my head. The creature's heads cocked up towards me. My eyes popped open. Too much. This stuff is too much. If it's just a head trip, then it's one I can do without. If it's cluing you into other dimensions, or into over-arching realities, then this has the potential to send you to dangerous places. Right? What am I doing fucking around with this shit? The 'Ask an Oracle, Save-a-Family' trope was really just a crutch. Something to hold on to, versus sliding into insanity.

Can this stuff even be called a drug? It's not like any drug I've ever experienced. At first, calling it a molecule instead of a drug sounded like wistful new age thinking. Like sidestepping facts to hit the loophole. But now I feel differently. I guess you could say that smoking this substance that occurs in thousands of plants and all mammals just makes you trip out. But then you probably haven't experienced it firsthand. This shit feels real. I'm not talking about daydreaming. I'm talking about seeing. My eyes were closed, but they became a canvas that showed intricate visions, full of wide-angle lenses and filtered views. It's too alien and intricate to dream up, impossible to dismiss. Smoking it is utterly convincing. Isn't seeing believing? This shit is not a drug. This shit is straight legit. And that's the most terrifying part about it. Imagine having a pocket-sized Stargate. Would you use it?

Friday – 1:00 p.m.

At it again. A single hit is all I managed. The body load is extremely heavy. Things get weird and it's a challenge to move. When you can see your arm in fractals, it's too hard to steer the pipe to your mouth. This time I found myself walking along an endless, red carpet. On either side of the fancy rug were lines of people. They had indistinct features, but they gave the impression of standing at attention. They were standing at attention for me. They say that you experience ego-death when you smoke enough of this. Well, these sub-breakthrough trips are all about me. Mega-egocentric, curated experiences. After I'd walked for a few minutes down the carpet, my entire field of vision was obstructed by an eyeball. A giant, human eyeball. It was looking at me. I opened my eyes. As the room settled back to normal, I contemplated the eyeball. It felt like it was my own eye. Neat and all, but I'm not the kind of guy who cares about image resolution or 3D color accuracy. I don't care. Taking a hallucinogen and seeing a giant eyeball that you think is yours doesn't fall into the earth-shattering category. I could be wasting my time. Okay, I'm definitely wasting my time. Or maybe I'm buying time? Biding?

I'm underwhelmed.

Yes, that's all there is. After all my huffing and puffing about secrets of the universe and Oracles and manifesting family reunification, I just got really fucked up all day. I bounced between patting myself on the back, and scaring the shit out myself.

That evening I was feeling despondent, low and lonely. I decided to take a drive. I drove for a few hours in a haze. I don't remember where I went, I was just letting the car follow street signals. After a few hours the fog lifted. I realized I had parked my car across the street from Albert's place.

What am I doing here? I wondered.

I found myself getting out of the car and walking up to the door. I opened the screen door and knocked. That was Albert's standard request.

"Cops won't open the screen door, yo. They just gonna knock on the screen. This way, I know it's safe."

Albert opened the door and did a double take.

"Been a little bit, bro."

I shrugged, embarrassed.

"I'm so sorry, Albert," I said.

Albert crossed his arms and looked back at me for a second, before dropping them and warming his face with a smile.

"It's cool, yo. I'm sorry about your boy. That shit wasn't right. Come in bro. Come in!"

Albert ushered me inside.

"Sit down. Take a load off." He gestured towards the couch. "I didn't expect to ever see you again."

Albert lowered his voice, avoiding eye contact. "I heard you lost your job, yo. I'm sorry. A man needs his job, yeah? How you holding up?"

He seemed genuinely concerned. I felt a surge of gratitude at human empathy. I realized just how lonely I'd been. I felt tears welling up and without thinking I said, "Man. I need a friend. I don't deserve one. But I need one nonetheless."

"That's me, bro."

"I'm beyond sorry for coming down on you last month," I said.

"Don't sweat it. I get it. What's been going on?"

And right there, sitting on his couch, I told him. I told him everything. I told him about Fire Day, the shoplifting, the kidnapping, the shed, the drugging, the murder, the bomb. Then I told him about Water Day and Higgins and Egypt. I explained how my marriage unraveled, and how Earth Day culminated with me losing my job, and how I got Benji's dog killed. It took me about three hours to spill it all. Roger's Decline is a brief debacle.

Albert was a wonderful listener. He sat and listened intently. He didn't interrupt once.

What a great skill, listening. I'm terrible at it. Heck, I even interrupt myself. Can't help it. I'm always jumping trains. Albert's round, jovial face went from wide-eyed shock, to fear and his eyes spilled a few tears as I told him about my loneliness. About how much I missed Abby and the kids.

It felt so wonderful to be able to tell someone. What a pathetic turn of circumstance that I never talked to Abby. I could talk to my drug dealer. But not my own wife. After I had finished, I felt better than I had in over a year. More human than I'd felt in over a year.

Albert shook his head.

"Wow. Wow bro. That's some fucked up shit. That's some wild, fucked up shit. I got two things to say. Okay I got lots to say. But. First of all, man I knew that guy. Jasper? I knew him, yo. I sold him the N-Bombs. I bet that's how they got to your boy. Secondly-"

Albert looked around conspiratorially and whispered, "Secondly bro. Do you have any more of the DMT?"

I nodded.

"How much more?"

"About a gram."

He stood up.

"Okay man. Let's go smoke that shit."

I hadn't expected this. I should have. Albert is the one person in this world that loves drugs as much as I do. Of course, he'd be interested in DMT. I hesitated.

He grabbed his keys.

"Let's go bro."

"But," I protested. "I'm not ready. I gotta- "

"Fuck that, yo. We are both ready. Right now, we ready."

He looked at me, smiling.

"I gotta lot of questions, bro. But first. We gotta try this shit. We don't pass go. We don't prepare. We just smoke that shit."

He stood over me for a few moments. I didn't move.

"Come on bro," he said gently. "I got a pipe we can use."

"Okay," I said, and got up. I felt a long-lost confidence in the wake of getting everything off my chest. And he didn't hate me. I told him everything and he didn't hate me. He was still my friend. It was time to smoke that shit and save the day!

He followed me back to my house. It was the first time he'd been here. I had been buying from him for over fifteen years and we'd never hung out.

"Damn player. Look at your place," he said after he pulled up.

"Yeah, well. I'm about out of here. Can't afford it. I'm no player now."

That's how we found ourselves in my empty living room, staring at the bowl and the DMT.

"Shit, yo," said Albert. He was sitting facing me. I tapped some shards of DMT onto a plate and set it between us. "Sitting here, looking at it. Now, I'm scared. You made this shit?"

"You go first," I said, thinking it was odd to be the one providing the drugs.

We were startled by a loud knocking on the front door. We both looked at each other, at the drugs, and back at each other.

"You expecting someone?" asked Albert.

I shook my head. No one ever came by. Ever. Probably a neighbor. Maybe Albert left his car headlights on.

I calmly pointed at the drugs and paraphernalia.

"Albert, can you take that shit down the hall and into one of the bedrooms? Close the door."

Albert nodded, scooped everything up and took off down the hall. Like me, he was an extremely heavy drug user. Heavy drug users are familiar with urgency.

It was with that mindset that I walked to the front door. Despite my extreme culpability, since my family left, my constant paranoia had subsided. I want to make the point that I wasn't nervous, or apprehensive in the slightest. I wasn't on the cops' radar; I had finally deduced. The previous month was so full of grief, loneliness, despair and pity, that I hadn't had time to be afraid of the police. But something checked me at the last minute. Right before placing my hand on the doorknob, I decided to peer through the peephole first. No harm in being cautious, I thought. I was eager to get back to the DMT. I had a friend! The crippling fear I'd felt at taking the drug had faded away once I had talked to someone. I winced, thinking that Abby was the friend I wanted most.

"You fucked that up," said Wally. "Just sat around and watched her slip away."

I put my eye to the peephole. It was Higgins' heavy, the German. He was looking around impatiently. I took a deep breath and answered the door.

Gunther pushed past me and walked into the living room, looking around, appraising the bare walls.

"So, they are all gone then?" he asked.

I stiffened my stance and tried to look confident.

"That's my business, man. What do you want?"

He turned in a slow circle, his eyes noting everything. The man was a giant, easily six and a half feet tall. Standing in my unfurnished living room, the tiny, unshaded bulb in the corner cast his shadow over the entire room, up the wall, and onto the ceiling. He was menacing in bright light, let alone with his face cast in darkness. His teeth glinted and I could tell he was smiling.

"The boss has one final job for you."

Yeah, right. I felt a frost spreading down my spine. Alarm bells were ringing everywhere.

Wally was screaming in my head. "DEFCON One! DEFCON One!"

"Why not text me? Why come here? What's the job?" I asked, surprised at my composure.

Gunther calmly reached into his jacket, pulled out a gun and pointed it at me. He did it in one smooth, non-hurried motion. He looked like he was in a movie. Natural, well-rehearsed. I've strolled into living rooms all across the globe and pulled guns. Another day, another dollar.

"You're to dig a grave. Your own." He waved the gun at me and continued in a dull monotone.

"We are going to drive up to The Wheel," he continued. *Ze Veel.* "And you are going to dig a nice, deep hole. Then I'm going to shoot you, and fill it back up. After that I'm going to go home and make a schnitzel for my favorite woman. From there maybe missionary, maybe doggy. I don't know. Depends on how I'm feeling."

Yes. He said schnitzel. The fucker. Unbelievably, my fear evaporated. And I began to get mad. Gunther may be a professional level home invader, but this wasn't my first time at the end of a gun. Hell, it wasn't my second time, or third time either. My quality of life had been desperate of late, indeed. I was getting used to facing death. In the absence of family, I felt defiant.

"That's stupid. Why would I dig my own grave? Or go anywhere with you?"

"Because I have a gun, and will shoot you if you don't."

"Just shoot me here, then," I said and pulled my T-shirt off in a brazen show of nothing-to-lose.

Gunther seemed confused. I wondered how many people told Gunther 'no' at the point of a gun. Since I've been through it a time or two, I'm guessing none.

"I don't want to dig my grave. Shoot me here." I tapped my chest. "Shoot me here, you fuck."

In that moment, I was truly ready to die. I don't mean I'd lost hope, or that I was afraid, or tired of living. I wasn't going to dig anything. That shit hurts your hands. Tears them up. I wasn't going to get in the car with another asshole and drive to my doom. I don't do that anymore. What Gunther wanted was not possible.

He shrugged and leveled the gun at my chest.

"Alright. Okay. I will shoot you here. Right. In. Your. Chest."

He said the last words deliberately and pressed the barrel against my sternum. I closed my eyes tightly, and imagined I was back in time, at the beach with

Abby. My wife.

When the gun went off, it was the loudest thing I'd ever heard. I was surprised I had time to hear it, considering a Magnum to the chest is instant death. Searing, chest bursting pain. But I felt nothing. I heard the gun fall to the ground, followed by the sound of a body hitting the carpet. I opened my eyes. Gunther was laid out in a growing pool of blood in front of me, his gun a few feet from his body. I looked around in amazement and saw Albert, gun in hand, step out from the hallway.

"Wha?" I barely managed.

Albert grinned. "Course I carry. I sell drugs, yo. You know?"

He walked over to Gunther's gun and picked it up. "Bro. Check this out. He said 'make a schnitzel.'"

The adrenaline in my body made my knees week, and I collapsed next to the Nazi. I could feel his blood on my naked shoulder. It was warm. I didn't care. I couldn't move. My body started to shudder. I flashed back to the floor of my garage. After I'd overcome Jasper.

I felt Albert's hands on me, rolling me away from the blood.

"You gotta calm down bro," he said. "We gonna try that DMT. You know?"

I started to laugh. The more I laughed, the more my body loosened and unclenched. I laughed for a minute or so and Albert joined me. After a few more breaths I was able to sit up. That was a surreal scene. Me shirtless, with a bloodied shoulder. In my empty living room. With a dead guy on the carpet. My drug dealer, wiping off his gun. A pool of blood expanding. And we were laughing.

"Do you think we already smoked it?" I asked.

"Yeah. This is a trip and half. This guy works for Higgins, I'm guessing?"

"Yeah. He's an asshole."

We laughed again.

"We should go off Higgins too," suggested Albert. "He's garbage, yo."

I nodded. And I meant it. It was a night for meaning things. And I meant for Higgins to die. I'd dicked around too long in my sadness.

"Well man," Albert continued. "We gotta get rid of the body. I've watched lots of Dexter. Got them all on DVD. I'm ready for this, yo. We need a large sheet of plastic, and we need it forthwith! You know?"

"I happen to have some," I volunteered, control returning to my body, along with a general lightness I hadn't felt in years. I'd bought a bunch of plastic tarps to use as painter's drop cloths. I'd put off the painting. Abby and I both hated painting. We always painted together, sharing the tedium. The thought of painting without her was enough to make me consider taking what was left of my savings and paying someone.

From the way I popped up from the ground, you would have thought I'd just won the lottery. I literally had a skip in my step down the hall. Just Roger heading into the garage to grab a plastic tarp to wrap up a corpse in the living room.

When I returned, Albert was going through Gunther's wallet.

"Dude has nothing in his wallet. Just an out of state

Driver's License," he said. "His name is Gunther Guntherson."

His eyes narrowed and he looked around conspiratorially.

"Mrs. Guntherson must have been a proper bitch. You know?"

We laughed like two old friends hanging out on a Tuesday night. With a corpse.

Albert helped push the body onto the tarp. We rolled him up like a burrito and used duct tape to tape off the top and bottom. Albert wrapped lengths of duct tape around the body at about twelve-inch intervals. That way blood doesn't leak from the sides, yo.

We used the keys we recovered from Gunther's pocket to pull his car into the garage. Popped open the trunk and heaved him in. Our quick plan was to drive him up to The Wheel and bury him. Hey, it worked once, as Albert pointed out.

I cannot fully articulate how great I was feeling at that moment. I attributed it to the first meaningful social connection I'd had in a long time. Wally said it was from the adrenaline. And that I was officially psychotic. But my confession had been cathartic. And sure, Albert was a heavy drug user, but he didn't think I was crazy. He understood everything. Look, I know that my drug use wasn't a good thing. But it wasn't evil. The shoplifting? I don't know what that was. Fallout from years of chemical abuses? I was a good provider, an engaged father, and a loyal husband. Bad shit happened to me. I improvised. Hey, the other drug addict in the room thinks I behaved reasonably.

After the body was loaded Albert told me it was

time to blast off.

"Bro. Look. I know we have a body. A goddamn body. You know? But that stuff. The DMT. Man, I need to try that shit. My moms passed last year. That shit hurts bad. What if I could reach her? Could it work that way, you think?"

"I don't know man," I said, shaking my head. I have a hard-core history with drugs, but even in my I-just-cheated-death-for-the-millionth-time afterglow, my instincts were to first rid the house of signs of murder. Then move on to life changing mystical experience drug use. I glanced at my phone. It was 1:30 AM. We had about four hours of darkness left and had to get going.

"After," I said.

Albert faced me squarely and grabbed both of my arms.

"Bro. I just saved your life. Give me 30 minutes. I want to blast off. Ask about my mom. You said this stuff was safe, you know?"

"Yeah. But- "

Albert cut me off. "Mr. Schnitzel waits, yo. Do this for me, then my entire schedule is cleared for improper disposal of dead bodies."

I couldn't argue with him, and that is how I ended up in Charlie's old room, sitting on the carpet, staring at the crack pipe again.

Albert picked up the loaded pipe, and lit his lighter. He artfully swirled the lighter under the glass, never touching the actual flame to it. The bell of the pipe filled with a cloudy smoke. I was amazed, in all my times with my oil-burner or the light bulbs, I never once got that much smoke.

"No replacement for experience, bro," Albert said. He put the pipe up to his lips, looked at me and smiled. "You're a good man, Roger. You're good. I'mma see you on the other side, yo."

He took a deep drag and cleared the pipe. He quickly exhaled and flicked his lighter back on and off again taking a second, deeper drag. His eyes met mine for a brief second and they were the most terrified, tortured looking eyes I'd ever seen. And then he collapsed backwards on to the floor.

Watching Albert lie there was scary. I worried I was going to have a second body on my hands. I asked him if he was okay a few times, but if he heard me, he showed no signs. His breathing was steady, but his eyes were racing behind the lids as if he were dreaming furiously. I grabbed his wrist to check his pulse. No, I don't actually know how to do that, but from what I could feel it was slow and steady. That was a good sign. Watching a friend lose consciousness after taking a drug is disconcerting at the least and Drug-Den Trainspotting at the worst. I was afraid he wouldn't wake up. Maybe what I made was bunk. Or some type of accidental poison.

"What if he wakes up and isn't my friend anymore?" I thought.

I had just connected with the first sympathetic voice I'd heard in months and what had Roger, Destroyer of Worlds done?

"I got him involved in a mess where he's already had to kill someone," I bemoaned to myself. I knew firsthand how painful that could be. "And on top of whatever torturous future the shooting is going to cause him, now I've poisoned him," I worried to myself. I was balancing two immediate pressers:

Re-thinking taking this extracted DMT tonight, or any other night, ever.

Wake the hell up Albert. Because we have a body to bury and stuff.

"He's going to die," offered Wally.

Albert awoke with a sudden fit of tears and sat up stiffly. I stood and cheered.

"Mrs. Guntherson is a good person, Roger. She was there. Oh my God. Okay, my moms wasn't there, but Ygritte was."

I knelt beside him, concerned.

"Who was there?" I asked softly.

"Mrs. Guntherson. You know? Mother Schnitzel?" Albert pointed toward the garage.

"Christ," I said.

Albert started laughing. It was odd to see tears streaming down his face at the same time. But his laughter seemed genuine so I went with it. I sat down against the wall next to him.

"In the interest of articulation, Albert, did you just kill someone, then meet his mother in a hallucinogenic trip induced by smoking DMT less than thirty minutes after the said killing?"

Albert nodded vigorously. "You are the champion of articulation, Roger."

He began to shudder fiercely and his teeth started to chatter.

"Oh shit, yo I'm cold, yo," Albert chattered. "Cold like a mother fuck, yo. Is this supposed to be happening?"

"Yeah I've read this happens sometimes. I cannot believe you did that, Albert," I said shaking my head. I got him a blanket. As much as I was grateful for his company, experience, drug-dealer guns, and urban chat, I was suddenly seized with an even stronger urgency.

"Albert. I want to know what you saw. I need to know."

"Man, oh my God, you gotta know Roger," interrupted Albert. "Oh my God."

"I know man. I do," I reassured him. "But we have to get the fuck out of here. Do you think you will be okay to drive soon?"

I winced as I said it, but surely that was softened by the massively understated 'we have to get the fuck out of here.'

Albert stopped chattering and nodded. "I understand, yo. I should be good in a couple."

I really liked Albert. It wasn't because he sold me drugs. That hadn't happened in ages. It wasn't even because he showed empathy for my fucked-up situation. Or because he saved my life minutes earlier. It was because he was pragmatic. A pragmatic bad-ass.

He said "oh my God" about a hundred more times then got to his feet.

"Wow," he exhaled. "That was some proper blotto shit, yo. Okay. So. Ready to go?"

We were startles by another loud pounding at the front door. We looked at each other.

"What the fuck, yo?" asked Albert. "It's like, two

in the morning."

He stepped close to me, lining our faces up.

"You are into some seriously fucked up shit, Roger."

I shrugged.

"You have a way with articulation too, Albert," I said. "I'll go see who that is. Hang back."

I glanced meaningfully at his gun as the front door was hit with another hail of insistent knocks.

Albert nodded.

I sped down the hall to the front door, my heart racing. I peeked through the peephole. It was Larry. I was overcome with two conflicting emotions:

Yeehaw! You stupid fucking hick. You're gonna die, you asshole. I'm going to let your ass in and then Albert is going to kill you. Yee fucking haw!

Christ! What's wrong with you? Don't open the door. Maybe he will go away. You don't need any more death. No more bodies.

"Open the door. This asshole dies tonight. Next, Higgins," Wally said. He snapped me out of it, god bless being crazy, but it just feels right when your inner voice agrees with you.

I opened the door with a smile.

"Hello!" I said enthusiastically. "What can I do you for, Larry?"

He looked surprised to see me.

"Of course, he is," reasoned Wally. "You are supposed to be dead and buried up at The Wheel already. Let him inside."

"Come on in, man," I said in a friendly tone. "How can I help?"

Larry stepped inside and I closed the door behind him. "Have you seen Gunther?"

"Sure haven't" I lied.

"He was supposed to, uh, stop by tonight. Before we leave, the boss asked him to leave you a little going away present. For your hard work."

Goddamn, these heavies were an arrogant bunch. I felt confident that Albert had my back. Confident enough to be curious.

"Going away gift? Is he going somewhere?" I asked innocently. I tried to be casual. As casual as you can be with a body in the garage and a second killer in the den.

"The boss is moving to Jersey. We're all going with him," answered Larry.

"Jersey?" I asked. "As in New Jersey?"

"Yep. More opportunities and the like. Gunther hasn't stopped by yet? Have you been home all night?"

I didn't answer him. I didn't think. I walked down the hall casually, and saw Albert pressed against the wall, with his gun readied. I grabbed the gun from Charlie's room wordlessly. Walked back down the hall with the gun and calmly shot Larry in the chest. Then I walked to his body as he collapsed and shot him in the face. Then I lost the thread. I don't know where I went, but I zoned out. All the way out.

I was brought back to reality by Albert. He was standing in front of me with a hand on my shoulder.

"You okay, yo?" he looked concerned. I realized at that moment I had never seen Albert with anything other than a smile on his face. It looked out of place.

"Whoa. Yeah. I don't know what the fuck is going on with me," I offered. I looked at dead Larry on the ground and remembered what had just happened. I stood, looking down at his body, and realized I could not muster a single negative emotion. I'm telling you friends that I, Roger Clines, shot a man. On autopilot. And I felt no remorse. Not one solitary tear over dumb, dead Larry. Even Wally was high-fiving me in my mind, congratulating. Yes, he had to die. And that is just a simple, no frills fact.

"You just shot this motherfucker, is what's going on with you, yo. He said some shit about New Jersey and you shot his ass." Albert laughed. "You and I are danger tonight, bro. Straight up danger."

"I don't want Higgins in New Jersey," I said.

"What do you think the chances? Your family out there, you know?" asked Albert.

"Don't care. I don't want Higgins in New Jersey, or anywhere," I said. I felt more confident at that moment than I'd ever felt in my entire life. I knew what I needed to do. I'd always known what I needed to do. I needed to kill Higgins and get my family back.

"Yeah, you can do it!" cheered Wally.

I don't have to tell you how out of character Wally's comment was. But I agreed. For the first time in the last few weeks I no longer cared about DMT. I didn't care about Oracles. Or answers. Or deep meaning. Or how I looked. Or how I was going to get my family back. Or how I was going to go about killing Higgins. Albert and I just took care of Higgins' goons. It had been child's play. Easy-peasy. And it felt good. If felt so good that I could no longer relate to my old, guilt-stricken self. Why had killing Jasper torn me up so much? He needed to die. That's all. Bad people need to die sometimes. That's not generally known these days, but that's how it is.

Albert looked from me to Larry's body and back. He shrugged.

"You got anymore tarps, yo?"

ROGER GOES TO THE MOON

I held the third hit in as long as I could. I don't know how long I held it. Before I could think about exhaling, or breathing at all, the room dissolved. All the trappings, beginning from the ceiling, melted away. Walls, then the carpet, then the floors, revealing a giant grid matrix of white electric lines. I tried to look around to see if everything had disappeared but my body felt too heavy, heavier than it had ever felt. I couldn't turn my head. I couldn't move a muscle. I was paralyzed! I had taken too much, I thought. Panic set in as the grid began to spin, wrapping itself around me, forming a tube of motion. I accelerated through this tunnel. I was travelling on my back, rigid and could only see directly above. The white lines began rushing faster and faster until they became a solid, defined mass. The tunnel had begun as an ephemeral mesh of electrical lines and morphed into a white, solid plastic-y silo that was blasting me backwards like a reverse ice luge run.

I heard a creaking sound that was so loud, I instinctively would have ducked from it, if I could have moved at all. This is what it sounded like: Imagine a giant tree. This tree is so tall that you cannot see the top. The top is shrouded in the clouds above. Next, imagine Paul Bunyan shows up and begins to chop at the base of this tree with his giant Big Blue Ax. He swings mightily for an entire day and night. The following morning he's worked his way through the massive trunk and he has one final swing left. He swings his ax and sinks it into the perfect spot to topple the great tree. He's done this a million times and knows exactly what he's doing. The Big Blue Ax breaks the last bit of resistance and the tree slowly, slowly begins to lean. At first the shift is infinitesimal and the tree hovers, momentarily defying gravity. As the lean becomes more pronounced, the fulcrum of bark at the bottom of the tree begins to creak as the tree falls from the heavens to the forest floor. If you were a teeny squirrel, watching this from ground level, imagine how loud the creak, creak, crrrrrrrrrrr-ack! of the tree would sound. The loudest sound you've ever heard. Form of, creak.

The creaking culminated in a mighty woosh that squeezed all sense of air and space from my body, followed by a sharp pop!

And I could move again, only I was no longer lying down. Or in my room. I was in a warm, white space. An opaque light permeated everything. I was standing on a bleached and weathered stone floor. I couldn't see a ceiling, just endless white above, yet I had the sense that I was inside. I was in some sort of immense, vague structure. A low hum began in the floor. The stones vibrated under my feet. Their buzz became so insistent that my body began to thrum along. I was a glass of water on top of a crate amp at a sweaty pizza shop show. The buzzing was causing me to spill. The hum rose until I felt emotions welling up, like a disturbed liquid. Happiness sloshed out from my head. Grief streamed from my nostrils. Joy burst from my mouth.

And then, the buzz stopped, and with its cease I had been transported to another location. I was now in a fancy study. The walls were paneled with a glowing, polished wood. There were two plush, high-backed chairs in front of a stone fireplace. The fire was roaring and I could feel the heat emanating, warming the entire room. I realized I wasn't standing on stone any longer. Now there was a deep, plush carpet. My feet sunk about an inch into a many-hued forest green shag. The room was shaped like a hexagram, with the fireplace taking up an entire wall. The other five walls were lined from floor to ceiling with overstuffed bookshelves. There were no doors or windows. How had I gotten here? I'd been tuned into the room. I was charged up and struck like a tuning fork, and popped in. I had an impression that the low key of G was the only way in or out.

I heard a startlingly close voice. It sounded like it came from directly behind my left ear.

"You're correct, to a degree."

I swiveled my head, but there was nothing behind me.

"It is the key of G. G minor seventh, specifically."

I turned back to face the fireplace and there was a yellow creature sitting in one of the chairs. His shape eludes my words. He was something like a banana, elongated and yellow. He was wearing a maroon fez.

"He isn't correct, to any degree," said the hat.

Yeah. A talking fez.

The yellow thing rolled his eyes. They weren't eyeballs, just three small Rorschach blobs of light. And they didn't exactly roll, they jiggled. Somehow, I knew what he meant. He meant: Shut up, hat. He's just an ignorant human. He's fragile.

"Come sit, Roger. We don't have much time."

I didn't question him. I didn't question how I knew the banana thing was a "he." After being buzzed in, literally, you stop questioning trivial things. I walked to the empty chair, which appeared to be Roger-sized when I was looking at it from across the room, and realized as I got closer, that it was much larger. I had to clamber up into the seat like a toddler. I sat, perched at the edge.

"Very good," beamed the banana.

"Very adequate. Why are you patronizing him? You embarrass us," growled the hat.

The hat was right. I was a fool. I didn't belong here. I was in a magic room, where even the hats are smarter.

"No time," continued Mr. Yellow. "I wanted to introduce us. You're here. We're here. Hello!"

A papery scroll appeared in my grasp. It was an ancient scroll, with two rods, and a fine paper wrapped around the side in my right hand. As I watched, the rods began to turn in my hands, the scroll unfurling from right to left. A series of images and information appeared on the paper. None of the data was static. It was almost like holding an iPad, embedded in a steampunk scroll. The scroll told me the story of the Mushroom People.

The Mushroom People were an advanced extra-terrestrial race, having evolved and refined over thousands of millennia. Their home planet, many light years away, had degraded beyond usefulness. Their population had thrived and was massive. But their people required an oxygen rich atmosphere and when they grew their neural network, they waste-output carbon monoxide. In a last-ditch effort to save their race, they launched into space in search of a new home. It wasn't going to be easy. They had specific requirements for advanced survival.

They consume oxygen at a high rate and expel carbon monoxide at a high rate. Finding an oxygen rich environment was not going to be enough for them to thrive. They needed lots of oxygen and a way for an atmosphere to absorb their massive carbon waste. They didn't have opposable thumbs – they had shed those as useless during their 245th epoch. They needed help in their new reality. They came upon Earth, shielded within microscopic vessels enclosed in chitin. They discovered humans and realized they found a match.

Over the years they formed both symbiotic and parasitic relationships with humans, plants, animals and other fungus. They contributed to the ecosystem, bridging critical gaps. They jump-started humanity's self-awareness, nudging them on to a track of advancement and also provided nourishment with their power strips. They call the mushroom fruit that humans eat "power strips." The scroll didn't contain that word, or that image, but that is how they were conveyed in my mind. Their vast mycelium networks spread for miles, and they can send messages and information from one end of the network to the other, faster than the speed of light. They are proud of our unwitting partnership and hope for many prosperous generations.

The scroll "finished" and then went dark. I surprised myself when I cast it away to the carpet like flicking a cigarette butt or tossing a spent casing. "You can't just throw shit on the carpet here!" worried Wally. He'd been silent up until this point- I thought I had shed him when I left my body back in California, United States, Earth, Milky Way Galaxy. I did not know where I was at that moment, but I was definitely the furthest I've ever been from home.

Mr. Yellow gestured at me dismissively. The chair gradually began to hum. It rose in tone and volume until the sound was all I could "see." I think it was G minor seventh. I learn fast, Mr. Hat. I began to float on the sound, blind to anything but The Hum. I felt myself bobbing up and down on cascading waves of vibration. The sound sawed through me violently and I thought I was going to get sliced apart. And then POP! And I open my eyes and I'm alone in the corner of Charlie's empty bedroom. In California. On Earth. Ah sweet Earth! Don't know what you got 'til it's gone.

ROGER GOES TO NEW JERSEY

We arrived in Ocean City, New Jersey around seven in the evening. It had been five days since what Albert and I referred to as either The Great Burial or The Great Reckoning. I want to point out that the guilt I had from killing Jasper faded away after I killed Higgins' hoods. That heavy weight lifted after I shot Larry. Kill one, crippling guilt. Kill two? Relief. Survival. Roger Clines is surviving and has no qualms about it.

Albert was a great travelling companion. He was relaxed, supportive, encouraging, fun. He made me miss Abby even more. She used to be the person who was all those things with me. But I welcomed his companionship. I hadn't realized how lonely I'd been and Wally makes for a very shitty roommate.

We decided not to take any drugs with us, except for the DMT. And we took our guns. Well, Albert brought his gun and I brought Larry's. We looked like outlaws, especially toting the guns, but when people are trying to kill you, you tote a gun. Albert passed a lot of the time pulling up fun facts about New Jersey on his cell phone: "New Jersey is the most densely populated state. New Jersey is considered the diner capital of the country."

"What's that mean?" I'd asked.

"It says they have 525 diners," he answered. And then after a pause he continued: "Atlantic City has the longest boardwalk in the world. New Jersey is the car theft capital of the world, with more cars stolen in Newark than in any other city. Even more than NYC and LA combined. New Jersey has the most shopping malls in one area in the world: seven major shopping malls in a 25 square mile radius."

Somewhere in middle of Iowa, Albert asked me a question.

"Whose place did Higgins take you to in Abu Zenima? Does he happen to have a house there? I was under the impression it was a no man's land."

"Good question."

Albert messed with his phone for a while and pulled up some photos. He showed me photos of the place Higgins used in Abu Zenima. I recognized the roof and front driveway. There were even pictures of the balcony and railing. The seaside views.

"Where did you find these?" I asked in shock.

"Dude, Higgins straight up got an Airbnb. Look. 85 dollars, US, a night. Yo."

We both started laughing.

"Ridiculous," I said.

"Ain't too scary of a dude," smiled Albert. "Renting vacation homes online and all."

Albert had booked us a room for a week at a place right on the boardwalk, The Flanders Hotel. Here is how that happened.

When we were about ten hours out, I asked Albert to find us a couple of rooms in Ocean City, near the boardwalk. Ocean City is an oblong island just off the coast of New Jersey. Abby's parents live off Bay Avenue, on the opposite side of the island. Their house is a block from The Great Gatsbian-named Great Egg Harbor Bay. The island is narrow, at about three miles wide.

"How about right on the boardwalk?" Albert giggled.

"Sure."

He snickered. "Right on the boardwalk is good?"

"Yeah, it's fine," I said, wondering if I should ask what he was laughing about.

"How does a place named The Flanders Hotel sound? Have you heard of it?"

"No, I've not heard of any hotels in Ocean City, New Jersey, but I'm excited to learn of them."

Albert laughed again. "Okay man. The Flanders Hotel."

Then he changed the subject to DMT, and in the fascination of contemplation I forgot about it. Which means I was late to the joke.

The hotel had a squat, white square design, wrapped around a central courtyard with a pool. It had ornate, red tile roofing at floor intervals across the outside, with wrought-iron fish adorning the spaces between windows. There was a green sign in front that read, in a fancy gold script: The Flanders Hotel:

Luxury All Suites Hotel, Restaurant, Banquet, Conference Center. Beneath that it read: Emily's Restaurant, Breakfast, Lunch and Dinner, 8am-8pm daily.

When we walked into the hotel's foyer, the first thing that struck me was its obvious age. It felt ancient. The ceilings of the lobby weren't exactly low, but they felt oppressive. You could tell that this place was grand at some distant point in its history. There were countless black and white photos along the walls. Photos showing the place in better days. The long great room wall was lined with fireplaces along one wall and sets of French doors on the other.

While it was nice, it felt threadbare. Worn. The elevator foyer was beautiful though. The ceilings were vaulted with ensconced pillars, and the halls were decorated with a palatial-chic look. While we were waiting for an elevator I commented on the stark difference between the lobby and this elegant hallway.

"The front felt almost haunted," I said. "But we turned the corner and suddenly it feels like we are in a different world."

Albert started chortling again, the same stifled snort-laugh gangsters sometimes do while saying something like "youknowit, youknowit, youknowit."

"What?" I asked, getting irritated. Sometimes Albert's ghetto-slang effect felt forced to me. He's the son of middle class Korean-American parents, raised in the suburbs outside of Seattle. He went to Arizona State. He graduated with honors in Biochemical Engineering. But if you spoke with him on the phone, you would assume you were speaking with someone from the Wu Tang clan. Sometimes it just doesn't seem genuine. While I'm grateful for his company and help, I want to ask him to just drop the act. Wally tells me this means I'm insecure and must have some sort of issue or I wouldn't care how Albert spoke. "Considering how you err, and massively so," is how he'd framed it.

Albert laughed again. The elevator arrived and he tabbed the second-floor button. I looked at my key.

"We're on the third floor," I said.

"But first, I want to show you something on the second floor, yo."

"Will you stop laughing once you show me?"

Albert smiled. "Sure."

We got off on the second floor and walked down an ornate pillar-lined hallway. It was truly beautiful. The walls had gilded wainscoting and the tops of the pillars were gilded with filigree. There was a marble fireplace, surrounded by plush, fine upholstery. Albert stopped in front of a painting of a red-haired woman. She was dressed in white robes and clutching a broom, in what looks to be an autumnal wind-leaf storm.

"That's her," said Albert, pointing at the painting. "That's Emily."

"So, the restaurant that's here is hers?" I asked.

Albert laughed his Flavor Flav laugh again.

"No, yo," he said. "No, this is a painting of Emily. And Emily is the ghost who haunts this hotel!"

He guffawed and slapped his knee.

"A haunted hotel? Seriously? You picked us a

haunted hotel for Operation Phoenix?"

Operation Phoenix is what we were calling the murderous mad-dash-lost-cause Hail Mary that is Roger restoring his family.

"Yes, and that's shit's dope, yo," reasoned Albert. "We could see a ghost while we are here."

We had gotten two rooms on the third floor. They were next door to each other. It felt wonderful to have a home base and to shower and rest. I needed a bit of space. We had been taking turns driving and sleeping in the car. We talked a lot on our drive. It was close quarters, but Albert was pretty good company. He was bright and entertaining. We talked about our families and our careers. But mostly we talked about DMT. Specifically, we discussed its function. Drug or Tesseract? Interior psychedelic trip or inter-dimensional voyage? Albert wondered about the military's involvement. I had not considered that.

"Fo' real. Not only is it documented, but it makes sense. I read an interview with Terence McKenna where he says that he initially heard about DMT from a friend of his who was a scientist with the Army in the bay area. His friend smuggled some out. The Pentagon is doing shit with this right now, yo! They've had this shit since the 40's, but only really got into it in the 60's. I'm telling you. There are rooms with PsyOp military personnel getting injected with the shit all day long. The soldiers are interacting with entities in this space, sending back bits of helpful data. DMT entities, whoever the fuck they are, are builders. Like elves, yo. Only they ain't cobblin' shoes, they are creating intricate machines that humans could never understand. No one knows what these machines do, yo."

"Machines?" I snorted.

"I bet they got the plans for the particle accelerator from them."

I laughed. "When did they invent Kevlar? What the fuck is Kevlar? Alien technology?"

"Everything in existence isn't good. Cancer. Female genital mutilation. Famine. All the cats they gotta kill. A lot of the shit we seen on DMT is closer to Greek mythology than reality. Fairies, hybrids. Satyrs? They are a thing? But say, you pop out into some godforsaken corner of the multi-dimensional universe, and 'they' aren't glad to see you? With DMT all bets are off yo. I saw a dead mom. She was sweet. She cooked for me. She forgave me. That's sweet. You know?"

Even though we were alone in my car doing 65 miles an hour, Albert looked around and lowered his voice.

"But if DMT space is real space, then it's not always going to be a friendly space, inhabited by friendly folk who are excited to see you. You could bob into a Hell, or interrupt an eternal demon's quiet time, or turn up in some intergalactic prison cell. Think of all the random shit you've seen, yo. If it's just in your head, you are one sick puppy. If it's not..."

He didn't finish his sentence. He didn't need to. DMT felt like serious business. Heavy, heavy stuff. But it had taught me nothing useful. The great DMT banana slug was mum on how to save the day, and long on the intergalactic history of mushrooms. DMT may be heavy in big picture sort of way, but my family is heavy in an immediate way. And I need to be with them. The distance between us is crushing me.

And like I said, Albert's great, but people need space. Yo.

Operation Phoenix, for all of our strategizing, was still in its infancy. "Roger Reunites with Family- A Second Chance," in addition to being obtuse, is also highly unrealistic. What was I going to do? What could I do? My situation was bleak. What do you say to someone after you watch them drown? Sorry, I turned away because I didn't like seeing you in distress? Sorry, I promise that the next time something mission critical happens I won't leave you hanging? Was sorry even appropriate in my case?

We had general plans of attack.

Option One: The Total Truth. Find Abby, where ever she is. Right away. Beg her to listen. Tell her every ugly horrible thing. Duck and see what happens. While this looks like my best option, it's the one I'm most reluctant to try. I know, I know.

Option Two: Albert could pose as a terrorist and kidnap my entire family. He could take them to the edge of a cliff and tie them up. I could show up at the last minute and heroically save the day. Hugs all around. Right? While this is a ridiculous option, it could work, providing Abby transitioned to a one-dimensional cartoon girl.

That's it. Those are the flimsy planks that support Operation Phoenix. Tell her the truth and accept the consequences. Or magically skate out of it by heroically saving the day from a manufactured crisis.

"What do you think she told the boys?" Albert had asked.

Christ. I didn't know. I had only gotten the one letter from Benji. I get why Charlie hasn't reached out. Mom is likely to be more forgiving if she blames it on me. Distance from his father is making his life easier. Gross. I doubt she told them too much. But her actions communicated volumes. Hey Kids! We are making a midnight run across country. Sans Dad. It's one a.m. and all is well! Benji has probably made a PowerPoint or two about divorce statistics. Poor Benji. I felt pounds of shame over the dog's death. It was just a quick, physical manifestation of my issues. I was insular, criminal, deceitful. Ugh.

I cleaned up and changed my clothes. It was about 10:30 p.m. I paced around in my room for a few minutes trying to figure out what I should do. I was so close to my family. I swear, I could feel them in the air. I could feel my heart's proximity. I decided to drive over to Abby's parent's house, just to take a look. See what I could see. Albert wanted to come with me.

"I'm down. They have White Castle out here," he said. First, we do recon, then we do feast. You know what I'm saying?"

We drove the three miles across the island to the residential strip on its inner coast. I parked the rental about three houses down on the opposite side of the street. I got out of the car.

Albert leapt out and grabbed my arm.

"Yo! What are you doing?" he hissed. "This isn't

in the plan."

I shook him off. "I'm just going to look around. They are probably all asleep."

"Dude. This is a bad idea. Let's get back in the car and talk about it," advised Albert.

But I knew what I was doing. Abby has never been a night owl, and her parents were the types who got up at three in the morning to start work by four. They were in bed for the night by six p.m. Every night. Everyone was going to be asleep and I was just going to do a little recon. A sweep of headlights cut up the street and Albert and I instinctively dove to hide behind our car. I don't know exactly why two sober middle-aged men, thousands of miles away from home decided to hide like crooks. Okay, well I hid because of the off chance the car coming up the street was Abby. I didn't want to look like a creepy stalker or a peeping Tom so I, uh, played it off legit by cowering behind my car, in the dark. Albert just hid because, I don't know. Maybe because he's a good sport? Or the drugs? But it was a good thing that we did, because to my shock, the car pulled up to my in-law's house. I watched as Benji shot out, and bounded up the walkway to the front door. Then, I watched as Abby exited the car. On the passenger side?! The driver's door opened and I could see a silhouette of man. She was out with a man? With Benji?

My vision faded to a solid red field. I could feel Albert grabbing my arm, holding me down. I was blinded by the red, and my lack of sight amplified my sense of hearing. When the man's voice floated down the street, I recognized it. It was Higgins!

"See you at the office tomorrow, Abby! Good night, little Benji!"

It was hard knowing Higgins was anywhere within fifty miles of Abby, but hearing him say my son's name literally made me wretch.

There I was, outside of my in-law's home, hiding behind a rental car, dry-heaving into the gutter. Thank god for Albert. He patted my back and shushed me.

"Shhh, Roger. And this is why we don't get out of the car next time. Right? Right homie?" he asked in a hushed tone.

I nodded. We heard the car drive away and Albert hauled me to my feet as my vision returned.

"Let's go. See where he goes."

We clamored into the car. Albert got behind the wheel. I wordlessly got into the passenger seat. I was in no state to drive. I was feeling alternating waves of dread, disgust and horror.

"He's a murderer, for Christ's sake!" hollered Wally.

"It'll be okay," said Albert, soothingly.

"And what the fuck did he mean 'see her at the office,'" demanded Wally. I appreciated his support but it wasn't helping to diffuse anything.

We followed Higgins for about ten minutes. As we drove, I felt pressure rising from inside my belly. My head was a barely seated cork, getting pushed up the neck by gathering gasses. It had been a while since I'd felt yawning panic like this. Well. A week, at least. We ended up off the island at a strip mall along the coast. Albert and I watched from across the parking lot. Higgins walked up to a store front that had a giant banner across its frontage that read "LEASE NOW, 2800 SQ. FT" and disappeared inside.

"Yo, how long has this fucker been here?" asked Albert. "He's already setting up shop. Man, let's go end this fool. He's buggin'. You know?"

I dropped my hand to my waist and felt the gun I'd forgotten.

Just an aside here, friends. Look how far I've gone into the underbelly. Drugs. Murders. And now I'm in another state, stalking my murderous nemesis. And I just so happen to have a gun on me. As does my friend. What types of figures would we cut for the law? Or for strangers? Less than ideal. I mean, if you guys didn't know me, how scary would we look sitting in that parking lot?

Asked and answered.

"Hold up, Albert," I said. We watched Higgins exit, lock up and get back into his car. "Let's see where he goes from here."

We followed him back across the bridge to the island and watched in disbelief as he pulled into the Flanders parking lot. My heart began to hammer even harder.

"He knows I'm here?" I asked. The dread flood from earlier had subsided but the angsty waves of panic were still lapping my feet.

We parked at the back of the lot in a dark corner. Albert tossed the keys to me. He put a hand on the door and turned back to me.

"He don't know me, yo. It's cool. Relax, I'll tail him."

He took off across the lot and into the hotel after

Higgins. I nervously locked the car doors. All kinds of horrors were marching through my landscape. Higgins knows I'm here. He's just gone in there to kill me. Higgins knows Benji. And talks to him. Unacceptable. Abby working for Higgins? Disgusting. 'He knows her social security number!' I thought. Through all of the threats, that felt significant to me somehow.

"He's seen her naked too," offered Wally. "Maybe that's another reason you're so steamed up right now."

"He's a murderer, though." I defended.

"So are you," my inner voice replied. Albert startled me by rattling the door latch.

"Open up," he mouthed at the window. I flipped open the locks. I'd dropped the keys to the floor board when he had frightened me. I dug them up from the fast-food wrappers and debris from a week-long road trip as Albert got in the car.

"It's cool, yo," Albert smiled. "He's just staying here too, that's all. Popular place. Fancy and shit."

The third flood of the evening washed over me. Relief.

"Yeah. It's good. You know? He's going to tuck himself into bed, pull one off over those damn photos of your wife and fall asleep. We should go back and check out his office."

"Check it out?" I asked, wincing.

"Get in and look around."

I dropped my hand to my waist and felt for the gun again.

"Let's go."

THE PORK ISLAND CENTER IN BARGAINTOWN, NJ

In the full spirit of ridiculousness, I'm parked at the north end of the "Pork Island Center", which is just off the Garden State Parkway, in a city that is actually named Bargaintown, with a lower case "t". This the place where Higgins is making his new base, and I'm at the other end of the lot in front of the Harbor Freight. It's 6:45 a.m. on a Thursday morning. Albert isn't with me. He's in a second rental car that we got earlier this morning, keeping an eye on my family. After what we learned last night, our battle has split into two fronts: Abby at her new "job", and Benji at his grandparent's house. I haven't forgotten about Charlie, but I'm guessing he's stays in bed until noon. Safe-ish.

I'm waiting for Abby to arrive for work. The payroll sheet we found last night indicated her start time was 7:30 a.m. I wanted to be here well before that. If things go according to plan, she will phone the police within moments of arriving. I'll explain.

We found a lot of bad stuff at Higgins' office. Albert labelled them "straight-up wicked." What we found there defies my imagination. I don't know what I expected. Maybe some surreptitious photos of Abby. Maybe he got his hands on my cellphone. You know, the one I disposed of behind Smiles Donuts back in California? I had been so naive and so careless back then. Ugh. The only difference between then and now is that I have nothing. And I'm less naive.

"Hey! You're sober now too. Off the drugs, don't forget," says Wally.

That was a rare moment of compassion from my hyper-critical voice. Too rare to discard. That's true. I'm sober now. That's something, right?

I'm a bit more violent since I gave the drugs up, but that's definitely a transient, situational thing. Am I more credible now that I'm not a drug user? No?

We were not prepared for Higgins' newly-moved-into strip mall office. Not at all. How do you prepare for apocalypse, madness, delusion, messianic visions and blood mysticism? Yes, blood mysticism is a thing! I hadn't heard of half of the things Higgins is into. Straight wicked, indeed.

We waited around at the hotel, keeping an eye on Higgins' room and car until we were confident he was in for the night. Then we rode out to the "Pork Island Center" in Bargaintown to see what we could see. I mean, to break in. Pork Island is a small island about 7 miles east of the hotel.

The Pork Island Center is a tiny strip mall, typical of Every Town, USA. It's anchored with a Harbor

Freight and a UPS Store. Higgins rented a space next to the UPS store at the west end. We looked around for a sneaky way to get in, but there was no back entrance so our options were limited. We looked for any signs of surveillance but saw none. We brute forced our way in. I waited with the running car in the lot while Albert hurled a brick through the front glass door. He ran back to the car and we took off, heading north up the Parkway. We figured we'd drive around for a bit and then head back, see if any security was alerted. Albert hadn't seen any signs of an alarm, but while Albert was demonstrably good at biochemistry, smoking freebase, and Googling things, I felt that there must be some limits.

After about thirty minutes we turned around and went back down the Parkway. We were both exhausted. Albert was uncharacteristically silent. He only said one thing the entire drive.

"You know why I picked us a haunted hotel? If ghosts are real, and I mean really real? Maybe that means I could see my moms again. I wanna see my moms again, yo. You know?"

We pulled back into the dark, totally non-alarmed strip mall about an hour and a half from the time we broke the glass. Everything looked the same. No cops. No alarm bells. No security guards. Figuring it was safe, I tapped out a few remaining glass shards from the door-frame with the butt of my gun, and we stepped in.

The space looked a lot like Higgins' office had looked in California. Banal. Typical. There was a modest waiting area that had a small coffee table in the front corner, stacked with magazines. There was an orange plastic chair on either side of the magazine table. Across from the chairs was a front desk. There was an interior door both on the left and the right.

"In there," I pointed left.

The door was locked. I looked around for a blunt instrument, and spotted a wrought iron book-end at the reception desk. It was a bust of an eagle head. I brought it down on the doorknob hard and the flimsy interior lock came away in pieces. Albert pushed the door open and we looked inside. The giant desk from California dwarfed the room. It was piled and overflowing with documents and books and scrolls. It looked like a medieval scholar's room from the set of a horror movie, complete with a skull ashtray at the desk's edge. Albert started to go through the documents.

"What the fuck?" he asked incredulously. He read from a few.

"This one says 'The Desposyni in the Twentieth Century.' What's The Desposyni?" he asked. "The fuck?"

I shrugged as I looked through some open packing boxes. Higgins hasn't gotten around to unpacking all his weird shit. There were books, creepy knickknacks like random bones, a shrunken head and New Age crystals. Higgins' shit test crystals. Yeah, the ones he said were hogwash.

"Don't know," I answered. "I'm surprised you haven't heard of it."

"The 'Historia Ecclesiae by Eusebius'," Albert continued. "Holy Blood, Holy Grail. The Handybook for Genealogists, Tenth Edition. The fuck? Yo?"

At that point, I had no idea what picture the titles were painting. It was ominous in the abstract, but even darker when we figured out what it all meant.

"The Dead Sea Scrolls Uncovered? James, the Brother of Jesus: The Key to Unlocking the Secrets of Early Christianity and the Dead Sea Scrolls?" Albert scoffed. "This book has like, one thousand, seven hundred and four pages, yo. Straight wicked!"

He grabbed a series of thin, leather bound books. "The City of God Book Two? The City of God Book Eighteen? Augustine's Confessions? The Occult Significance of Blood, An Esoteric Study? Yo, he's a wizard? You didn't tell me the dude was a wizard."

He dropped the books back on the desk, knocking a precarious stack of magazines onto the floor. We both shrugged. While we didn't have a plan, neither of us cared about making a mess at this point.

"I'mma Google," said Albert. He looked down at one of the thin leather-bound books. "Hey Google, what is Augustine's Confessions?"

"Confessions is the name of an autobiographical work, consisting of 13 books, by Saint Augustine of Hippo, written in Latin between AD 397 and 400," intoned Google's female robot voice.

"The work outlines Saint Augustine's sinful youth and his conversion to Christianity."

"Homie ain't no Christian, yo," quipped Albert. "What else?" he mused, rifling through the paper mess. His eyes settled on something and they lit up. "Hey Google, what is Historia Ecclesiae?"

We got another strange response.

"The Church History, of Eusebius, the bishop of Caesaea was a 4th-century pioneer work giving a chronological account of the development of Early Christianity from the 1st century to the 4th century. It was written in Koine Greek, and also survives in Latin, Syriac and Armenian manuscripts."

Google could not give us an answer to "What is the Desposyni?" It kept responding with: "Desposito means surly in Spanish." I checked my watch. It was 3:00 a.m. I walked out of the office into the lobby and peeked through the empty door frame into the parking lot. All was quiet. No wonder so many cars are stolen in New Jersey, I thought. They don't have video surveillance.

I stepped over the broken glass of the door pane, through the lobby and back into Higgins' mad world. Albert was sitting in Higgins' high-backed chair with a manila folder opened on his lap. He looked up at me, and his expression was serious.

"Come see this, bro," he said. He handed me the folder. "Look at the first page."

The top page was a blank sheet of paper. "Clines Family Tree, Rex Deus?" was scrawled across the top. The next few pages were session notes. They were of our first interview where Higgins had asked the boatload of random, Dr. Seuss questions.

"What months were your parents born in?" Higgins had asked.

"Both parents born in November" was noted at the bottom of one page and he'd drawn a box around the sentence. The last ten pages were a family lineage. My family lineage. It started with Benji, from Roger

Clines and Abby Clines (formerly Abby Hillsdale) and worked backwards. I didn't even know my Great-Grandfather's name, but Higgins did. I thumbed through and stopped at the last page. There were three names: son of Phinehas, son of Eleazar, son of Aaron.

I looked at Albert. He had been looking things up on his cell.

"Get this," he said, reading from his phone, "The Rex Deus attribute their lineage to Jesus, back to King David and even further back to the High Priest Aaron, Moses' brother. Speculation exists that they have kept their bloodline pure throughout the centuries and wield the secret power of Jeshua God."

"Huh?" I asked, not expecting an answer.

Albert shook his head. "This is wack. Higgins has traced your ancestry all the way back to Moses' brother. Bible Moses. And he's got lots of creepy books about magic."

He bent down at the bottom of a stack and read titles, moving upward: "Ritual of Blood, Blood Ritual in the Hebrew Bible, Blood Sorcery Bible, Baphomet Spell Book, The Black Scriptures: Foundational Rituals of Maegzjiran Majick."

They were ominous sounding books. "What is Maegzjiran Majick?" I asked, as Albert scrolled through his phone.

"It's a Black Magic Cabal for the Disciples of the Left-Hand Path, led by Grandmaster Somnus Dreadwood. Sounds like a Dungeons and Dragons character. This is what they posted as their biography: During the 1100's A.D., the first blood pact was made between the Drujziya family and The Black God,

Cernobog in Veszprem, Hungary. Through this, the Archdemon joined his blood with the gypsy's tribe, thus leading to all and their progeny to be born with an (un)natural affinity for magick and the black arts. In 1436, at the hands of the Fra Giacomo and the Inquisition of Hungary, nearly every last gypsy of the Drujziya tribe was slaughtered. Those who survived abandoned their heritage and adopted a new persona and lifestyle, blending back into the social weave. Sybastien Drujziya, our Patriach, was visited by Cernobog in the winter of 1436. The Black God formed a second blood pact with Sybastien, granting an aspect of his infernal divinity. In return, a Cabal would be founded, a movement made, and all enemies of the Cabal would be decimated. Thus, came the Maegzjiran Cabal from the fires of Hell, Maergzjirahl; the Underworld, Keraktes; and the plane of shadow, L'Oima Isto."

"We are an ever-expanding, studious order of Sorcerers and Sorceresses from a wide array of spiritual backgrounds and scholarship. Our mission is to destroy ignorance of the arcane, venture further into the occult so as to learn its most intimate secrets, and to reach our apotheosis: perfection and power absolute of the soul. Godhood, Lichdom, Vampirism, Omniscience, and Immortality is not just a fantasy or a dream. For Disciples of the Cabal, it is merely a step along the grand journey into the multiverse. It is a reality for those who are diligent enough to remain focused and to always drive hard toward their goal when the world would otherwise crush the flame of their ambition."

Albert exhaled hard. "Damn."

I glanced at my watch. It was four a.m. Shit was getting weirder.

Albert shook his head and sighed. "Man, all this is nuts. Two weeks ago, I would dismiss it all as crazy. But after blasting into hyperspace and meeting a dead moms?" He shook his head again. "Now, I don't know what to think. This shit scares me, yo."

I agreed with him completely. You only need to leave your body once and talk with cartoon spirits in hyperspace to know all bets are off.

"I hate that he's been anywhere near my family."

"What's his deal with Benji, do you think?" asked Albert. He opened the desk drawers, pawing through the contents. I had opened all of the moving boxes, but didn't see anything that struck my interest.

I pointed at a large armoire that was up against the south wall. The doors were still taped shut from the move. "Let's see what's in there."

It was a hulking antique mahogany armoire, decorated with bunches of grapes in relief. I ripped the packing tape off and opened the doors. That's when a new wave of horror swept over me. The inside was a shrine. To my boy. Ugh. He had pictures of Benji taped to the back walls, like a high school girl tapes pictures up inside her locker. He had cut random letters from magazines, and glued them to the back wall like a ransom note, to spell out: Benji Clines, the Blood of Christ.

"The fuck?!" exclaimed Albert, as he looked inside, wide-eyed.

"My life is a Dan Brown movie?" I asked,

incredulously.

"Doesn't matter. Doesn't matter what this shit is about. Benji's in trouble. Higgins has got to go. We gotta do something forthwith, yo."

He was right. Suddenly, America was the Wild West. It may be a new millennium for most Americans, but for Roger, it's Frontierland. A place where violence is everywhere. A place where someone is always lurking around the next corner, plotting. A land where people want me dead. People literally want Roger Clines dead. That's not a good feeling. It generates ill-will and leaves you in a kill or be killed position. The twenty-first century American Dream. Prosaic, huh? Well, it's more poetic and romantic than the truth. I broke the law and now I was outside it's protection. My bad.

We huddled in the lobby and came up with a rough plan. It was rough because we were stressed out and exhausted and it was 4:30 a.m. We both needed sleep, but with the blood and the magic and Abby and Benji so involved with Higgins we had no time. We left the strip mall office in shambles and drove to pick up another car rental. Albert split to go park at my in-law's place back on the Island to keep an eye on Benji, and I came back here.

It's 7:15 a.m. now. We are betting that Abby arrives before Higgins, and that she will call the police when she does. If she ventures beyond the broken glass, she will see the creepy armoire-shrine to Benji and be appropriately aghast. Higgins will be mud. Albert and I will quietly kill him and then I will appear cap in hand, and beg Abby to talk to me. I will tell her everything. I know I've said that before, but this time my life is in free fall. No job, no family, and an empty house I can't afford in California. There has always been a safety net before. A perceived way out. But now I know that the way out is the way through. Maybe I won't look so bad next to a blood worshiping, black magic voodoo doctor. Maybe I'll look normal.

So, that's the plan. It's flimsy, but it exists. I've got one ally in the field. I've got the moral fuel I need to put it into action.

"He's vampire-gay for your boy, yo," Albert had said.

I don't know what the fuck Higgins is planning. But it ends today.

THE END

Abby pulled into the parking lot at 7:25 a.m. My heart jumped when I saw her. It looked like Benji was in the car with her. She got out and took a few steps towards the office when she noticed the shattered front door. I could see her look back at the car and yell something. I was about five hundred yards away- it sounded like "stay in the car."

She stepped inside the office, her cellphone in her hand. She disappeared from my view. I started counting, wondering how many seconds it would take for her to see the armoire/Benji shrine. She had been inside for seventeen seconds when I saw Higgins' car pull in. It slid up to Abby's car and blocked my field of view. That was too close for me. I got out of the car and started sprinting across the mostly empty lot. Where the fuck was Albert? I wondered.

I couldn't see what was going on but I could see Higgins' head above the car. I was pushing as hard as I could but it felt like I was running through deep water. I'm a 56-year-old recovering drug addict. I don't run much. As I got closer, I saw Abby come out from the office.

"Get back in the car, Benji!" she yelled. "Stay away from him!"

I was about two hundred yards out. From that distance, I could see that Higgins was leading Benji by the hand, mostly dragging my son across the broken glass and into the office.

"No!" I yelled at about a hundred yards away. It was a hoarse cry that Abby must not have heard, because she ran into the office after them.

I was exhausted and felt faint as I closed to twenty yards. I was almost to the office and I didn't have any plan. I was just going to charge in there and shoot Higgins, and save my family. When I got to the front door I paused and pulled the gun from my waistband. I was panting and drained, but I was in a suddenly serene head-space. I even had two smug thoughts that I would regret once inside. First, I considered that Higgins probably bought this gun that I'd taken from Larry and I found that poetically fitting. Second, I thought that this was a pretty lucky setup. What better way to re-connect with my family, than to charge in and save the day! A non-manufactured crisis, hurrah!

"Maybe your life is a Dan Brown novel after all," offered Wally.

I entered the office, gun out and ready, and swept the lobby. It was empty.

"Abby?" I called as I approached the side office. "Benji?"

I darted into the office gun-first, like they do in the

movies. The room was empty. Papers and books were strewn everywhere, the door-less armoire shouting its creep love for Benji, but no one was there.

"The fuck?" I asked aloud and called out again.

"Benji? Abby?"

I exited the office and looked behind the front desk. Nothing. There was one other door to the right. It looked like it was to a bathroom. We had missed it last night. Where the fuck is Albert? I wondered again.

I stood in front of the door, one hand hovering over the knob, the other stiffly aiming the gun, straining to hear any sounds. They had to be in there. I tried to visualize the bathroom. Maybe Abby and Benji huddled against the sink, Higgins training a gun on them? The thought broke my heart and emboldened me. I flung the door open and charged in.

The charge was met with a blinding strike to the head.

My vision exploded with bursts of sharp yellow pain. As I fell to the floor, my consciousness began to fade. The last thing I heard before I lost consciousness was Benji. Even in this dire moment it warmed my heart. I heard something I hadn't heard in months.

"Daddy!!!!"

And then all went black.

I woke up in stages. The first thing I was aware of was pain. My shoulders were on fire. The second thing I realized was that I couldn't feel my hands. Next, I became aware of a soft moaning. A low, feminine whine of grief and helplessness. I had no context for the sound, but it made me deeply sad. Then I was aware that I couldn't see anything. My eyes were closed. I tried to open my eyes and couldn't. No hands, no eyes! As I wondered where I was, frantically trying to remember what had happened, my eyes popped open. They had finally gotten the message. I took in my surroundings and everything flooded back.

I was in an underground room of some sort. Maybe a basement? The walls were cinder blocks and there was a long stairway that led up to a door. I discovered that I was strapped to a chair, my arms tightly bound behind the back, the wood cruelly digging into my joints. The soft moaning was Abby. She was in a chair a few feet to my left, quietly sobbing. Her hair was disheveled and her pretty mouth was turned like an upside-down rainbow. A sad rainbow. Her makeup was smeared down her face and snot dangled from her nose, and saliva-tendrils hung from her top lip to her bottom like glistening spider webs.

She noticed I had come to.

"Roger!" she cried. "Oh my god, Roger!"

My eyes were instantly full of tears. It would have hurt to see her after all this time under the best of conditions, let alone seeing her in this cluster fuck along with me. This was all my fault. Holy shit, Roger Clines the Destroyer.

"He's got Benji over there," she whimpered and tossed her head to my right. I followed her glance and saw the worst sight yet.

My little boy was blindfolded and strapped to a crudely built wooden chair. It vaguely resembled an old electric chair with leather straps at the ankles, waist, neck, elbows and wrists. His arms were strapped along the wooden arms of the chair and he was bucking his body, straining against the restraints. There was a goddamn IV in his arm that led to a bag, filling up with his blood.

What the fuck? I thought for the millionth time in a week. Where the fuck was Albert?

"Benji?" I called to him. I looked around the room for Higgins or a heavy, but it was only the Clines family. "Benji? Calm down and breathe Benji."

"Daddy?" He stopped moving and his blind head cocked to the side.

"It's me, son. I'm working on getting you and your mom out of here. Okay kiddo?"

"What is happening to me Dad?" His little body calmed a bit and he began to breathe evenly.

"Something very strange, Benji," I replied. I had no idea what I was doing but the words kept coming. "Just hold still and try to breath. I need you to focus on breathing while I work through this."

"What are you working through?"

"Just hold still and breathe, Benji," cried Abby. "Your Daddy and I need a minute to work things out."

"Are you having therapy?" Benji asked innocently.

Even though we were doomed and this was the saddest shit, Abby and I both laughed.

I strained against my ropes, but my arms were completely numb and didn't respond to any will. The ties didn't budge. Feeling helpless I looked over at Abby.

She was smiling broadly.

"I knew you'd come for us."

"I did, but I fell short," I choked out, feeling a flood

of emotion hearing her kindness. I had been afraid I would never hear that sound again.

"You came for us, Roger!" She tried her best to toss her hair out her eyes and beamed. "Now. What's the plan?"

Minus the fact that we were tied up and that Benji was getting leeched, that was one of the best moments I'd had in the last two years. She still believes in me! I thought excitedly.

"She's desperate, champ," snided Wally. "You're her only option."

I tried to hop my chair over to Benji. I was able to bunch my body together slightly and then flex up and my chair would bounce. Each bounce threatened to rip my arms off my body. I was getting closer. When I was about ten agonizing "body-hops" away the door at the top of the steps swung open.

I'm too late, I thought.

Then I saw a familiar face peek in. It was Albert!

"There you are, yo," he said as calmly as if we were at a dinner table.

He closed the door behind him and trotted down the steps. He began to undo my binds, but I stopped him.

I cocked my head towards Benji.

"Get that shit out of him first, man."

His eyes widened when he saw the blood bag hanging over Benji's head.

"What the fuck, yo?" he said in wonder. "I told you he's vampire gay for him, man. So fucked up."

He gently removed the needle from Benji's arm, pulled the blindfold off his little head and began to undo the leather straps. Abby was sobbing with relief, her head hanging forward. I was laughing myself.

"Daddy!" exclaimed Benji when the blindfold came off. He looked haggard and had dark circles under his eyes. I glanced up at the blood bag and tried to gauge how much he'd lost. Albert freed Benji's right arm and moved down to undo his leg straps when the door at the top of the stairs opened again.

Higgins stepped into view. My elation sunk. The hope I was feeling drained away. The emotional seesaw was becoming too much. One moment things were good, the next, devastating. The next few seconds played out as a slow-motion event. I saw Higgins raise his gun. He aimed it at Albert. Albert was kneeling at Benji's feet- he followed the look of horror on my face and turned to see the outstretched gun.

"And who is this?" Higgins asked with a far too comfortable grin. The words stretched out like taffy, each syllable low and drawn out. It was like bullet time from The Matrix. It was Doom Time. In that eerie space, I swear I heard the click of the trigger before the bang of the gun. Albert turned his head to look at me. And then a bullet took him across the side of his face. His eyes popped wide as part of his flesh and top jaw were sheared away. He wobbled and his remaining lower jaw worked like he was trying to tell me something. He collapsed at Benji's feet.

Benji's scream broke the slow-motion fugue and time caught back up to its regular pace. Only his left leg was free and he was kicking wildly. He looked down in horror at Albert's body. I turned to look at

Abby- that was the absolute worst moment. The most hopeless moment. We were doomed. Part of me had actually thought I was going to save the day here. I dropped my head, unable to look at the horror of my family's full-stop. My wife restrained, my son bleeding out, my friend dead at his feet.

Higgins began to laugh. It was a horrible sound.

"I'm surprised to see you here, Roger," he said, like he had all the time in the world. We could have been at church, passing in the halls.

I didn't say anything. I was defeated. For the first time in my life I was utterly defeated. I've never been in a moment so bereft of hope. Certain death. Certain death for my loved ones. And God knows what torturous things they would have to endure before Higgins disposed of them.

"Killed your stupid henchmen. You thought we'd be dead!" Wally tried, but I wasn't having it. We were fucked. It was all my fault. And we were fucked. I fucked my life up. Then that fucked my family up. Then I led them right into the arms of a sadistic killer. I'd delivered them to the firing squad. I might as well have tied a bow around their necks. I had no bravado left.

Higgins made his way down the stairs, almost sauntering.

"Where are Gunther and Larry? Any ideas?" Higgins asked.

I couldn't respond. Abby was sobbing. Benji was crying. Wailing.

"Daddy?! Momma?!" he screeched out in heart-rending bursts.

He must have been so terrified. Abby must have been so terrified. I've got a pretty solid notion of terror now, folks. And that was terror maximum.

"Quiet, little one," shushed Higgins. Abby began screaming.

"Don't touch him! You stay away from him!" she shrieked fiercely.

I kept my head down. I couldn't bear to look. I'm ashamed of this, but in that moment, I'd given up. I even thought: Kill me first. That way I don't have to witness any more pain.

Yuck, huh? Big man wanted to go first, I wanted out. Roger Clines couldn't even raise his head and look. Would you have? If your family was getting tortured to death by a madman, would you look? The sudden jerk from fear to relief to final fear had taken every bit of my strength away. I couldn't look, I couldn't speak.

"At least you won't be wondering 'why me' anymore, Roger," said Higgins. "You are Rex Deus. And a terrible representation at that. If you hadn't been so pathetic this could have been you."

I heard him make a tapping noise. It must have been Benji's chair because he cried out again.

"Could have been you here in this chair." I heard him step away from Benji and approach Abby. "Such a pretty girl," Higgins continued. "Such a naughty girl. Oh yes, I've seen the pictures. Who hasn't?"

"Fuck you," Abby spit at him. Her defiance encouraged me. It lifted me slightly. Lifted me just enough to raise my head.

"Yeah, fuck you," I chimed in.

Higgins laughed. "You aren't completely pathetic Roger. I'll give you that much. Gunther would not have been an easy man to kill."

"I'm not either, asshole," I retorted. Abby's strength had buoyed me. "How many times have you tried and failed?"

Higgins laughed again. "Truth. At least twice now. But in the end? I win."

"You're insane. Cuckoo. What, the manna not making your dick any bigger?"

"The manna is crap. It has no effects. Roy Stacks is a washed-out hillbilly. His stuff is crap. But truly, Roger. Who needs manna when you can have the blood of Christ? I know it's hard to believe looking at you, but you are part of a long lineage. A very special lineage. It's clear to me that your family's greatness skipped you. But Benji! Benjamin! He's lovely!"

"His name isn't Benjamin," snarled Abby.

"Benji, Benjamin. It makes no difference. He's got the juice." Higgins shivered. "Oh, I gave myself the chills just then."

"Shut the fuck up!" screamed Abby.

Higgins trained the gun on her. "I had hoped to keep you around for a while. I was thinking after all of this is over, we could recreate a certain photo shoot. But you need to quiet down, or I'll have to end you."

"Shut. The. Fuck. Up!" I raged, pointedly adding periods between the words.

The gun swiveled to me. I liked it better on me than on Abby.

That's when a miracle happened. Higgins was standing next to the blood-chair, pointing the gun at me. Abby quietly sniffled, "I love you, Roger. I've missed you so much."

Oh my God! The angel said the words I was supposed to say! I immediately burst into tears. She looked so beautiful.

"I love you, Abby. I'm so sorry. I'm so sorry, honey," I said between sobs.

Higgins groaned. "Pathetic. I'm done with you Roger."

He straightened his gun arm. And that was the absolute final moment of my life. He was seconds away from blowing me to pieces. Right there. In front of my wife. In front of my son. But. But, friends. She loves me! Abby loves me! After everything, she loves me! Her love filled me with a roar. I opened my mouth and out came a long, loud, spontaneous roar. I roared wordlessly at Higgins, staring him in the eyes. In the last moment, Abby's love gave me my final courage. A defiant roar. I expected Higgins to shoot me right then, but he paused. I ran out of breath, took a deep one and roared again.

Higgins shrugged. "At least you won't die like a complete pussy."

And then! A second miracle! The door at the top of the stairs flew open for a third time. In stepped a shirtless man. He was wearing a ragged pair of jeans, combat boots and a red sweatband around his head. He was holding a machine gun of sorts. And I recognized him. Roy Stacks?!

Roy let the bullets fly. He aimed down from the top of the stairs and fired. The impact of the bullet assault lifted Higgins off the ground and bowled him over.

Roy walked down the stairs, stepped next to where Higgins had fallen and shot him a few more times. A large pool of blood spread within seconds.

"Close your eyes, Benji," I yelled. "I'm almost to you! Close those eyes, son."

Roy walked to Abby and began to untie her. She looked at me.

"Is it over?" she asked, through her tears.

I nodded. Unbelievably, improbably, maybe it is? I thought.

"It's over," answered Roy. He then went to Benji and undid the remaining straps. Abby came over to me and put her hands on my shoulders. Her touch sent all the screaming agony away. She was kissing my neck and my face saying, "Iloveyou. Iloveyou. I love you, Roger!"

I was crying again, afraid to believe my eyes. "I love you so much, baby. I'm so sorry."

Roy finished with Benji and moved behind me to undo my bonds. Benji ran up to me and climbed on my lap, his arms around me and his mom.

"Daddy! Daddy! Daddy!" he cried.

After Roy untied me, he looked at Higgins' body.

"You guys should get out of here. I will take care of this mess."

I hugged him. "I can't believe you saved us! How did you know?"

Roy grinned. "I didn't. Not about you. I managed to turn the tables on the goons Higgins installed at my home and escape. I've been coming for him. After what he did to me and my family, to Tarek and Mido, his days were numbered."

Mr. Roy Stacks' arrival wasn't completely off the wall. His story was the same as mine. He had also been kidnapped; his life hijacked. He had also been forced into servitude for Higgins. And just like me, he found a way to turn the tables on Higgins' goons. And most reassuringly, just like me, had hightailed it across the country coming for blood.

Benji climbed down and wrapped his arms around Roy's waist.

"Thank you for your help, sir" he said in his best little man voice. Oh, that voice melts me.

Roy touched his forehead. "It was my pleasure."

Benji came back to Abby and I. We were clinging to each other for dear life. Our arms around each other, our faces touching. My face touching her face. My wife's beautiful face.

"You guys better get out of here," said Roy. "Go!"

And we did. I paused at the foot of the stairs briefly and looked back at Albert where he lay on the ground. His once animated face ripped in half. I couldn't think about that. We had to go. Roger Clines and Abby Clines and their son Benji Clines headed up the stairs.

"Where are we, anyway?" I asked as we climbed. I had no idea where Higgins had taken us.

"We're at the beach, baby," answered Abby. She grabbed Benji's hand and put her other in mine. I paused for a second at the landing, took a deep breath and we all stepped through the doorway.

EPILOGUE

Drug-addled family man begins shoplifting from grocery stores, then gets kidnapped and unwittingly helps some punk kid build a bomb. Then he kills the kid. That's quite a story. Said man then searches for manna in Sinai, in an attempt to alter his DNA to outwit the police- that's an even bigger story.

DMT? Oh my God, friends. This is the penultimate story. What the fuck is it? A Stargate in a molecule? The Philosopher's Stone? The answers regarding life after death? A phone to God? To quote ethnobotanist Terrence McKenna on DMT:

"Why this is not four-inch headlines on every newspaper on the planet I cannot understand, because I don't know what news you were waiting for, but this is the news that I was waiting for."

It's a big deal. Other than any accompanying messiness or pain, I no longer fear death. Not for myself or my loved ones. I don't want anything to happen to any of us. But I'm no longer afraid. I believe in cosmic joy and all that jazz. Seeing is definitely believing. And I saw all kinds of shit. I literally saw the continuum and how I fit within. How everyone fits, minus some bad apples. But in the end, the most important thing is family.

My family.

They are all asleep right now and it's the most amazing scene. Abby is curled up on the sofa, Benji passed out across her feet. Charlie is sprawled on his bed, on top of the covers. Brian is asleep on our bed. Ugh. When did he go in there? That kid, I swear. He is always living all over me.

And I love it. I can't remember the last time we all slept under the same roof. I have a true sense of peace. That moment where all your tasks are done for the day, and all the kids are fast asleep. It's bliss.

Can you believe it? A happy ending for Roger? Does he deserve a happy ending? Oh, hell no! Not in the slightest. But that's what he gets. A bona fide happy ending. Hey, this isn't entirely without precedent. I want to explain. I haven't had the luxury of digression since things went south. Thank you for indulging me.

When I met you I was in a dark place. I know it looks really bad, but the Roger you know isn't wholly representative. I am not always a self-serving narcissist. Just sometimes. Do you remember the traumatized cop who became a compulsive shoplifter that I told you about back when we first met? The guy's name was Karl Hettinger and after being kidnapped, watching his partner get killed, barely escaping with his life and being ostracized by the police force he loved, he snapped. I was scared back then and I didn't tell you the rest of the story.

After Hettinger is fired in shame, he leaves Los Angeles and moves about 90 miles north to a city called Bakersfield. He met a really nice man named Trice Harvey. Trice had heard of the disgraced cop's story. He'd seen the movie and had sympathy for him. He felt Hettinger had been mistreated and deserved a second chance. Trice happened to be on the Board of Supervisors for Kern County and offered Karl a job as his administrative assistant.

Karl Hettinger flourished. He shook his demons, straightened up, and delivered a stellar performance day in and day out for a decade. He had a new reputation. Hettinger was kind, patient, and he got things done. When Trice Harvey was elected to a State Assembly seat, Governor Deukmejian appointed Hettinger as Trice's replacement. When he ran for the seat officially, he was elected to stay and served an additional term.

What a great story! And a great ending. Karl Hettinger made it out alive, and thrived. Why can't I?

Now, I've got to go. I'm waking Abby up, and then we are kicking Brian out of our room. I know that's selfish and that she needs to sleep. I don't care.

Made in USA - Kendallville, IN
1182692_9781735516233
10.20.2020 0844